# THE GLASS-FACE MAN

## MICHAEL PARK

FOX POINT BOOKS

The Glass-Face Man

Print edition ISBN: 9780999771532

Published by Fox Point Books; foxpointbooks.com

# Also by Michael Park

*Kentucky Dragon*

*Good to Grave: Why Some Human Hosts Succeed and Others Burn*

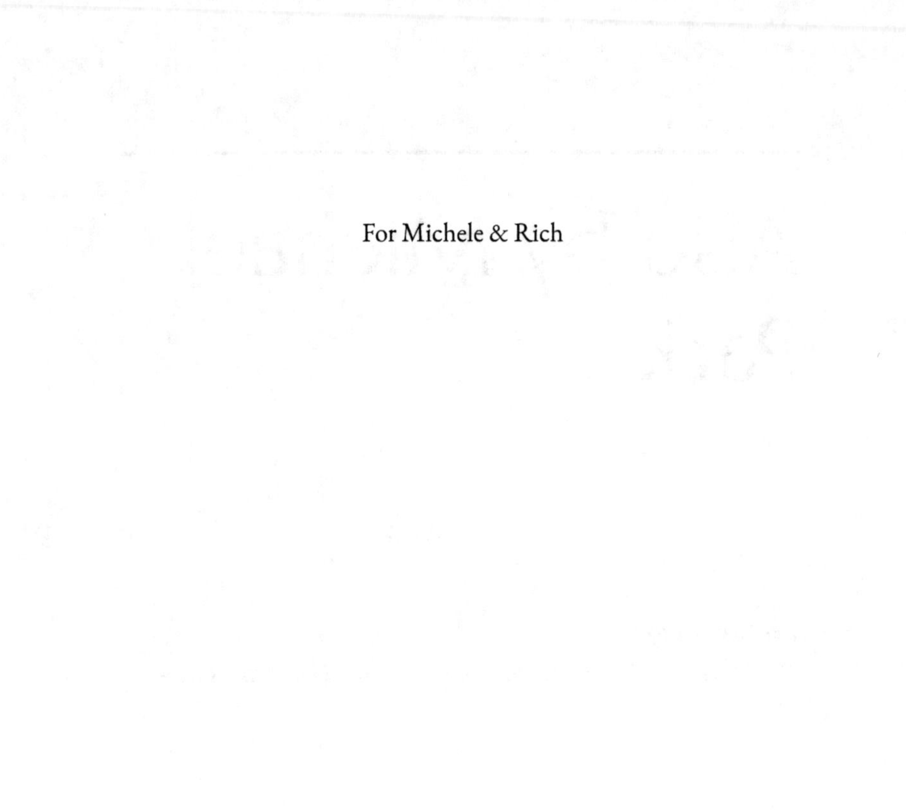

For Michele & Rich

# Chapter One

J osie's dead father watched from the back of her high school graduation ceremony.

*Not again.*

She closed her eyes, and when she opened them, there was no Dad ghost at the far wall, just a shadow between display cases of taxidermy wildlife. *Nobody there. Not him, not anyone. A trick of the light.* The central auditorium of the American Museum of Natural History at West 81$^{st}$ Street shimmered ocean blue over the assembled crowd of several hundred people—parents, friends, relatives—all watching the front stage. An immense blue whale replica hung overhead. From her place in line at the edge of the stage, Josie squinted to be sure the gray, imaginary version of her dad was gone. *I'm imagining things, because, well, nerves. Don't tell Mom. She'll go into panicked, cross-examination mode, maybe call Dr. Laymon. Four years since my last panic attack looking at an ordinary gas station on Flatbush Avenue. I'm off the happy pills. Focus on the end of high school, right now.*

Josie spotted Clara in the line of maroon graduation robes that led off stage right, behind her. When their eyes met, Josie felt a familiar rush. Clara's freckly face loosened into a smile that tugged at her high cheekbones, creating half-moon dimples around her lips. Her red hair sparkled in the stage lights, like Elvis in a Vegas spotlight.

Neon cape-wearing Elvis was Clara's favorite. She'd been Elvis-obsessed ever since Mom snuck them into a New Jersey casino for an Elvis impersonator show back in Sophomore year. Josie's first concert. Standing in a pit below the stage, eyes watery from cigarette smoke, she remembered seeing the awe on Clara's face. A full-on Christmas morning glow. In a flood of adrenaline, Josie wanted—*needed*—to see Clara smile like that, again and again.

Josie fidgeted with the flat, circular shape of Clara's lucky fossil in her right pocket, under the robe. As long as Josie had known Clara—all four years of high school—Clara had been *so* into rocks. Well, no—not *rocks*-rocks. Rocks, as in the same million-year-old shells and stone squiggles that Dad sometimes talked about, with bourbon in one hand. Faux superstitious, Clara prized the lucky fossil she'd found by that Kentucky riverbank way back when they first met. Usually under her bed. Only now, she let Josie slip it into her pocket like a talisman for the transition nerves that made Josie's heart tremor a little too fast.

*I can't believe high school is over. So glad you're here. Love you.*
Clara winked.

The principal called the name of a boy two spots ahead of Josie in line. Thick-necked Jonathan Marshall crossed to receive his diploma. *Where is Mom sitting? There.* Past a bobbing helium balloon with the words, *'Congratulations Graduates!'* Wedged between an old woman and a toddler, Mom held up her cellphone, already recording. Mom's long blonde hair was drawn back tight, and she wore a formal navy jacket and skirt. High-end stuff. Made her look older, pretty too, but like a banker chick. As if she was playing an earlier version of herself, Mom 2.0—from her corporate lawyer days, when they could afford to live on the Upper West Side, just a few blocks from this museum. Before things got bad.

Another student crossed the stage. Josie was next. Mom waved and mouthed something, probably 'I'm so proud' or 'we did it.' Mom and Josie had persevered through four years of latch-key afternoons, Clara-packed weekends, and late-night study sessions to wrap up high school.

And as the principal turned to Josie and said, "Josephina Elizabeth ..." the lights went out.

Total blackness.

For a moment, Josie's perception swam, the stage and auditorium replaced by solid nothingness, as if she were deep underground. The air felt too close, as if the walls, ceiling, floor even, were shrinking. Irrational claustrophobia. Of course, it was, but Josie's breath caught, tightening. She needed air. *Stay calm.* Her heart pounded, and she tasted the ozone air conditioner smell of the great room. A square of light from someone's phone blinked on, then another, and more. Backup lights flashed to life around the walls, illuminating museum displays of endangered animals. The audience clapped. The principal joked about Con Edison and the weather. Not a hurricane outside, but Mom had talked about the storm all morning and said she might even have to go into the office tonight to help. City flood prevention and all.

The principal said, "... we New Yorkers aren't deterred by a little rain!"

*Does that include me?* Even though she'd lived in New York through high school, longer than anywhere else, Josie didn't identify as a native. Home wasn't a place. It was wherever Mom and Clara were, right? The white backup lights turned the audience into hard edged shadows. The faux-underwater lighting had been annoying, sure, but now the crowd looked like a student art project, black-and-white bunker people.

The principal nodded to Josie. "Let's continue. Josephina Elizabeth Morris."

With everyone staring, Josie crossed the stage. Her legs felt stiff, clumsy. Josie's cheeks went hot, as they all watched. Unlike Clara, who owned the stage in every high school play, Josie had spent the last four years avoiding spotlights. She knew she was too lanky and pale, with hair that always popped wrong, as if she'd just rolled out of bed. *A girl most of you would look past on the street. I'm here, too.* What if she twisted her ankle, like three months ago on the subway steps and last year at the ice-skating rink at Rockefeller Center and ... Josie pinched a strand of sand-colored hair out of her eyes. She shook the principal's hand, took her diploma, and ...

... Dad's ghost was back. Dressed in the same white button-down shirt and dirt-streaked pants Josie remembered from that railroad bridge over the Ohio River four years ago, he watched with a friendly smile. His coarse jaw and receding hairline hadn't changed either. It wasn't real, but there he was. Her dead, deadbeat father.

"Ten days, Josie," he said.

No one else seemed to hear.

*No. He isn't there.* Josie's pulse throbbed in her ears, and she gripped the podium hard to steady herself, closed her eyes. *My head doesn't hurt, and I'm not sleepy. 'Ten days'? Stop. Remember Dr. Laymon's mantra: think of solid things, real things. The smell of the antiseptic, recirculated air. The heaviness of my fingers and toes. Unclench my jaw and when I open my eyes ...* She took a slow breath. The principal repeated her name, asking if she was okay. *When I open my eyes, Dad's ghost will be gone. But what if he isn't? What if it's like in Kentucky?*

Josie looked. The back wall was empty again. She let out a shaky breath and coughed, still balanced on the podium.

"Josie, are you all right?" the principal asked. "You can return to your seat ..."

*I'm not crazy.* The microphone buzzed, when she breathed too close to it.

"I'm sorry to interrupt, everybody," Josie said. Her voice wavered. She felt her pulse in her neck. So many people stared. "My dad's not here." *Stop. Don't do this.* But the words came out: "He isn't here today, because he was an asshole." *Childish and selfish to do this. But he was right there. No, I am not losing my shit.*

*You are, though,* a part of her said. *You literally are, right now. Halting the graduation ceremony to show everyone how collected and composed you are. Center of attention.*

"I'm sure I'm not the only one to grow up like this. But my dad left my mom and me ..." Her throat caught, but Josie coughed, kept going. "Then he died. In the most selfish way possible. I just want to say this *isn't* for him."

Josie's voice echoed. Nobody spoke. Back between the toddler and old lady, Mom sat rigid, her shadowed face unreadable. Her excitement a moment ago was long gone, but she still aimed her cellphone camera at Josie. *Still recording.*

"Thanks, Dad," Josie said. "Stay gone."

Murmuring in the crowd, as Josie left the podium. Half-smiling with a focused look of concern, Clara's expression meant she knew. *She knows I saw something.* Somehow, Clara always knew. Around the edge of the audience, Josie walked straight back toward an exhibit hall, where a grizzly bear posed in mid-snarl over a pair of deer. Her tongue tasted like coppery adrenaline, and she checked the empty spot where Dad's ghost had been. Of course, he wasn't there. Mom stepped into her path, but Josie didn't stop. Behind them, the principal read another name.

"I can't believe you did that, Josie," Mom said. "After everything…"

Mom followed her into the hall, the backup lights casting long shadows up both walls. *Makes this all so dramatic. Storm outside, storm in here, too. 'After everything.'* Moving to a smaller, shittier apartment in a sketchy neighborhood of Brooklyn, barely seeing each other most nights, because Mom worked late. The flipside of 'Team Mom and Josie.' *That 'everything'?*

Josie whirled to face her. "I'm not pissed at you, Mom …"

Mom's eyes and nose were swollen red, as if she were fighting back tears. *Shit.* In the rush Josie had felt at the podium, she hadn't thought it through. Impulsive and self-sabotaging. But Mom should understand. She resented Dad as much—maybe more—than Josie, didn't she? Except now, Mom looked like she'd been slapped. She shook, hugging both arms together, with a scrunched-up graduation program in one fist. *I did this, hurt her.*

The thought made the exhibit hall sway off-balance, and Josie hugged her mother tight. "I'm sorry."

Mom's reassuring skin and lavender shampoo scent was so specifically *her* that Josie's tension melted.

"I was just angry," Josie said.

*And—don't say it—scared. That's why I saw his imaginary ghost again. My brain is in desperation mode, because of course I'm terrified about the fall.* Last week, welcome emails started arriving from New York University with the dates of Freshman orientation in September. Just a subway ride away, but NYU still meant swapping the apartment with Mom for a dorm—and what if Clara moved, too? She was taking a gap year, still hadn't picked a college. *Or maybe she has and didn't tell me.* In high school, Josie had developed predictable rhythms for the first time, without worrying about packing up her room for a new school. Before that, Dad moved them constantly. *And now, boom: over, sorry, move on. Find a new island to settle. Catan is full up.*

"What possessed you up there?" Mom asked. "Seriously, Josie. That wasn't like you."

Josie leaned away again. Mom kept her arm close, like she didn't want to let go, as if she were worried she might need to fend off the dead animals in the exhibits around them.

"I don't know. I was thinking about Dad, and standing up there ..."

"And standing up there, you decided to let everybody know ..."

Closer to the museum lobby, they passed an evergreen forest scene, displaying large, black-necked birds, with distinctive white-black heads and ruffly brown feathered bodies above white bellies. *Canadian geese, obviously, I recognize them without even checking the birding app.* A dramatized scene from Mom's suburban Toronto childhood, maybe? It didn't look real.

Mom shook her head again, as if she still couldn't process what just happened. "I wouldn't call your father 'selfish'."

*Really?* Everything related to why that alcoholic dick did what he did was usually off-limits, as far as Mom was concerned. Josie had learned to avoid Dad questions and ignore her memories. Neither of them even attended the funeral. When a 'Dad thought' surfaced, Josie had tried to stuff it down, focus on something else. Except he'd once made her laugh until she snorted milk out her nose by imitating a Canadian goose, just like the one in that museum exhibit. Josie had tagged a goose in Central Park on the app, and when she showed Dad, he'd stretched out both arms like a bird, pretending to be lost in New York and asking for directions in an absurd French-Canadian accent.

"Josie!" Waving her rolled up diploma, Clara rushed over in a swell of fabric—a maroon goddess of freckly sex. *She looks amazing in literally anything.* It wasn't fair. She came in for a quick kiss and took

Josie's hand. "The vice principal is looking for you. I don't think he was a fan of your speech." And to Mom, "Caitlyn, I'm sorry I put Josie up to that. I encouraged her."

Josie squeezed Clara's hand. *She's still throwing herself in front to protect me, always.*

Mom looked back into the auditorium, where the principal's voice echoed with more students' names. "It's okay, Clara. I didn't expect my daughter to yell 'asshole' in the Natural History Museum, but if that's her big act of teenage rebellion, it's not the end of the world. Lord knows, I said worse at your age. Are Bill and Kate here?"

Josie tried to imagine a dyed hair and grunge-makeup 1990s high school version of Mom pumping her fist on a graduation stage in Ontario. Didn't seem plausible.

"No, they couldn't make it." Clara's fingers tensed, just for a moment, on Josie's.

*She always pretends it doesn't bother her. Even if her foster parents deserve a microphone slam, like Dad.* Bill and Kate had skipped out any chance they got as long as Josie had known Clara. *Since we met right before freshman year, when Clara helped me up from that flooded riverbank. The first time I saw his ghost.*

*Stop.*

"Clara, we missed you last night," Mom said. "My office got comp tickets, but Josie said you were out of town visiting schools?"

Clara was usually all-in for Broadway tickets. But not this time. Totally unlike her ... but also not—if she planned to dump Josie now that summer was here. *You still won't talk about what you're going to do during your 'gap year' next year.* Now, before Clara could respond, the vice principal appeared at the edge of the auditorium, glaring.

"Crap," Clara said. "Go, Josie."

As Mom and Clara moved to intercept him, Josie darted to the end of the hall. A rope line separated the graduation ceremony area from the veiny-pink marble lobby. Flooded with natural light from the front windows, the wide room echoed with the laughter of tour groups and families. *Dad's ghost isn't real, of course. The other time I saw him, I was suffering from heat exhaustion, and ...*

And Josie's dad waited for her under the yawning skeleton of a Tyrannosaurus Rex.

# Chapter Two

Josie stopped. The sounds of the lobby quieted, and the movement of people fuzzied around the sharp focus of her father. He smiled, totally calm and ordinary-looking. Just like the last time.

*No, Dad wasn't in the auditorium, and he can't be here. He's very gone.* Josie closed her eyes, concentrated on her breathing and the swell of her heartbeat, and then checked again.

Dad waved. "Josie, can I talk to you for a second?"

His voice lilted with the same veiled southern accent she knew from a thousand childhood dinner-table conversations. Dr. Laymon had helped her wall over the memory of their last conversation. *Because it wasn't real.* 'Put it in a safe space you can visit,' he'd said. 'Where it can't get out on its own. You control the memory.'

*I don't control this. I'm losing it.*

Slowly, Josie approached her father. A nearby informational placard read, *'The Worst Day in 66 Million Years: How Dinosaurs Went Extinct.'* Maybe that day was number one, but today was on track for a close second.

"Even if you're here," Josie told her father's ghost, "I don't think you're real."

"It's good to see you, too, sweetheart," he said. "But let's play that out. Okay, suppose I'm not real. What then?"

*I don't want to hear this.* The lobby beyond Dad and the dinosaur bones felt vague, as if Josie needed eyeglasses to make it register. *Contact lenses for my senses.*

Of course, she'd worked all this out with Dr. Laymon. The last time, four years ago—when she met Clara and saw her father's ghost—a part of her must have known that he was in trouble. A part of her exhausted, panicked lizard brain created an imaginary conversation with her father on a riverbank bridge, below a highway overpass in Kentucky. It wasn't uncommon, that's what Dr. Laymon said. People had virtual conversations with loved ones all the time. The only difference: unknown to her, Dad had killed himself twelve hours earlier.

*No. That was four years ago. He bailed, and Mom panicked. We went to find you, too late. I'm better now.*

"What do you want?" she asked.

"If we play this out—"

"No," she said, concentrating on the Tyrannosaurus display, not her imaginary Dad. She flattened her palms on the railing around the exhibit and looked up at its small front arms and bulging ribcage. Its jaws were lined with teeth the size of chop-block steak knives. Never mind the movies, it didn't seem possible this monster was ever alive—and with feathers. *Focus on the dinosaur.* "I'm not 'playing anything out,'" Josie said, "because you're not here."

"Okay," Dad said.

He always did that. Sidestepped, when she expected him to go straight. Josie glared at him, and yes, he was still, stubbornly there, solid as ever.

*"Okay?"*

"Yes," he said simply. "I can't convince you otherwise. And maybe I'm not real. But then that means you're talking to yourself. Anything I tell you, you already know, right? Things you don't want to acknowledge, until you hear them from someone else."

"Like my dead father."

Dad smiled, his eyes wrinkling and bright for an instant. "Yes, like him. The dead deadbeat. Ballsy, by the way. I like what you did back there. Your mother must have been pissed, though."

"Why are you here, Dad?" Josie asked and forced herself to look away again. *Don't get sucked in. This is what delusions do. They make you want to burrow down the rabbit hole.* "The last time I saw you—the last time I *imagined* I saw you ..."

"I know. I wasn't in a good place then. I am sorry about that, Josie."

"I don't want to hear this." She closed her eyes again, heartbeat too loud in both ears. Her sinuses clicked and cleared. *Slow breaths. Calm down.* "Not like this. You said ten days—why?"

"Okay, that's how you want to play this. I respect that. You don't believe in me, I understand. We'll skip the sentiment and jump in. Ten days is how long you have until this all goes away."

That was pure Dad. A vague, depressive proclamation that managed to be grandiose and trivial at once.

"You want to tell me what that means?" Josie asked.

"Open your eyes, Josie." She did, and he gestured at the dinosaur skeleton, then pointed to a display with a giant, mollusk fossil near the far wall. "Remember when I used to talk about 'extinction events'? Do you think they had any idea what was about to happen to them? That they'd be in a museum like this someday? Cautionary tales, right? Josie, monsters are waking up. Deep underground, almost to the surface, and they do not mess around."

"You were always the crazy one, not me," Josie said and spotted a security guard. "Unless I *am* talking to myself. Will he see you, too?"

"Please, Josie," Dad said. "Even if I'm just here telling you what some part of you already knows, you have to listen to that, right?"

"No, I don't." Josie waved to the security guard. "Hey, excuse me? Can you help me?"

The guard perked up, already approaching.

"They're called 'blacklegs,'" Dad said quickly, as if he were running out of time. "The Kentucky dragon found them in the limestone. In ten days, they'll reach the surface. They're afraid of you, Josie. They know you can hurt them, if you go back."

"Go back where?" Josie asked, smiling at the security guard, still out of earshot.

*I know where. I'm not going back to Kentucky. Not ever.*

"The early ones, some of the blacklegs are already here. Like hungry cicadas. They'll start with your family, now that the tree is gone. Please, Josie, listen to me ..."

A tour group in neon yellow shirts surged between Josie and the security guard, blocking him in a swell of excited shouting and selfie sticks.

"This sounds insane, Dad." Josie looked at her father. He didn't flicker or lose substance but that word—'insane'—withered his expression a little. He knew it, too. Dead or not, of course he did.

"It's complicated," he said quietly. "Maybe I'm not here. Maybe. I know why she didn't, but I thought your mother would bring you to the funeral."

"Mom was a wreck, Dad." *Both of us were.*

"I know." He smiled sadly. "Or maybe I don't. But which way is worse? Really? Which do you want to believe?"

"Which what?"

"The reality that you're talking to yourself right now." He glanced past her to the nearby security guard. "Or that you're not?"

Josie followed Dad's stare to the guard, started to ask if he could see—but Dad was gone. No smoke or fade out, just erased. Josie turned in a slow circle. *They'll start with your family.* And there was Clara, stepping around the hallway rope line, with Mom behind her.

Josie apologized briefly to the security guard and went to meet Clara. "Don't ask."

"About the security guard," Clara said, and then, too quietly for Mom to hear, "or what you're pretending you didn't see right before your impromptu speech earlier?"

How did Clara always know? She understood Josie too well, that's how. *Don't think about any of it. Just tell me it's going to be okay.* This wasn't a riddle to be solved. It was just neural noise.

Josie squeezed her hand. "How about don't ask about both?"

"No deal."

Mom came closer behind them, and past the lobby, they stepped outside into a press of wet wind. On the surrounding blocks of apartment towers, people hunched into rainy gusts, most behind umbrellas that flapped and bucked. The air smelled charged and alive, like a damp electrical wire. *Maybe not far off.* Down the museum steps, Josie saw six lanes of taxis, cars, and delivery trucks stopped on Central Park West. High, leafy tree branches thrashed in the park past the stone perimeter wall. The sky looked like rotten soup. *Cream of mushroom—the worst.*

*But no more high school!*

*So, there's that.*

*I'm not getting hung up on an imaginary conversation with Dad's ghost or that nonsense Kentucky shitshow. And why did Dad's ghost have to skew so reasonable? 'Oh, I'm not real? Okay, no problem. Let's play that out and talk about monsters anyway.' Real or not, that was him, though. Always.*

When they crossed the Williamsburg Bridge into Brooklyn on the subway ride home, the New York City skyline glowed like fuzzy almost-stars in the gray rain.

"Which means they'll need me late tonight," Mom said, at their stop. "There will be flooding and more outages."

Climbing the subway station steps, Josie held Clara's hand and tried to tune out Mom's storm warning. Four years ago, Mom had swapped corporate law for long hours and less money in a city government office managing environmental preparedness. 'A contradiction in terms,' she'd said. Only once, last fall, when Mom came home late to find Josie still watching TV did Mom really explain why she did it. 'I owe you more than *this*.' Mom had gestured at their cramped apartment, with mice behind the oven, no sunlight, and a leaky toilet. 'If we don't have a home that lasts, you should at least get a planet that does.' Josie had nodded and said she understood. *If you can't fix our family, try to repair the world. Yeah, good luck with that.* At NYU, Josie planned to study something—*anything*—that looked in, not out. Focus on people, rather than the unfeeling mess of the environment. Human beings were messed up, sure, but not like the oceans and forests Mom cared so much about. And anyway, wasn't the point of school, a job, all of it, just to be safe? Josie would never say it to Mom, but adventure and striving—that all felt too much like a performance for an audience that didn't care. *All played out, as Dad would say.*

Lots of Josie's and Clara's friends were having parties or elaborate dinners in the city tonight. Yvette even got a corvette—'Yvette's little red corvette,' Clara said—as a graduation present. Cliché of a cliché. *Not us, though. And I wouldn't want it any other way.* They walked from the subway and hiked up three flights of stairs to Josie and Mom's apartment. Inside, Josie squeezed between overstuffed bookshelves and drying racks in the entry hall to change out of her graduation robe in her bedroom. A glorified closet, her room was decorated with hanging glass birds and finch-shaped windchimes, and was just big enough for a mattress and dresser. Back in the kitchen, the room smelled like the garlic and red wine tomato sauce that had been simmering in a crockpot all day—Josie's favorite. And now Mom found a Ziploc bag of raw, marinating steak in the fridge to prep for the spicy tacos Clara loved.

"We're doing Frank and Joan, if you're good with that?" Clara asked Mom.

Frank Sinatra and Joan Jett was a music playlist of oldies from Mom's youth mixed with the oldies-oldies from decades earlier that Clara liked. Drum machines and orchestral swooning, Josie could relax to either. She'd never been picky, as long as they were happy.

"Play it loud," Mom said. "Clara, do you want to be our sous chef?"

Mom handed Clara the short, high-end cutting knife that always made Josie uncomfortable. 'Sharp enough to cut paper,' Dad had said, when the shipping box arrived from Europe at their old apartment in Boston. When he started to explain the differences between American, German, and Japanese knives, Mom had tried to change the subject. Josie remembered Dad fell silent, staring hard at his reflection in the blade, as he said, 'Don't. *Cut* me off.' Then a smile broke across his face. 'That's what the knife is for.'

A Dad joke *par excellence.* Now, as Josie went to set the table, she pictured his contagious grin. He'd known he frightened Mom on his bad days, couldn't control it, but still he played it up back then with a pun. Pretended to be moody for a laugh. And it had been funny, so corny it worked.

Dad had good days, bad days, and 'workdays.' Not normal office workdays, like Mom, although he had those, too. Mom's job as a lawyer was easy to explain. But Josie never knew exactly what Dad did at the construction sites where he worked. When she asked about those jobs, he always shrugged off the questions with 'electrical wiring, building, tear downs—you name it, Josie,' as if it were all the same. And they didn't last long. His jobs were incidental, like clothing that he swapped to keep warm across climates. At home, Dad huddled over notebooks and folders, the kind that used to clutter their living room. 'Research,' he'd said. That was his *real* work, manic scribbling. Over the years she'd decided it was related to his therapy, which explained the parental radio silence. Better not to know.

"... too much saline in the water tables," Mom said, as she tasted the pasta sauce. Josie had missed the first part of the conversation. "They're cutting down the ghost forests in Central Park."

As Josie arranged the plates and silverware on their too-large table—a tag-a-long from their Upper West Side apartment, like most of the furniture—she asked, "Ghost forests?"

"Oh, I'm sure you've seen it." Mom's cellphone buzzed.

*Already? Is she getting called in before we even eat dinner?*

"Because of all the fallen branches, the city is getting rid of dead trees. Like Mark's old maple."

*Mark's old maple. Dad's tree.*

Mom answered her phone, and Josie realized she was grabbing the edge of the table. *The tree in Central Park.* She'd deliberately avoided it since the impromptu phone burial four years ago. Mom still didn't know about that, of course. Back then, Josie had returned from their flash trip to Kentucky with a new best friend, who seemed to effortlessly get her. Clara. And in a spike of fourteen-year-old rebellion, Josie snatched Dad's old phone. The bastard was buried hundreds of miles away anyway, right? No one would call. So in Central Park, Josie and Clara stashed it inside a shoebox in a shallow grave by Dad's tree. 'To mark his passing,' Dr. Laymon had said. Which still made Josie smile. To *mark* Mark's passing. Not 'haha funny,' but Dad would have appreciated it.

Clara didn't look up from the cutting board, where she sliced green peppers and onions.

Mom ended the call and sighed. "I need some help downstairs. Josie? That was the building manager, the basement is flooding."

While Clara manned the kitchen, Josie followed Mom to the laundry and storage basement.

"Their roots can't grow with so much salt in the soil," Mom said, when Josie asked about the ghost trees—careful not to mention Dad. Mom was right, Josie had seen dead, bare-branch trees in parks and along sidewalks. But not Dad's tree, not the shoebox grave.

Sure enough, in the basement, there was already a couple inches of standing water, and more dripped down the stone-cut walls. So, Josie and Mom splashed into the rear storage closet and found the three boxes of crap that had been stored here since they moved in.

"You want to grab that one, and I'll—" Mom slipped and went down in a splash of muck.

Josie shouted and grabbed Mom's arm to help her up. Gasping, Mom braced her right leg. The water wasn't deep, but Mom's ankle had twisted the wrong way. She always said Josie had that side of the family to thank for her weak ankles. *But I'll take soft joints over alcoholism and schizophrenia any day.*

"I've got you." Josie draped Mom's left arm over her shoulders. Carefully, Josie helped her hop with a dragging slide of her leg, all the way back up to their apartment.

Inside, Clara was on her cell and quickly ended the call when she saw them. Beside her, ribbons of onions and peppers simmered in a meaty pool with the steak on a stovetop skillet. "Sorry. I have to get home."

"No, you don't," Josie said. "Clara, it's graduation, and our favorites."

"I know." Clara prodded the skillet fixings with a wooden spoon, and they spurted white smoke. "Save some for me?"

Mom collapsed into a kitchen chair. "I think I just twisted my ankle. Before you run, do you mind ... the boxes?"

"We'll get them, Mom," Josie said, still frowning at Clara.

On the stairs down to the basement, Josie stopped. "You're not really leaving, are you?"

"They got me a cake."

*Amazing.* Still, a cake from Bill and Kate was rarer than a corvette. *But, of course, they didn't invite your girlfriend.*

"But does it have to be tonight?" Josie asked.

Clara touched Josie's cheek and traced her jaw. "You're amazing to look at when you're upset. So *severe.*"

Josie's cheeks got hot. "Don't do that. This isn't funny."

Clara sighed and started down the stairs again. "You know I'll see you again tomorrow and whenever you want."

"Just not tonight, I guess, when we planned to be together. Here." She found Clara's lucky fossil in her pocket and gave it back. "Ceremony is over now."

It was childish, but Clara didn't argue, just took the fossil back. Josie shouldn't have to be alone now. Not after high school ended and the hallucination at the museum. With the open expanse of summer and no classes to organize their weeks, what if this was how Clara ended things? Not like a light switching on-off but a lamp with a dimmer. *My girlfriend just fades out ... end scene.*

They lugged up three waterlogged junk boxes from the flooded storage room, and when they neared the apartment with the last one,

Clara said, "You have to tell me, you know, what happened during the ceremony."

"I was going to, but you're leaving early."

Clara let the box drop.

"Seriously, stop." She nodded her forehead against Josie's, so their eyes were blurry-close, and Josie tasted Clara's tomato-garlic breath. "Josie, nothing is changing. Not with us, okay?"

Josie's pulse jittered. She started to answer back with a snarky retort, caught herself. *Stop. She means it.*

"Okay," Josie said.

"I'll call the moment I'm outside." Clara stood straight again, and they lifted the box. "And you'll tell me about the thing today?"

The thing. After so many years, why did I see—*imagine*—Dad's ghost today? Telling Clara would make him feel a little less like a hallucination, because then there would be questions. And he said that in ten days—*stop.*

"Yes," Josie said. "I'll tell you all about it. Just not with Mom around. And you have to promise not to freak."

"No, I don't."

They arranged the musty boxes on the TV room floor.

"We can sort them tomorrow," Mom said. "Anything gross, we'll toss. I have to head into the office, too. Clara, I can walk you to the subway or, I should say, you can walk me."

"No, Mom," Josie said. "Your ankle is hurt. You shouldn't be going out."

"Sorry, no choice. I'll try not to be too late." *Yeah, right.*

Mom hop-limped to shrug on a raincoat and grabbed her briefcase in the hall. At the table, Clara kissed Josie. The gentle touch of Clara's lips blotted out the nagging at the back of Josie's mind, but when she pulled away, tension came back. *Everyone's leaving. For work and graduation cake, but still.*

When she was alone, Josie finished cooking the tacos, then the pasta. With her phone tethered to a wall socket charger, she tapped through apps onscreen, only half-thinking.

She flipped past icons of games, news, and the birding app. The Christmas before Dad left, he'd bought her a lifetime subscription. The program could identify local birds by their songs and tag locations in a global database, with other birders. At the time, Josie had even thought she might reconnect with Michele and Tom in Chicago. After all, they'd gotten her into birding in the first place back in middle school. Dad's eyes were wide and excited when Josie unwrapped her new phone. He'd helped her use the app to take a picture of a sparrow on a window ledge outside their old 10th floor apartment. Then, he had spotted a crow and downloaded the app for himself to tag it. 'We can bird as a team,' he'd said. Mom watched from the edge of the room, arms crossed, monitoring him. 'Team Pigeon,' Dad said.

'Should I make you guys shirts?' Mom had asked.

'Shirts and hats,' Dad said. He'd placed his phone alongside Josie's to compare the birds. 'When Josie learns to drive, we can get bumper stickers. 'Bird Nerd 4 Life.'

*Yeah, right.*

Josie hadn't used the app in months. And, of course, she never tried to contact Michele or Tom with the app. It had been too long. For two years in Chicago, Michele and Tom accepted Josie, as if the empty chair at their lunch table had always been hers. They didn't laugh at her southern twang or mock her as the new girl. She'd been born in Kentucky but only really remembered their houses in Tennessee and Indiana, before the two good years in Chicago. Weekend sleepovers were packed with gossip, board games, and neighborhood bird hunts across Lincoln Park. Until Dad told Josie they had to go—all the way to Boston. And even then, facing Michele and Tom amid a pile of U-Haul boxes in Josie's railroad apartment, she swore to stay in touch. Michele and Tom promised to visit her in Massachusetts, and Josie could come back on holidays. They'd stay best friends.

Except they didn't. *Because we were kids.* Josie sent emails and even mailed three old-fashioned letters. Nothing. At first, Josie cried at night and kept quiet at her new school. She hid the hollowed out feeling in her guts from Mom and Dad, until it slowly scabbed over. And when they moved again, this time to Connecticut, the numb act became real. By then, Michele and Tom felt less real, like characters in a movie, not kids she'd actually known. And Josie stopped trying to make friends. *Until Clara.* But she kept birding, until the bird numbers became so uber-depressing, she couldn't deal.

Dad had hoped the birding app would make the two of them a team again in New York. *We were a team—until you left.* Mom taught Josie to drive, not Dad. And she didn't do it to show off a birding slogan—they didn't even own a car—but so Josie could be prepared. Always. 'It's part of leveling up,' Mom had said. Not 'growing up'—'leveling.' As if skills like driving, swimming, cooking, even birding, advanced Josie's character in one of the ancient video games Mom and Dad had played before she was born.

The phone screen flashed to display an incoming call, with Josie's contact photo of Clara laughing, vanilla ice cream on her nose. Two summers ago, Josie had taken that photo on a fossil hike in Connecticut. They'd missed the Amtrak train back to New York and found an old-fashioned ice cream truck on the New London waterfront. No fossils, though. Josie remembered Clara grumbling right up until Josie smushed a waffle cone into her face—hence the shocked laugh in that profile shot.

She tapped to answer the call and put it on speaker. "Hey again."

"So," Clara said, her voice muffled by wind and street sounds. "Tell me what happened at the museum today."

Josie ate a mouthful of noodles. "Sorry, are you going through a tunnel? You're breaking up."

"Breaking up is hard to do," Clara said. *She loves her retro songs.* "Fess up, Josie. Come on. You saw something. What?"

Josie sighed. *Don't think, just talk.* "It was my dad."

A long pause, and then Clara said, "What do you mean? Like you imagined ..?"

"Of course I imagined," Josie said, but the tremor in her voice called BS. *Maybe. That's the word he used, right? Maybe-maybe.* "Obviously, he wasn't there, but I saw him anyway." She sighed, tried to smile. "Your girlfriend is nuts again."

"Wouldn't have you any other way," Clara said. "What did you dad's imaginary ghost want?"

"I'm not supposed to fixate on this stuff, right?" *I'm talking too fast.* "The last time, Dr. Laymon told me to try to put it in a box, like lucid dreaming. You know you're dreaming, so you can control it."

"The last time was a long time ago, Josie." Clara's voice dipped, worried.

"Four years, that's not ..."

"What did he want?"

"He wasn't there, Clara," Josie said. *He wanted to warn me about monsters called 'blacklegs' and a countdown. Something to do with dinosaurs and mollusks.* A slow tug of muscley panic formed in her chest. *What if it is real somehow? It isn't, and in ten days I'll know.*

Someone knocked on the front door.

The tension uncoiled beneath Josie's ribs. She smiled. "Is that you?"

"Is what me? What are you talking about?" Clara asked.

Josie left the phone to charge on the table and went into the hall. Clara had done this before—the sneaky double-back, after Mom left. Clara wasn't really ditching Josie tonight. That had been a ruse. Annoying earlier, but amazing now.

"I'm on to you." Josie reached to unlatch the chain.

From the kitchen phone, Clara said, "Seriously, what are you—"

The door banged open. *Not her.*

# Chapter Three

A white orb, flat like a dinner plate, hovered in the doorway. It had gray eye indentations that streaked down, like it was crying. No mouth and only a nubbed nose. Not hovering, it was a mask on a shadow figure. Josie stepped back, knocking into the drying rack, and the figure clomped in. *Hooves, it has actual hooves.* A warped Josie reflection squiggled on the mask. Behind the glass mask, its head and neck were dark flesh, veined and slick. Hard insect wings folded down against its bare back, and tangled fur was matted along its waist and crooked legs.

It was dragging a chain with one arm that caught, and something heavy thumped in the hall, around the corner—a woman, pale and naked, being dragged by the neck, with a shaved head, duct-taped mouth, and frightened, wild eyes. *Why isn't she fighting?* She didn't have any arms, just bandaged elbow stumps, and past her shivering stomach and groin, both of her legs were severed at the knees, with stained towels tied tight by rubber-hose tourniquets.

Behind Josie, Clara called on the phone, "Josie? What's happening? Is someone at the door?"

*Yeah.*

*This is real. This is happening now.*

Josie backed away, past Mom's bedroom and the bathroom. From the apartment stairwell outside, she heard faint singing and flute music, with a steady drumbeat underneath. The glass-face man huffed and sniffed, like a dog. He jerked the cut-up woman by the chain into the entry hall. She saw Josie, eyes wide, and murmured into the duct tape. The wrongness of it numbed Josie's mind, but she felt her hand shaking, as she braced on a bookshelf. *Move. Help her.*

Clara's voice was tiny on the kitchen-table phone. "Is everything okay? Josie, seriously, answer me."

*No.*

"Burn," the glass-face man said, his voice hoarse.

Josie tried to speak, couldn't. Her throat caught. When he came closer, she smelled an iron, oily stink. Blood, that was a butcher shop smell, like when she and Mom went downtown last Thanksgiving and stopped to get a duck. No turkey that year. It was just the two of them since Clara celebrated Thanksgiving with her foster parents. Josie had been surrounded in that cold shop by the hanging pink flesh of birds and pigs. And as the friendly owner helped Mom pick and weigh a duck. Josie had watched a kid—maybe ten or eleven years old—chop up a slab of meat on a table behind the counter. The kid had looked right at her, a wet butcher's knife in one hand. Then he picked up a foot—a pig's hoof—and wagged it at her, smiling. He set it on the table, still grinning, and hacked it open, so the hoof split to expose joints and blubbery pale muscle. That was this smell, the same open-animal taste in her mouth.

The glass-face man pressed closer. She could still run. *Where? No door in the TV room. My room.*

*Help the chained woman.*

Clara's voice turned to static on the phone speaker. Josie's bedroom was close, three steps back, almost to the kitchen. *Go.*

"Burn," he huffed again.

Something moved behind her, and Josie spun. Across the kitchen, by the stove, a second, smaller figure watched, the window wide open behind it. The figure's face was swollen—a fish—and it raised a knife. *Our knife.* The dangerous, short knife Clara had used earlier, still streaked with steak juice.

"She needs rest," the fish man said. Its voice gurgled with phlegm. "Give the treatment plan time to work. Trust the prescriptions."

*Talking to me or the glass-face man? Either way, it's impossible. That has to be a costume.*

The fish man cocked its head to aim a vacant eye at Josie. "Where do you think you are right now?"

Josie held the bookshelf. *Now. I have to.*

"Don't worry," the fish man said. "You are safe now. None of what you see is real."

Josie shoved off the wall and into her bedroom, slammed the door, and stabbed the doorknob lock button. *I left that woman out there.* No sound from the hall. If they were following, they weren't loud. Josie's fists tapped against the door. She couldn't hold still. *My phone. I left it on the kitchen table.* Josie rubbed her shaking arms and heard her own breathing, too fast. She felt her pulse in both ears, but with a strange, tense calm. *Survival mode. I have to get out of here.* If she climbed across her bed, she could adjust the blinds, knock out the window screen, and—*and what?* Her bedroom window opened over a side alley, three stories up. No ledge and nothing but a sheer fall. *Far enough to break my leg at least.* The fire escape was in the kitchen, out the open window behind the fish man.

Still, no sound past her door. *That thing—a person, a person in a costume—had a woman on a chain, and … stop. Just listen.* Time swam with the steady rhythm of her heart and breathing. For a long time, she waited. No one. The front door slammed, and footsteps pounded into the hall. Josie's bedroom door bounced against her arm. Someone knocked. "Josie, are you in there?"

*Clara.*

*What if it isn't her?* Josie kept her hand on the latch. *Of course, it's her.*

"Josie?" Clara asked again from the other side of the door. "We were on the phone, and you cut out. Something was wrong. Open the door."

*Don't.*

Josie fingered the doorknob, took a slow breath. *It is. It has to be her. Don't lose it completely.* And she opened the door.

Clara grabbed her, and Josie stared at the empty hall.

"What happened?" Clara asked.

*What happened?*

*A man in a glass mask broke in, dragging a woman on a chain who was missing her limbs. A fish man held your knife and told me none of it was real. That.*

"Did you see?" Josie asked. "Are they gone?"

Clara shook her head. "Who?"

Slowly, Josie leaned out, gripping Clara's hand, probably too hard. No one in the hall to the left, empty kitchen on the right. Her phone was still on the table. *I did not imagine it. It happened.* Before Clara could ask again, Josie told her. The trembling in Josie's arms turned to a cold shiver, as she went to shut the kitchen window, then knelt by the floorboards at the front door.

"Look," Josie said. Fresh scratches and streaks from the woman and the chain. "They were here." Clara examined the marks, too. *She doesn't know what to say. What do I want her to say? 'We're safe now?' We aren't.*

Josie locked the door again, and after checking the apartment, she found the kitchen knife—the blade the fish man had been holding—on the counter by the cutting board, the counter and stove still packed with uneaten spaghetti and tacos. She forced herself to sit at the table. Still, Clara hadn't spoken.

"You're missing your cake," Josie said.

Clara leaned on a chair across the table, her hair a damp, reddish swirl around her right cheek that frizzed down to the top of her chest on the silk graduation robe. *I want to hold her. Throw her onto my bed and never let go.* But what if their relationship was running out of time, too? Just like the calendar. The thought made Josie imagine Clara on the sidewalk with another girl, laughing and holding hands. *Don't. She's here now.* Josie willed the image away.

"Thank you for coming back," Josie said. "This wasn't a trick to get you here."

"I know. I believe you."

Of course, Clara believed her. Whether or not it was real.

"But you have to be more careful," Clara said. "Let's say for a minute you saw all that, and those people were here. Opening the door like that, without checking? Something could've happened. There are some crazy, dangerous people in this city. That's not okay, Josie."

"I thought it was you. I feel so stupid."

"You're the smartest person I know. Careless, though." Clara half-smiled. "And maybe in desperate need of spooning?"

The way she said 'desperate' made Josie look down at her phone. *Because she's right. I do need her.* The table between them made Josie breathe harder, like a block between two magnets. *I'm just wired from the break-in. If it happened, that's what it was, right?*

"I should call Mom." Josie found Mom's contact on her phone. It dialed and went to voicemail. Josie left a short, stuttering message, without any details to spook Mom, but ended it, "Please, just call when you can. Love you …" And clicked off.

"The police?" Josie asked Clara.

Clara's cheeks were flushed, probably from running back in the rain outside.

"Maybe a good idea," Clara said.

"Do you have to go again?"

A slow smile started across Clara's face, and she rolled her fingers up and down the chair-back, as if it were an instrument. "Why? Is there something you want to do, now that we're alone?"

"Yes," Josie said. "I really do."

She went to Clara and kissed her, with her tongue pressing to open her lips wide, a hand on her chest to cup one breast.

Clara murmured, almost a purr, and then pulled away slightly. Her eyes were glassy calm. "What about the police?"

"In a minute."

In Josie's bedroom, she kicked the door shut, and as Clara yanked up her graduation robe, Josie rolled to lock them in. *If the glass-face man comes back, he'll have to wait.*

But only about twenty minutes.

When they both lay sweaty and naked under Josie's bedsheets, she traced the outline of a mole on Clara's right shoulder. Her freckles stood out like polarized stars against the pinkish white curves of her skin.

"Spend the night?" Josie asked. "This qualifies as an emergency, and Mom won't mind."

She might, though, because Josie hadn't asked permission. But who's to say that wasn't why Josie called her?

"Only if you promise not to shut me out," Clara said. "And talk."

That was code for 'no getting defensive.' Their only real fight last year left Josie crying into her pillow and Mom frantic, after Clara asked too many questions about Dad, and Josie made her to leave. That mini-break up lasted exactly one day. One fight in four years. They'd been together since October of Freshman year. After the final bell, Clara had walked Josie to the midtown Shake Shack decorated with Halloween pumpkins and cut-out witches, near Times Square.

Back then, across from Josie in a corner booth, Clara had lowered her voice. 'Two things,' Clara said. 'Promise you won't be irritated.'

Picking at her fries and sipping a vanilla milkshake, Josie had said, 'No deal.'

'Thing one: I like you,' Clara said. 'Two: I got the part.'

She'd auditioned for Juliet in the fall play.

'Wait,' Josie said. 'You're the lead? That's amazing.'

'You'll have to wait for me after a lot of rehearsals.'

The first point registered in Josie's mind. 'You're probably my best friend,' she said. *Probably.* Of course Clara was. Nevermind they'd only known each other for five months, they both knew it.

'No.' Clara leaned in. Her eyes shadowed in sexy pockets in the right light—any light, really. Even in a phosphorescent fast food glow. 'Not like that, Josie. Well, like that, but also ...'

She kissed Josie on the lips, slowly at first, as if waiting for Josie to pull away. Then, Clara's mouth opened, so their tongues touched, and the noises, grease smells, entirety of the restaurant softened around the hot tingling in Josie's body.

When Clara pulled back, her eyes misted. 'And?'

'I do, too.'

Clara's face lit up, and she half-slumped back in the booth. 'Thank God! I didn't know if you ... for certain ...'

'Me neither.' Not really true, though. Josie knew, but never had a girlfriend. Never even kissed anyone except William Samuelson in Indianapolis, during first grade recess, when a group of kids had pressured her into truth-or-dare.

'This is our first date then,' Clara said, raising her hamburger to toast. 'Will you be jealous of Romeo?'

Josie tapped her milkshake against the burger. 'Absolutely.'

Now, alone in Mom and Josie's Brooklyn apartment, Josie kissed Clara's shoulder as they lay in her bed. "I won't shut you out," Josie said. "Deal."

Clara looked up at her with a mock-serious frown. "Well, then you probably shouldn't be alone right now. Tell Caitlyn in the morning?"

"Of course."

But they didn't, because Mom didn't come home.

# Chapter Four

In the morning, it was tough to tell by the wet shadows in the back alley, if the storm was completely over. The kitchen window just showed a narrow courtyard of brick buildings past the fire escape. As Clara got out cereal and Josie finished cleaning the dishes from last night, she called down the hall to ask if Mom wanted anything. No answer. Josie went to rap on Mom's door. It opened to a neatly made black comforter bedsheet and still bedroom, with window blinds closed tight. No sign of Mom's shoes or the coat she wore last night. The air smelled dusty, without a trace of Mom's lavender shampoo or familiar body scent. *She didn't come back.*

*They'll start with your family.*

"Weird." Josie headed back into the kitchen. She tried Mom's cell. Straight to voicemail. "She's never done this before."

Bleary-eyed—not a morning person—Clara set out two cereal bowls and dumped nut-and-wheat crumbles into hers. And she always picked the cereal that looked like gerbil food. Josie found a box of kids' marshmallow cereal in a cabinet by the fridge and sat to eat.

"Her phone probably died," Clara said. "I'm sure she'll be back any minute."

*That's right. Mom will be back soon.*

But she wasn't. Not that morning, while they finished breakfast, showered, and watched a dumb reality TV show past the row of oversized basement boxes. Or later, after Clara left, when Josie lay on her bed, aimlessly scrolling through her phone, reading entertainment news, solving crossword puzzles—anything to take her mind off how quiet the apartment was.

When Mom worked late, she always called to check in, which meant her phone must be broken or out of battery. If Josie left the apartment, she might not know when Mom came in. Besides, with this slow-ramping tightness in Josie's chest, what was she supposed to do? *I should stay in until she gets back.* But by the evening, as daylight shadowed outside, still no Mom, so Josie called again—for the third time—left another message, and then looked up Mom's main office number.

A man told her Mom wasn't there.

"After the storm, do you know what time she left?" Josie asked.

"Caitlyn didn't come in," the man said. "She was supposed to, but she didn't. We tried calling."

"Are you sure? I know she went in last night."

"No," he said. "I was here. I promise you, she wasn't. Sorry."

Josie pressed him for a few more minutes, then finally clicked off. *Okay, stay calm.* She paced from the kitchen into the TV room and back. She called Clara and told her.

"I'm coming over," Clara said. "She's fine, Josie. Really. I'm sure there's a totally ordinary-boring explanation."

"I know," Josie said. *But I don't.* "Should I call ..." *The police. Missing persons. My mother disappeared. No, that makes me sound hysterical, doesn't it? Mom isn't 'missing.'*

"Yes. Just to be safe," Clara said.

*Right.* Josie slumped to the couch, facing the dark television. A yellow playbill for *All in a Day's Work* from a theater in Hartford was framed on the wall to the left, and a circular coffee table jammed against the bookshelves on the right. Josie had moved it to fit the basement boxes. All three were lined up in the middle of the floor. They made the room smell wet and faintly sweet, like mold. *I should get rid of them. Mom said we'd do that today. Something productive, to occupy my time.*

But first, she dialed the police. It didn't help. After a long time on hold and transfers across departments, a tired-sounding woman asked more and more skeptical questions, then said that, of course, this must be disorienting. But Josie's mom would be back soon. There was no evidence of foul play, was there? And no indication that Mom had gone off the rails. Probably, her phone battery just died, and she was delayed. Simple as that.

*Tell her about the glass-face man.*

Josie didn't. The policewoman promised to follow up.

"Best thing to do is stay calm," the woman said. "Nine times out of ten, she'll be there the moment we hang up."

Josie clicked off. She called Mom's professor friend, Susie, who hadn't heard from Mom either, and then finally, Josie put her phone away. *Best thing to do is stay calm. The policewoman sounded like Dr. Laymon. And why didn't I mention the break-in? Oh, the glass-face man and fish man who appeared and vanished from the apartment? How would the police have reacted to that? I'd be the suspect in Mom's disappearance, wouldn't I? Totally unreliable.*

*Dad warned me. He told me they'd come for my family.*

*Stop it.*

Josie leaned forward to peel the tape off the top of the first basement box. *And maybe I should be back on the happy pills, meeting with Dr. Laymon again. I promised Clara I'd talk.*

The thought made her stop, hands poised on the box flaps. For years after what happened in Kentucky, Dr. Laymon had helped her to control the anxiety dreams and stop fixating on delusions. 'It's rare,' he'd said at their first visit, 'seeing things like you did. But it's not unheard of, given the circumstances ...' *Now, I'm in new 'circumstances,' and I want someone to tell me what the hell is going on. Why is my brain doing this again? Where's Mom?*

Josie opened the first box. *Clara will be here soon. She'll know what to do. Check the boxes to be sure Mom didn't stash any gold bullion or whatever first.*

No such luck.

The first box was full of old clothes, all musty and damp. Maybe not trash-trash, but half of the flannel shirts were men's. *No way Mom would wear those, and I'm not putting on a shirt if there's any chance Dad wore it.* She sniffed a blue-and-white striped shirt and smelled the sugar-rot pinch of old whiskey. Josie's stomach clenched. As she dropped the shirt back in, snatches of memories bled into her mind. Dad wore this shirt once when he slammed a bedroom door in Mom's face in Boston, both of them shouting. Again, in the same shirt, Dad watched his favorite movie, *Fight Club*, on the couch beside Josie, when she was still in the second grade in Indiana. He had talked her through confusing, scary scenes, until he heard the sound of Mom's car in the driveway. 'She won't think you're old enough to watch this. Let's not tell her, okay?'

Josie closed her eyes and waited for the scent memories to dissipate, like early-morning dreams. Then, she dragged the box aside and checked the second one. It was stuffed with electrical wires, power cords, and an ancient DVD player. *Even less interesting.* The last box opened to reveal rubberband-lassoed papers, folders, and books, streaked with black mold. All this junk had clearly been soaked. There were water lines along the inside. *Great.* The top batch of papers were printouts of newspaper articles—*garbage*—and under that, a pile of wet hardback books, hiding a black folder. It had a yellow legal pad inside, covered in Dad's blue-ink scribbles. Josie recognized the writing from the notes they'd passed, when she was little. She'd used joke notes to shake him out of his bad days, long before she'd ever used the terms 'manic depressive' or 'self-centered alcoholic.' 'Do you like clouds?' she'd written. 'Check Yes or No.' Dad wrote back in mish-mash cursive, with lots of strike-outs, abbreviations, and shaded doodles around the margins. This was his.

The first handwritten line of the legal pad was dated May 20th, four years ago. The day before Dad left, and Mom took Josie to look for him in Kentucky. Where Josie met Clara.

> *'One of the blacklegs looked like a fish. A small man with human arms and legs, but the head of a giant fish. The thing was talkative, but anybody would be after so many years underground ...'*

A knock at the front door, and Clara's voice in the hall. "Honey, I'm home!"

The paper shook in Josie's hand, the words going blurry. She forced herself to set it down and went to let Clara in.

At the doorway, Clara's smile snapped into taut concern, when she saw Josie. "What's wrong? What happened?"

"Nothing."

"Josie ..."

*Right. 'Talk to me.' Time to talk.*

"I just started going through the basement boxes, and I found ..."
She led Clara to the couch. "Look at this. Please tell me I'm not crazy."

"You're not crazy," Clara said, and she read beside Josie. The letter
continued:

*'The fucker stalked me last night. He tried to trick me. 'You're so unstable,
Mark,' he said, 'that when we kill your family, it will be your fault.
We're your delusion.' That's what he said.'*

Josie looked at Clara. It was only the first page of the legal pad, no
telling how much more there was. "You see this, too, right?"

Clara nodded, her face serious, as she concentrated on the words.
"What is this?"

"It's my dad's handwriting."

Josie read on:

*'He was here to collect. The dragon still claims her. Even after all this
fucking time. I have to go back to Kentucky, don't I? My mom and
Don won't understand. They remember the last time, and before,
with Dad and the blizzard. Looking back, it's still hard to believe that
you forgave me, when my own mother wouldn't. But the trees have
been the answer all along.'*

"I don't understand," Clara said quietly.

Josie kept reading:

*'And Don just shut off. My older brother, who is always so brave for
everyone. I can picture him standing by our mom's bedside, saving us
all from ourselves. Noble Don. Screw him. I don't want to see them.'*

Josie read the paragraph twice. *Who's 'Don'? Dad had a brother? And his mom—I thought she passed away when I was a baby. But this was four years ago. He's talking about my grandmother like she's alive—and an uncle who doesn't exist. Mom and Dad never talked about Dad's family.*

Clara finished reading and rubbed her face, but Josie still had more to go.

*'So, who is this for, then? This. This thing I'm writing now, trying not to smear with my palm. This is probably for you, Caitlyn ...'*

"He wrote this for Mom," Josie said.

Clara didn't answer. She held Josie's hand and sat very still.

This was how Mom knew to go to Kentucky back then, wasn't it? This was why they'd jumped on a plane to the South to track down Dad. Because he left a note.

Josie read faster, all the way down:

*'Because even if you don't want to, you know, Caitlyn. You saw it too. I have to go back to Kentucky, not because I want to—because if I don't, they're never going to stop. Josie is still marked by the dragon. He still thinks he owns her. He's sniffing her down, the same way the Chicken Man did, like a dumb wrinkly bloodhound. A million-year-old bloodhound with scales and claws. Most of the blacklegs are down in the rocks, I think. But some are already here. That's why they won't see it coming. They think the caves are safe, dead places. But they're not. Roots grow there. I can use that, Caitlyn. I can save our daughter.'*

No more on the page. *'Save our daughter.'* Dad wasn't well. That wasn't news, of course, but it was easy to second-guess her memories of Dad laughing or crying—usually one or the other. Especially when Mom shut down every conversation about him. But there it was, evidence for what he had been. Mom tried to hide his illness from Josie. *Protect me from it, not hide.*

*Except.* This echoed the museum. A dragon in Kentucky was hunting Josie. No big deal, of course, because it wasn't real.

"What do we do with this?" Josie asked.

"I'm not sure," Clara murmured. "Do you have any idea what it means?"

"He wasn't well," Josie said, but too quietly. Just an excuse, flimsy. *Dad knew.* These scribbles nailed what she'd seen.

"They're just old papers," Clara said. She closed the folder to hide the legal pad and set it back in the box. "See? Gone. That has nothing to do with us now."

Except Dad used the word 'blacklegs' in his writing, just like in Josie's imaginary conversation with him. Whatever that meant. And he wrote about the fish man. The thing that stood in this apartment last night, with the glass-face man. *These papers are real. They're right here. 'Burn.'*

"I really saw those things," Josie said. "Even if they weren't, you know, actually there."

*Dad's ghost at the museum, no Mom, and now this.*

Josie dug deeper into the box, shoving the notebooks aside, exposing moldy papers, and at the bottom: a small stack of envelopes held together by a rubber band. Curled at the edges, the envelopes were grimy gray, but Josie took them out. All were addressed to her and had been torn open.

*What the fuck?*

Carefully, Josie tugged the rubber band off. The first envelope listed Josie's name and their old Boston address in Back Bay. From six years ago. The return address was Chicago, with two names: 'Michele Greenwood' and 'Thomas Kantowski.' *Michele and Tom.*

Josie realized she was squeezing the envelope hard in both hands. It was already opened. *Dad opened all of them.*

"You see this, right?" Josie asked.

"What are they?"

"Remember I told you I had two close friends in Chicago, before we moved," Josie said, her voice soft. "They never wrote me back."

"Apparently, they did."

Nausea bubbled at the back of Josie's throat. Somehow, this was worse than the blacklegs letter. This was betrayal. *Dad hid this from me.*

Josie flipped over the envelope to open it, and as she pulled out a folded sheet of notebook paper, it split and crumbled around her fingers. "Damn it."

Blue ink streaked illegibly on the mushed paper.

"Why would he hide this?" She started to open another envelope, and it dissolved into black crud on her fingers. Hands shaking, she tried the next one. It split down the middle, too soggy. "They're useless now."

"Josie, please ..."

She let the ruined letters drop back into the box, wiped her hands on the couch. *Stop it.* A familiar tug in her stomach made her want to curl sideways and cry. She closed her eyes and bit her tongue. A snap of pain cleared her mind. When she looked again, Clara rubbed Josie's arm, studying her expression.

"You think your dad hid those letters," Clara said.

Not a question.

"He did," Josie said. "I don't know why, but he—"

"Let's focus on now," Clara said. "Maybe you should call someone. Dr. Laymon? If your mom doesn't …" Clara smoothed the hair out of Josie's eyes. "She'll come back, though."

*But what if she doesn't?*

When Mom's bedroom was still quiet and dark the next morning—*day two, eight days left*—Josie called the old number she had saved on her phone. A receptionist answered, started to say how busy things were, until she recognized Josie's voice.

"So good to hear from you," the woman said. "Dr. Laymon had a cancellation. How soon can you be here?"

*Now. I can be there right now.*

# Chapter Five

J osie walked with Clara to the subway, where a gray pool of floating bottles and plastic bags flooded the street. But the sky was bright blue and the air light and easy to breathe, even now. They took the subway into Manhattan and switched trains up to Columbus Circle. Clara said she would pick up a frozen pizza during Josie's appointment, so Mom wouldn't have to cook. *If she ever comes back.*

Josie left Clara at an indoor mall and walked uptown. The crowded sidewalks and construction scaffolding hadn't changed. *When was I last here? Two years ago?* The area was still loud with cars and jackhammers, a neighborhood of apartment towers perpetually under construction. She passed tourists, joggers, dog walkers, and women pushing strollers, all hustling faster than her. Dr. Laymon's office was still on the ground floor of an old stone-brick building at 70th and Broadway, with animal heads carved over the front door. *A little like our old apartment building. Stop it. Be here right now.* A doorman let her in, then waved her back through a mirrored lobby to a side hall, where she was buzzed through a second door.

In a carpeted waiting room, a large woman—*what's her name?*—in a red-and-black, table-cloth-looking dress jumped up to hug Josie, then laughed and made her promise not to tell Dr. Laymon. "Not professional at all, but you look great, dear. He's ready for you."

Josie went in. The built-in bookshelves hadn't changed. They were still loaded with intimidating color-coded spines, and the wall behind Dr. Laymon's desk was jammed with diplomas. A room puffed up with authority. Except every flat surface was also decorated with cat photos. Where other people might have displayed family shots or vacation photographs, Dr. Laymon framed cats. The smell of licorice—he kept a glass container of it beside his computer monitor—brought a flood of not-quite-visual memories. Feelings from this place. Strong, contradictory emotions, like a roller coaster she'd ridden with her eyes shut but could still recall in the muscle memory of her stomach and tensing limbs.

Thin and with ashen circles under both eyes, Dr. Laymon had gone solid gray since Josie last saw him. He slowly circled the desk and gestured to a couch, then sat across from her in his usual chair. No notepad, though. He said how happy he was to see her, then trailed off.

"It has been almost two years, Josie," Dr. Laymon said. "How's your mother?"

"I don't know," Josie said. *And we're in it. Just like old times.* The rollercoaster feeling made her shift on the couch to try to loosen her leg muscles. Didn't work. "It's why I'm—it's part of the reason I'm here. I need someone who's an expert to tell me I'm not crazy."

Dr. Laymon crossed his legs and planted both hands on his lap. *But still no notebook and pen.*

"You're not going to write anything down?" Josie asked.

"You're not my patient anymore, Josie. We haven't caught up in a while. The last I heard, your mother said you were doing well. I can't remember the last time I called in a prescription refill." He hesitated. "Is that still accurate?"

"Yeah."

"Why don't you tell me what's happening?"

"My mom is gone. I don't know where." Her voice fluttered, rasping a little at the edges, the way it did when she was overtired. "I've tried calling, I've tried ..." *Stop. Choose your words.* Josie forced her hands open, so they wouldn't clench. "She left the night before last."

"I'm not sure what you're asking me, Josie. If your mother is missing—"

"It's not just that," Josie said. "I saw him again."

The room was still, the hum of pipes in the walls suddenly trembling enough that Josie could sense them. But no real sound. Dr. Laymon stared back at her and very carefully, uncrossed his legs.

"Who?" he asked.

*Who.* He was going to make her say it. *I'm not supposed to believe it's real. I'm supposed to be past that.*

"My dad," Josie said. "His ghost, like on the bridge the day he died."

Dr. Laymon's frown hardened, as if he were reading for a tell, something in Josie's expression to tell him this was a joke.

"Let's back up," he said at last. "It's been some time. Why don't you walk through what happened the first time?"

He didn't believe her. *Let's circle back to the incident we agreed was a fictional memory.* So, he could convince her to question what she'd seen.

"That's not what I'm talking about," Josie said, her voice rising. She smelled her own sweat in her armpits and around the curl of her collarbone. "I mean now—I saw him again two days ago. Then I went off in front of everyone—made a real scene—at my high school graduation."

"Okay, but tell me what happened the first time."

Josie started to object, then willed herself to stay calm. *No. I came here. Play along.*

"My dad and mom had a fight, a bad one," Josie said. "We had just moved to New York, and I didn't know anyone. All my friends—well, you know. We moved so many times that I grew up like an army brat, without the army. Except after this fight, Dad left. Like for good. Then Mom took me on a trip to Kentucky, where I was born." A memory hit Josie of a wide, gray jut of rushing foam that crested over the floodwalls below a concrete overpass. "Anyway, she didn't tell me at the time, but it's pretty obvious we went to Louisville to find my dad. We didn't find him, though. Instead, there was a climate protest at a baseball game."

Josie remembered hundreds of people dressed in black—like for a funeral—locking arms, filling a minor league baseball field. The team was called the 'Louisville Riverbats.' 'But your father refuses to call them that,' Mom had said. 'When he grew up here, the team was the 'Louisville Redbirds.' Mark always liked the old name better.' Back then, Josie had imagined a beautiful cardinal doused in black oil, fluttering into the sky as a bat. During the protest, a small, freckled girl in centerfield had caught Josie's eye, both arms up to hold a *There Is No Planet B'* sign, decorated with a red hourglass. The first time Josie saw Clara, she was protesting to save the planet.

"Mom and I got separated during the protest," Josie said. "I walked back to the hotel along the riverfront." A knot formed in the center of Josie's chest. A hard ball of tension tugged at her lungs when she breathed. She recalled waves pounding the floodwall, leaving a haze and industrial, rotten smell. *Until. Say it. Say what he wants to hear. I imagined my father. I passed out from heat exhaustion and woke to find Clara helping me up, with her lucky fossil. But Dad's ghost wasn't real. That's what he wants me to say.* Like a performance she'd rehearsed through therapy sessions and antidepressant medications years ago, Josie was supposed to remember her lines.

"Take your time," Dr. Laymon said.

*I don't want to talk about this again.*

"That's where I imagined I saw my dad," Josie said.

He had been waiting for her on a railroad bridge. No sign of train tracks, the bridge had been retrofitted with concrete in its metal joints, and she hadn't seen Dad right away, only after the river waves drew her attention. Except he *was* there. Not imaginary, even if she'd convinced herself later. Even if she said it now. Just like the museum.

"He was on the railroad bridge." Unsteady breathing made her wince. *Stupid chest pain. Anxiety.* "I didn't come here to talk about that."

"Okay," Dr. Laymon said. "But just to be clear, you imagined a conversation with your father?"

"Back then, my dad told me he was going to take a boat ride to kill a dragon." Dad had pointed down the riverfront to a paddle-wheel steamboat. Painted red-and-white, the ancient boat was fixed to the shore under a highway overpass. "But really, I passed out from heat exhaustion. Then I met my girlfriend—not my girlfriend at the time—Clara."

*Dad was there. It wasn't a fucking dream.*

"And then what happened?"

"Nothing," Josie said. "The river was flooding. Clara was also from New York, starting high school at the same school I was in the fall. Crazy coincidence.

"Dr. Laymon waited. "And then?"

And then Josie and Mom flew back to LaGuardia on an overbooked plane, and the next weekend, Josie met Clara at the Bethesda angel fountain in Central Park. They walked past the duck pond and dug a hole in the turf in broad daylight to bury Dad's cellphone in a shoebox under his tree.

Every place they'd lived, Dad had claimed a tree, usually in a public place near their apartment or house. Weird maybe, but it was one of his things. Mom called it a 'Mark ritual,' an eccentricity she had complained about but, Josie suspected, secretly found endearing. Until it got to be too much.

*His tree in Central Park is the last one. Was.*

"It's still buried," Josie said.

"As I recall, you chose to *bury* your father's phone near a tree that was important to him. Is that right? What association did that tree have with Mark?"

*You know this already.* Again, he was mimicking a stagehand poised out of view, holding a copy of the script. From the back seats of their high school auditorium, Josie had watched Clara rehearse just like this. 'Line,' Clara said, when she needed a prompt. Then a whispered voice from stage right: 'O happy dagger ...'

*I'm supposed to follow along.*

When Josie didn't answer, Dr. Laymon said, "Listen to the words: his phone was 'buried'—laid down as dead—near a symbol of your father ..." He watched her, as if he expected Josie to finish the sentence.

*Sorry, no script.*

Josie buried on the phone on blind impulse, only later shading in her motivations. Why she *really* did it. Because Mom skipped the funeral? Check. Because she never saw his body? Check. Because he didn't say 'goodbye' or call or love her enough to stay—not just in New York, but breathing?

"Your father," Dr. Laymon said, "you imagined a conversation with him, after he left, when it couldn't have happened. Mark was already ..."

*Yeah. Already.*

Dr. Laymon nodded to himself, as if he were impressed by the connections he was making. She'd forgotten how pretentious he was. Dr. Laymon was supposed to convince her this wasn't real, but the longer she sat here, the more solid the museum encounter felt. The more this therapy routine felt like the lie.

Still, Josie didn't speak.

"What did he talk about this time?"

"Monsters," Josie said. "A dragon. I don't know."

"Our minds have ways of trying to protect us," Dr. Laymon said. "From change, uncertainty."

"You think this just happened, because I graduated from high school?" *Is this a joke?* "Seems a little fucking dramatic."

Dr. Laymon stiffened at the F-bomb. *Oh right, he hates swearing.* They'd gone back-and-forth about that for twenty minutes at least during her first appointment years ago. Now, though? *Fuck that.*

"Many times, the most challenging dilemmas we face have ordinary names. So our minds create mythic terms to frame them—to match our feelings."

"High school graduation is boring, but end-of-the-world monsters aren't?"

Dr. Laymon leaned in, as if suddenly interested. "Is that what you imagined he talked about?"

"I don't know."

"Josie, I honestly don't know what you want me to say. I care about you and your health. Right now, I'm not impressed with what I'm seeing."

Josie stiffened. He said it as if she were a child again. "Not *impressed*?"

"No," Dr. Laymon said. "You cut off the treatment plan we agreed on, and you stopped taking the medications I prescribed."

"Because I was fine."

"We're always doing fine, until we aren't," Dr. Laymon said, his voice suddenly flat and lecturey. "Did you know that I treated your father? Did your mother ever tell you that? It's no big secret."

*Dad came here? Dad sat where I'm sitting? Dr. Laymon knew him?* Josie felt a chill, as if he'd suddenly cranked up the A/C. *That's how Mom knew Dr. Laymon to start. Why didn't she tell me? What about the notebooks?*

"Did he tell you—did my dad talk to you about things he saw? Do you have any idea why he might hide letters from me?"

*"Letters?"* Dr. Laymon said the word, as if it weren't English and he expected a translation. "What letters?"

"When we lived in Chicago, I had two close friends, Michele and Tom ..."

"Yes." Dr. Laymon nodded. "You told me about them. Long-distance relationships can be challenging, even for adults."

"Turns out, they wrote back, but my dad didn't show me the letters. Why would he do that?"

Dr. Laymon started to answer, then stopped himself, as if the question were a trap. "Trying to make sense of that type of behavior can be counter-productive. Mark could be very stubborn and convinced of his own reality. Intelligent but difficult. And I worry that's what's happening here. You're determined to be well, without doing the work."

Which meant what—that she should let him talk her into questioning her memory again? *But how could it be real?* Not the right question, anyway. She was older now. Real or not, she needed to understand *how* to figure this shit out, not be talked into memorizing old antidepressant ideas. "I have to go," Josie said, but she didn't get up.

"You might benefit from a break."

"A break?"

"There's an excellent clinic in Connecticut. I can write you a referral."

*A mental hospital? Dad went there.* Josie remembered Dad standing at the front doorway of their house in Hartford, holding a rolling suitcase with one hand. His eyes had been bloodshot, nose swollen, but he was smiling. 'Your father is taking a break,' Mom had said. She'd used the same words back then, hadn't she? Mom knew the script. *Are you joking right now?*

*But what if he's right? What if that is what I need?*

Josie pushed up off the couch, legs stiff. *Feet, time to move.*

"My dad talked to you about monsters, too, didn't he?" she asked.

"I don't like ..."

*That's a 'yes.'*

"I know. You don't like what you're hearing right now," she said. *Insane.* "I shouldn't have come here."

"You're a lot like Mark," Dr. Laymon said. "Just try to think about what this looks like from the outside. The bridge in Kentucky was empty, wasn't it? We talked about that. To anyone else watching, it would have been empty."

*Clara was watching—or anyway, she found me after. Right after.*

Josie's pocket vibrated with her phone, and a ringtone played. Dr. Laymon frowned, started to say that his 'no cellphones' rule hadn't changed, but as Josie murmured an apology and took out the phone, the ringtone clicked. 'House of the Rising Sun.' Dad's favorite song. She took out her phone: onscreen, Dad grinned in sunglasses, with a red-and-black University of Louisville hat. The call was coming from ...

"Josie? Josie, you know I don't allow phones ..."

It was from the fucking grave.

# Chapter Six

J osie banged back through the waiting room and lobby, without looking at the friendly receptionist or doorman. On the street outside, a young couple argued, traffic was jammed, and over it all, Josie heard that same ratchety pounding of construction. Turning back downtown, Josie tripped and caught the stone wall of the building. *I'm not paying attention. Watch where you're going. Think.*

*Smartass, Dr. Laymon.* She never should have come back here. She wasn't Dad.

Josie looked at the open blue sky above the street noise and car exhaust smells to steady herself. It didn't help. She returned to Columbus Circle and called Clara. "I'm done."

"I got a margherita pizza," Clara said. "Comfort food, right?"

On the busy sidewalk by the Columbus Circle traffic, Clara came out with a weighted plastic grocery bag, bulging with a square pizza box and the cylindrical shape of *Ben and Jerry's* ice cream.

"Great," Josie said. "But what are you going to eat?"

Clara kissed her cheek, and they walked to a crosswalk that led to the park. "How did it go?"

They hurried to catch the light and dashed across to the edge of a crowd of tourists watching acrobatic street performers at the park entrance.

"Oh, you know, totally normal," Josie said and showed Clara the new missed call on her phone: *'Dad.'*

"I don't understand." Clara pulled her to a stop.

A Fleetwood Mac song played from the street performers' stereo, as the crowd applauded a complex cartwheel routine. Mom loved that song, had once half-joked that if it weren't for Stevie Nicks records and *Law and Order* reruns she never would have moved to the United States to become an American lawyer. That was before she met Dad. It was hard to imagine them as anything other than Mom and Dad. They met when Mom was interning at a big law firm in the city. Josie didn't know what Dad was doing or even why he was living in New York. Probably so he could drink whiskey and write paranoid nonsense about blacklegs fish men. Setting a good example for the next gen.

"I got a call, while I was with Dr. Laymon," Josie said.

"Right, but that says it was from your dad's number."

"Correct."

Clara swung the grocery bag higher. "Here, before it melts. I bought you ice cream."

"Cherry Garcia?"

"They were out. Chocolate Chip Cookie Dough." She dug it out of the bag and popped off the circular top, gave Josie a plastic spoon. "See how much I love you?"

Josie scooped a quick bite, and the rush of cold sugar and chocolate loosened her jaw. Maybe dessert was all she needed right now.

"I tried to answer, but the call dropped," Josie said. "I called back and got nothing."

"So it was a glitch. Or someone else has the number now."

But they followed a path into the park, already headed toward the duckpond. *No mystery where that leads. I have to know it's still buried.*

A woman with a cute nose ring and braided pigtails offered them a red hourglass pamphlet.

"Do you have a minute for the environment?" She blocked their path, somehow eager and solemn at the same time. "Did you know, in the last forty-eight hours, the Greenland ice sheet crossed a tipping point? It's losing one-million tons of ice every minute—oh, hi, Clara."

They went in for a quick hug, Clara introduced Josie, and then the girl asked if Clara planned to attend an upcoming protest. Josie ate more ice cream, while they chatted.

A red hourglass meant extinction. Another climate change protest. People had worried about the environment as long as Josie could remember, but those Earth-size problems were so big they *just were*. Clara had convinced Josie to skip classes for climate walkouts and demonstrations, even though Mom grumbled about signing the detention slips. Most of the time, getting mad about global warming felt like being upset about the color of the sky. Plenty of other things to stress about.

Finally, when they continued into the park, Clara dropped the flier in her grocery bag and said, "I know you don't think we can save the planet, but we can't just give up, can we? It matters."

"You know I'm not as well read as you on melting icecaps or how much carbon is in the atmosphere," Josie said.

"You see it with your birds, though," Clara said. "You know there are only *half* as many birds in North America today as there were when your parents were growing up?"

Josie tried to ignore the pressure in her chest. So much for the ice cream solution. Why did Clara have to say 'parents?' *My parents.* Mom grew up outside Toronto, only came to the U.S. for law school, and Dad ... Dad was from Kentucky. *Like me. And if we're already past a tipping point or whatever, what's the point?*

"I'm fine not living in the same world as my dad," Josie murmured. "I'm not him."

"That's not what I meant," Clara said. "And that call—it's just shitty timing. I'm sure it's a coincidence that someone found the phone or hacked the number."

*I'm nothing like that asshole.*

They passed a jogger in a sweaty blue-and-gray NYU shirt.

"Can we talk about the fall?" Josie asked. "This week, you were gone before graduation."

Clara held Josie's hand but watched the path, not her. Sunlight dappled through the trees in perfect oversized-diamond-y patterns across the lawn, almost too pretty. She wasn't sure she'd believe this, if she saw it in a movie. CGI and lens-filtered sunlight effects. So maybe it wasn't real, like the fish man said.

*Stop.*

"Say something," Josie said. "Get me out of my head, please."

"We'll talk about it," Clara said, "just not right now, okay?"

Lately, that was her thing. "When?"

They rounded the duck pond, where a cluster of kids were steering remote-controlled sailboats in rippling circles, while their parents and nannies talked on the benches. *Almost there.*

"I don't want to talk about next year, while your mom is missing," Clara said. "And when we're about to do this."

*This.*

Past the benches and a few picnic tables, the trees were skeletal gray. In the backdrop, foliage still bloomed bright green but not here. Here, it all looked dead, the first row of trees all chopped down to uneven stumps. Dad's tree was gone.

"They cut it down," Josie murmured.

She crossed wood chips and shredded leaves in the wet lawn, closer to the ruined tree-line. And there it was: a faint carving at the base of one stump that read, *'Josie.'* Her name was still there. Somehow, the chainsaws missed it. Josie was breathing hard, her fingers tingling as she approached the crumbly stump. It really was gone. *This isn't right. Dad's trees are immortal.* She froze.

Behind her, Clara asked, "Are you okay?"

*No.*

A muddy, crumbling shoebox was centered on the stump, and as Josie turned in a slow circle she recognized the raw, chewed-up dirt pile nearby. *That's where we buried it. Someone came here to dig it up. No, to leave it for me.*

Clara stepped beside her. "Is that it?"

Josie scanned the ordinary couples, families, and joggers in the park. No one noticed them. No one waited in ambush. She crouched, planting both hands on the box. *Don't tell me this is nuts. I know, okay?* The wet edge of the top was rotted off, part of the bottom of the box, too. When she started to lift it, more cardboard disintegrated in a mushy paste.

"Someone dug it up," Clara said quietly. "This is bad."

"I know."

Josie took off the lid. A huge black centipede was coiled inside. She shook the box, but the centipede didn't move. *Dump it out.* The centipede flashed out the side hole and disappeared in the grass. And there was the small glass rectangle, right where it should be. Dad's phone.

Clara's face tightened. "Maybe leave it there, Josie."

Josie nodded. "I can't, though."

She lifted it out, and the screen blinked on, with a photo of Josie and Mom, both younger, their faces crammed together, with a bright blue sky behind them. From a trip to Watch Hill beach, years ago. *Shit.* A message popped up to display one failed call to Josie, placed thirty-four minutes ago.

"That's …" Clara said, shaking her head. "That's not …"

But it was. It was possible, all of it.

# Chapter Seven

All the way home, Josie clenched Dad's phone in her left hand, too tight, as if to prove it was there. Four years since they buried it, until someone dug it up to prank call her. Why put it back? *Because they wanted me to find it again.*

"Maybe it's magic," Josie said on the subway. Standing beside Clara in a packed train car, she still didn't put the phone away, just kept it in her field of vision, with both arms looped around the standing bar for balance. The train swayed and rattled toward Brooklyn.

"Tell me everything he said at the museum," Clara said.

Josie checked the distracted faces of the crowd. No one listened, and even if they did—so what? Josie and Clara were anonymous here, could speak freely about ghosts and monsters—mental illness—undisturbed. And Dad did go to a hospital in Connecticut for this. Just like Dr. Laymon said. Mom lost it when Dad got wound up drunk about imaginary things. *Of course, she did. But I have to tell Clara. Can't hide this from her.*

"He said ..." Josie caught herself. "No, I *imagined* my dad said that something is going to happen in ten days."

"That was two days ago," Clara said.

"Right, so eight days left, I guess." *Until what? Until the 'blacklegs' reach the surface.* "Monsters are coming to get me," Josie said. "I don't know. It sounds batshit crazy." Josie felt her arms trembling again, looped them tighter on the subway pole. The train slowed into a station stop. People got off and on in a shuffle around them, and when the train rolled on again, Josie said, more quietly, "He said they'd come for my family first."

Clara stiffened, crossed her arms. "Why didn't you tell me earlier?"

"Because it's not real."

"It isn't?" Clara asked. "I believe you saw him, Josie. And now Caitlyn is gone. Sounds real-ish enough for me right now, monsters or no monsters. What did he say is going to happen?"

"He didn't." But that wasn't true, was it? *Dad pointed at dinosaur bones and said the clock is ticking. My delusions are a little on the fucking nose.*

"What did Dr. Laymon—"

"Dr. Laymon wants me in a mental hospital. A drugged-up vegetable." She heard the impatient rise in her own voice again and sighed. The subway car lights felt overly bright now, hotter, too. Sweat beaded on Josie's brow. "You don't always have to worry about me."

She met Clara's concerned stare.

"I do, actually." Clara kissed Josie's cheek. "Sorry, I can't turn it off. Unlike that phone."

"We both see it," Josie said. "I'm not imagining this, right?" *I wish I were.* "I *was* hallucinating, though. Stress, I get that—but this? How is it possible?"

*Thank God, you see it, too.*

"It isn't."

*Someone dug up the phone to call me. Makes no sense.* A loud family boarded at the next stop, with kids squealing and laughing. *None of these people have any idea what just happened. The world is upside-down, and they're all blind. Or I'm losing it. But not alone.*

Clara helped Josie out at their stop into a subway tunnel of hustling commuters and peeling billboard ads.

"Your mom will know what to do," Clara said.

*If she's back.*

She wasn't. Not when they returned to the apartment, or later in the evening, or even the next morning. Day three.

*Seven days left.*

Josie glared through a dirty window at the always-dark buildings outside the kitchen. "We can't just wait."

Clara motioned to the kitchen table. "Caffeine first."

Josie sat and adjusted a cup of steaming coffee. A flutter of movement out the window caught her eye. A blue jay landed on the fire escape outside, its stripy head jerking and bobbing. It fluttered both wings but stayed put. On a Sunday morning like this, Mom should be asking if they wanted blueberry pancakes or eggs. She might suggest an obscure, off-Broadway show for that evening, since hockey season didn't start until October. Mom would ask Josie how she was feeling. *As if I'm always about to break.* Maybe they would walk to the farmer's market on Van Buren in the early afternoon, and then Clara would suggest a new street taco restaurant before the play. But Mom and Clara wouldn't notice the birds, like that blue jay out the window right now, with its symmetrical white neck plumage. Only Dad would have seen that. *That would've been our shared secret at this moment, the beauty of a totally ordinary little bird.*

Josie found her cellphone and opened the birding app.

"I thought you stopped birding," Clara said.

"I did. Mostly."

After Dad bought the app for her, Josie had chased him through Central Park in a puffy coat. 'I got a pigeon!' Josie had shouted, tagging an ordinary New York City pigeon. 'Pigeon!' Dad called back, from across the lawn. It became an inside joke for the season. Every day, when Josie showed him a photo of another bird—a seagull or raven, anything—he smiled and said, 'Nice pigeon.'

Now, she swiped through app menus and took a picture of the jay. *Not a pigeon anymore.* The phone blinked: *'Congratulations! You tagged a cyanocitta cristata (North American Blue Jay). Share with your friends?'* Josie tapped *'Ok,'* and the app brightened with the names of other birders, who had logged species recently. There weren't many. A message told her that in this area the average number of species identified daily was eight. When they moved in, after Dad left, that same message had said there were an average of twenty-five daily bird species sightings in this part of Brooklyn. A user comment underneath read: 'TFA.' *'They Flew Away.'* It was how the birders on the forums talked. Fewer sightings and less birdsong, because there weren't as many birds. Birds were dying, pretty much all of them. And sure, it might take a few lifetimes to happen, but it still sucked to see extinctions tracked on the app.

*It's why I stopped using this damn thing.*

She started to close the app, then paused. One of the recent birder contacts was Mom. *What the hell?* Mom had downloaded the app, too, but as far as Josie knew, she'd never used it—and certainly not in years. The bird wasn't tagged locally. Mom had tagged a bird yesterday at a different location. *This isn't possible.* Josie set her phone on the kitchen table by her coffee mug.

"What's wrong?" Clara asked.

Josie tapped to access a photo Mom had uploaded of her tagged bird: an image of a male cardinal standing in the grass alongside a stream, with a name carved into a nearby tree: *Josephina Elizabeth Morris.'*

A red bird, like the baseball team, before they became bats.

Josie showed Clara.

Clara frowned and then slowly seemed to understand the picture.

"That ..." She watched Josie, not the phone. "What does that mean?"

Josie's fingers jittered. She tried to close the app but couldn't steady them.

"Someone took a picture of a bird standing by a tree with my name carved on it—yesterday. Using Mom's phone." She felt the sudden urge to smash her phone—Dad's, too—against the wall. *Break the damn things. No more mysteries.*

"Where? Is the location marked?" Clara asked softly.

*'Marked' is what Dad said. In that note to Mom, he said I was 'marked,' didn't he?*

Josie tapped out of the birding app fast, poking the screen to download the photo. She found a technical file menu, and there was the bird picture's info. Taken at 4:30 PM Eastern Time, at specific numeric coordinates. Not a city, just latitude and longitude. She looked those up, and a dot appeared on the green plot of a zoomed-in map. She widened the view until a road was visible alongside a location label: *'Perryville Battlefield State Historic Site.'*

"Where's Perryville?" She zoomed farther out.

Clara opened her own phone, grunted. "You don't want to know."

More shrinking the map, and a larger city came into view north of the marker, against the horizontal curl of the Ohio River. The southern side was labelled, 'Jefferson County.' *Mom is in Kentucky. No, her* phone *was in Kentucky yesterday to take that photo.*

Josie let her phone go dark. "None of this makes sense."

Clara was still scrolling on her own screen. "Whoever took that photo picked a messed-up place to go birding. The Battle of Perryville happened October 1862 ... not great." She stopped reading. "Ugly Civil War carnage."

*Someone took that photo so I would see it. Which made not sense. But it's right there. The photo exists. It's real. A trick to make us return to Kentucky.* "I don't want to go back there."

"I'm not saying we should," Clara said. "Maybe the police will find Caitlyn, now that we have that photo."

But Josie didn't call, not yet. What would the police say? A bird in Kentucky beside a tree with my name on it? *The only person who would do that is dead.*

"What if it's real?" Josie asked. "They don't have to be monsters, but what if there are people looking for me, and that imaginary conversation—that happened, because somewhere in my brain I already know."

They stared at each other. *We can't wait in this apartment. These things know where I live, the glass-face man and the fish man. Dad's Central Park tree is gone. They'll come back.*

"We have to do something then," Clara said.

Josie nodded. "Maybe the cardinal photo isn't a trick. Someone could be trying to help us."

Josie checked airfare on her phone. The flights weren't cheap, but she had Mom's credit card for emergencies. And wasn't that what this was? As Clara watched in silence, Josie checked Mom's credit card statement, then logged into her bank account. Another 'leveling up' skill, Mom had drilled the basic of financial literacy into Josie 'just in case.' Back in Hartford, a week before Josie turned thirteen, Mom drove her home from swimming lessons at a chlorine-drenched YMCA to find Dad alone in the kitchen, staring at open cabinets.

'Where did you hide it?' Dad had asked. 'Did you think I wouldn't notice?' Red-faced and jittery, he stank of sweat. 'My notebook was right here, and now it's gone.'

When Mom and Dad started arguing, Josie had returned to her room. She heard the front door slam, then a knock, and Mom came in.

'Hand me your phone,' Mom had said. 'I want to show you how to level up and access my bank account.'

So functional and no-nonsense. Josie remembered almost laughing. *Ignore the paranoid man who just stormed out and let's learn about interest rates.* But she had listened. *Just in case something like this happens.*

Now, Josie saw that Mom's account total was low—less than one-thousand dollars—and it was linked to two personal loans, both with past due payments. The credit card, too, was racking up interest charges. They were in trouble. Mom's head was barely above water, and she was sinking, because of Josie. *My college plans for the fall caused this.* She stared at the numbers on one account, then the next. No recent transactions, though. No one was using Mom's cards. Was that better or worse?

"The flights are expensive," Josie said. Two one-way plane tickets would clean out most of their money. But she couldn't go alone.

Clara leaned in to inspect the bank screens. "The bird photo is all we have. She's been gone three days. But maybe try the police again first?"

Josie did, and, as expected, after another twenty minutes of department transfers and waiting on hold, the same policewoman she'd spoken to the last time told her to come in for paperwork.

"It's a formality," the woman said, "but they'll want to run background checks on anyone who might have a history."

"What history?" Josie asked.

"Somebody has her phone. So they'll want to know about your mother's relationships with people who have criminal records, histories of substance abuse, mental illness—you name it."

*A Dad-Dad-Dad checklist.* Josie remembered how he shouted at Mom in the park, sneering and slapping a tree trunk to mock her in the moments before he left the last time. Even then, his jaw trembling, a small bourbon bottle in one hand, Josie never feared him. Mom did. Josie remembered the way Mom stepped between them, as if Dad might grab Josie's wrist. *Mom didn't know him like I did.* And because Dad hadn't been terrible all the time, that made him *more* of an asshole, not less.

"One other thing," Josie said into the phone. "There's a box my girlfriend and I buried in Central Park a few years ago." Beside her, Clara shook her head, mouthed 'what are you doing?' but Josie continued. "Someone dug it up, and we found my dad's old phone inside."

The policewoman cleared her throat.

"That's fine, bring that in." Her voice was distracted, only half-listening.

"I'm not explaining this right," Josie said. "Someone used the old phone to make a call."

A strained silence, and the policewoman asked, "Any calls to your mother on the phone?"

"No, it was to me."

"They'll sort it out," the policewoman said quickly. "One question. Are you on any medications yourself? Drugs or alcohol?"

"What? Why?"

"There's no need to get upset. I'm only trying to understand the situation," the policewoman said. "Are you currently in clinical treatment?"

*What kind of unprofessional, illegal question is that? She thinks I'm making this up, calling for attention.*

"My mother has been missing for three days," Josie said, her voice steady. "What am I supposed to do?"

"I'll transfer you to support services, and they can schedule an appointment."

On-hold background music came back on, and Josie ended the call.

"They can't help." She set her slim phone beside Dad's clunkier block. Not that much older, but his phone looked like an artifact. "They want me to go in and fill out paperwork."

"If they ask, what are you going to tell them?" Clara asked. "About the other stuff, I mean?"

*The glass-face man and fish man, my father's ghost—that other stuff?* Josie pressed the two phones together, side-by-side. "I guess I won't."

"They're the police, Josie. Their job is to spot bullshit."

*They'll know I'm not telling them everything, and when I do, they'll call Dr. Laymon. And then I'll get my break, just like he suggested. A shared room in an institution and a cupful of pills. And Mom will still be missing.*

Josie eased both hands back to her coffee mug, and as she raised it, the handle slipped. The mug spun sideways out of her palm. Clara caught it. Smiling, she wiped a little spillage from her fingers.

"I'm too jumpy. We can't just sit here," Josie said. "No more coffee."

Clara took the mug to the sink. "I agree."

"Is it crazy to go based on one photo?"

After dumping and rinsing the mug, Clara leaned back against the counter, arms braced behind her. The pose tugged her 'Save the Humans' T-shirt and short-shorts tight. Josie felt warmth in her chest, her pulse quickening, just watching her.

"Yes," Clara said. "But that's okay. If we have to be a little crazy right now, we can."

"Don't leave."

Clara smiled. "Stop thinking I'm about to disappear. It's not a good look."

"Fine, then come along." Josie grabbed her phone again. Not a question. *Do it before I change my mind or Clara's foster parents call.*

On the travel website, Josie tapped to buy two one-way tickets for the next morning, direct to Louisville. Expensive. Almost nine-hundred bucks.

Clara approached Josie and saw the price. "We'll figure it out. Maybe your uncle is rich."

*My uncle.*

Josie opened Dad's phone again and checked the contacts. Bingo. There was a 'Mom' entry—*Dad's mother, my grandmother*—and a 'Don' entry. Long-lost Uncle Don. Josie showed Clara and tapped the screen for more info. The contacts were identical. Same number, same address on 'Tyler Lane' in Louisville. Either they lived together and had the same phone number, or it was old info.

"We can start with the coordinates at the battlefield," Josie said.

*And if there's nothing there? If it comes to it? Will I cold call strangers in Kentucky?*

Josie crossed back into the living room to dig through Dad's moldy box again, until she found his manic-scribbling notebook. "Airplane reading," she said.

Clara shook her head. "Just so long as you keep track of which bits are in there ..." She nodded to the notebook. "... and which are out here." She tapped her scalp.

"That's why I need you."

"Oh *that's* why?" Clara came in for a kiss that stopped Josie from opening the notebook and loosened the pull in her chest. When Clara pulled away, she rested her forehead against Josie's again, so close Josie tasted her coffee-spit breath. It was perfect. "I won't let you go off the rails," Clara said. "Much." And before Josie could answer back, "Seriously, it's going to be fine, Josie. It doesn't feel like it now, but I bet you any amount of kisses that there's an ordinary, boring explanation for that photo—and everything."

"Ten thousand," Josie said.

Smiling, Clara eased back to look at her, rubbing Josie's clenched shoulders with both hands. "Ten-thousand kisses. Deal. Payable upon receipt of a boring explanation for all this."

*And if it's not? If you're wrong, and we never know what happened to my mom? Or we do, but it isn't…*

"It won't be like the other time," Clara said. "Okay?"

The other time. The last time Josie went to Kentucky to find someone who was missing. *There was nothing we could do.*

"I know," Josie said.

But that wasn't true either.

# Chapter Eight

*'The government tracks guns, but not fertilizer. Not diesel or Styrofoam or A/C circuits or pocket batteries. That's a relief. I'll need guns, sure, but no amount of bullets will end this. I learned that last time. Guns aren't the reason I have a 'second shot' at him. Blame dumb luck, Caitlyn. Like always.*

*'I suppose if this works, I'll go to prison. Destruction of property. People may even get hurt or die. I don't want them to—I hope they don't, I really do, you know I do—but they might. Something this complete, there could be casualties. Will they lock me away again? You should probably shred these papers, honestly. I'm only writing this now to explain, so you know—you know already, but so you really know—why I have to finish this. He won't stop. I can't count on the trees to protect her forever. In a few years, the blacklegs will be here. Then there will be no chance. I can stop that. Save our daughter and keep the world breathing. Two birds. Chirp-chirp.'*

"It makes sense," Clara said.

Josie looked up from Dad's notebook. She'd only just started reading, but already it felt so off-kilter. Unhinged—what the hell was he talking about? Fertilizer and gasoline? Was Dad building a bomb?

*He was more dangerous than I ever knew, wasn't he? That's what this means.* More than imaginary monsters, he had planned something.

"Josie?" Leaning across the empty middle seat from her window seat, Clara tapped her phone. "I said, the cardinal bird makes sense. The battlefield is a nature preserve now."

On Clara's phone, Josie saw photos of sunflower fields and a vast hillside of pink and white flowers surrounded by high grass. A dense flock of geese soared overhead in mid-takeoff.

"The Cincinnati Series juts down there, too," Clara said.

*Trying to distract me. Anything—birds, the Civil War, even fossils—to take my mind off what we're actually doing right now.* Josie's phone was synced to the plane Wi-Fi, but no message from Mom. Any minute now, Mom would text or call to say she was so sorry to scare them. And not to worry about the travel costs. Everything was fine.

No luck. This flight from LaGuardia to Muhammed Ali International Airport marked four days since Mom disappeared.

Scrolling on her screen, Clara launched into a mini lecture about the 'Cincinnati Series.' Fossils. More rocks. Josie tried to listen, but Clara's fossil itch wasn't new. And it wasn't like she could help it. It was part of what drew Josie in, the way Clara's face swelled with excitement. 'Interest' wasn't really the right word. 'Clara-splaining' was more like it. An obsession. She hadn't stopped until she downloaded *all* of Elvis's concerts from his Las Vegas years. And she learned everything—books and books of everything—about these old-beyond-old rocks. Clara talked about famous fossils in the same reverential tones other people used to describe the canals of Venice or Coral Reefs before they bleached out. Cincinnati Series fossil shells, trilobites, and other, spongy-looking worm shapes were all more than 400 million years old, perfectly preserved in areas near Cincinnati, Ohio. Hence, the creative name. Origins of life and all that, before the first mass extinction, when almost all life on Earth nearly flickered out, only to bounce back again. The same way it had four other times, too.

"I need to find my mom, Clara," Josie said. "not look at rocks." *Shit, did I say that out loud.* "I'm sorry, I didn't mean ..."

Clara stiffened, a quick flash of color in her cheeks, but she tried to shrug off her annoyance. "*Rocks*, huh? Fossil aren't organic exactly, but they're not all just *rocks*, Josie." Before Josie could cut in, Clara continued, "I know, I know, you don't love these prehistoric memory stones the way I do. But that's what they are. People used to think a rock is a rock is a rock, like you do. But do you know they've found DNA in fossils? It's true. Most of the time, the organic stuff swaps out for minerals, but they found wooly mammoth DNA—more than a million years old—in a *rock*. So."

"Sorry," Josie said again.

"And speaking of, I read the other day about a piece of quartz—a *rock*—that can store terabytes and terabytes of digital data for *billions* of years. Rocks aren't always just rocks is all I'm saying."

"So Perryville is a fossil park?" Josie asked.

"No, Perryville is a Civil War battlefield," Clara said, and she read: "'*... the iron storm passed through our ranks, mangling and tearing men to pieces. The very air seemed full of stifling smoke and fire ...*'"

Josie watched a ramble of solid-looking white clouds out the window. *Are we doing the right thing? Yesterday, it made sense. Sort of.* But after the police call, she'd still slept hoping, half-expecting Mom to be there when the alarm went off. Now, leaving New York felt like another move. Another dive into unknown streets and faces, smells, and accents she didn't recognize. And there was that old-school shakiness in her hands. Just like Illinois, Massachusetts, Connecticut, upstate New York—*too many times, I learned to deal.*

"'… *which seemed the very pit of hell,'*" Clara read, "'*peopled by contending demons.*'" Clara looked up, smiling. "Anything interesting in your dad's notebook?"

"He was still writing to my mom," Josie said. "It almost makes it worse, though, reading what he wrote here."

"Worse how? Because he wasn't well?"

*Because he didn't know he was gone.* No hesitation in Dad's jagged handwriting, he'd been convinced—he'd *known*—that he had the answers. Whatever his plan was to stop the monsters, Dad wrote to explain, not justify or defend. *Reality doesn't have to be proven, does it? It just is. That's what Dad thought this was. As real as this airplane.* 'Belief' wasn't even the right word for these scribbles. If this was madness—actual pills and soft-spoken nurses madness … *Is this what it looks like?*

"I don't think it matters anymore," Josie said. "He wrote all this four years ago."

"Hey." Clara reached to take Josie's limp hand. "We got this."

*Unless Mom's not there. And why would she be? Waiting in a Civil War nature preserve?* Josie had tried calling Mom's cell again and again, but she didn't bother with the police after the last call. They had packed in a hurry, one backpack each, and no hotel reservations either, just a rental car waiting at the Louisville airport. Clara even brought her lucky fossil, and maybe it was weird to bring along, but it felt weirder somehow to leave it behind. *Why? Because we don't have tickets home or the money to pay for them. Because what if we never go home?*

The captain came on the cabin speakers and said they were making their final approach. "It's a hot one down there, folks. Fasten your seatbelts."

After they landed, moving sidewalks zipped them through the terminal into a network of restaurants, gift shops, and bourbon displays. The familiar labels and bottles stopped Josie in mid-step on the slow-moving walkway. Clara followed her stare to the passing liquor kiosks. Josie knew Bulleit from the top of the kitchen fridge, squarish Woodford Reserve from Dad's living room side table, and there was Maker's Mark with a red wax cap at the top. The same type of bottle Dad used to keep at his bedside. *This is a trap.*

Clara asked if she needed a drink of water and said Josie looked pale. Josie closed her eyes. When she looked again the world stuttered. It felt like the frames of a film jamming for an instant, then playing again.

*Someone's watching.* The air changed, and Josie's mind throbbed with a steady beat. *Leave.* She knew, somehow, that if she spun, she could spot a shadow at the edge of her vision. Someone hunting her. But as they took the escalators down to a car rental office, Josie glanced around, and of course, nothing. Only people waiting at baggage claim carousels and others dragging suitcases.

"Tell me what's wrong," Clara said, but when Josie met her eyes, Clara nodded. *She knows.*

"We shouldn't have come back here," Josie said.

At the rental car kiosk, a guy at the desk smiled at Josie. "Welcome home."

She started to ask what he meant, and he tapped Josie's birthplace—Louisville—printed on her passport. She'd had to bring two forms of ID for the car.

"Don't worry," he said. "Kentucky remembers you."

When Josie had the keys, she hustled outside to a hot airport parking lot, with the sun reflecting on all the car windows. The air here was heavier than in New York, strong with pollen, like a close-up inhale of dandelion weeds. Past the lot, a tangle of concrete highways cut them off from chain hotels and a distant amusement park. But that tense pull wasn't going away. Something knew they were here. She counted the parking spaces, matched the number on the keys to a red sedan.

In the driver's seat, she turned the key to start the engine. A newscaster was talking about political scandals. Clara climbed in, changed it to music. Angsty indie music, something Dad would have cranked up, while Mom rolled her eyes.

"You know how to operate one of these, right?" Clara asked.

Josie adjusted the mirrors. How long since she'd driven? More than a year, not since the mini-disaster last August, when Mom rented a car to take Josie to see a modern-day retelling of *Pride and Prejudice* in Western Massachusetts for Josie's seventeenth birthday. Clara had been sick with a head cold.

In jammed traffic returning to the city, Josie remembered Mom shouting at her to use her turn signal and 'watch the side mirror!' Until, at a rest stop on interstate I-95, Josie was so rattled she somehow lost the car keys. They spent an hour searching the parking lot, arguing and exhausted.

'Why didn't you leave them in the car?' Mom had asked.

'I didn't want someone to steal them.'

'Really, Josie? This isn't a car heist movie.'

After a tow truck finally carted off the locked car, Mom and Josie sat together in the back of a taxi, drained from their fight. Josie had asked quietly, 'Since when do you watch car heist movies?' And they burst out laughing.

That evening, when Josie knocked on Mom's door to apologize, Mom cut her off. 'You didn't do anything wrong,' Mom had said. 'We're home safe. I'm sorry for that kerfuffle. And we managed to avoid car thieves.'

That became a running joke for Mom and Josie for months. Except now, Mom wasn't here to over-react. Mom wasn't anywhere.

"Take it slow," Clara said and changed the radio to a Boomer music station. More oldies. "We'll know soon."

Holding the steering wheel helped, but Josie filled her lungs with the remnants of faint cigarette smoke and a greasy fast-food smell from whoever had rented it last. As she backed out of the parking lot, Clara touched her arm. The warmth of Clara's fingers helped order Josie's thoughts. *Be here, now. Clara is right. We'll know soon if this is a waste of time and money.* What was the plan? Find Mom, or—failing that—aim for some kind of clue, anything, at the battlefield park and regroup. *Foolproof? Not so much. But until we know-know, we can't think about how to get home. How much debt to rack up.*

"I haven't been here since," Josie said.

"I know. Me neither." When Josie met Clara four years ago, Clara had been visiting Louisville by piggy packing on a business conference with her foster dad. He'd agreed to bring Clara along so she could hit up the baseball field climate change protest. *Where I first saw her.*

"I'm so glad I'm not trying to do this alone," Josie said.

Clara kissed her. Still driving, Josie kept her eyes on the road, but in that instant, the tension in Josie's ribs was gone—back again, when Clara leaned away.

Out of the lot, they merged onto Highway I-65 headed south. Past identical-ish suburbs and strip malls, the houses became farmland. They passed a wooded trailer park and blasted-out mining ravines.

*And someone is watching. We aren't safe.*

They talked about the flight, the radio music—anything but this place. An hour and a half dragged to the interstate exit, where they followed cornfields and horse pastures to the Perryville Battlefield.

Opposite the park turnoff, a ruined barn displayed by a huge Confederate flag.

"Guess that means we're not in New York," Clara murmured.

"My dad grew up here."

*Explains a lot.* The reflexive thought made Josie shift uncomfortably in her seat. *I was born here, too.*

They pulled onto a long, empty road between fields of high, rippling grass that led up to a mostly empty parking lot near an aluminum-sided visitor's center. Historical plaques at the edge of the lot overlooked a scenic crest of hills, with more monuments along the hedges and fence lines.

Not ominous, though, the park was calm, peaceful even.

"Let's get a map," Josie said. "In case we lose the phone signal."

She grabbed her 'one personal item'—a travel bag just small enough to stow under the plane seat but large enough to fit two changes of clothes, and Dad's notebook and phone—and got out. In the humid parking area, she breathed in florist flower smells, with the mulchy taste of plants and gardens. Inside the visitor's center, they wandered into a wood-paneled gift shop, with racks of books, antique military bric-a-brac, and clothing displays.

*We don't need a map, not really. I'm stalling. We came all the way here, and now I'm hiding in a gift shop, because I'm afraid.*

Josie followed a camouflaged college-age group back to a dark theater room, with a high-end flat screen monitor. The front theater benches were full, so Josie and Clara sat at the back. A narrator launched into a monotone description of battle tactics, while blue and gray squares surged along arrows on a computer-generated map. The video cut to a panorama of the park grounds at sunset. Solemn music and that same narrator droned on about the horrors of war.

The place where Mom tagged the cardinal was right outside. They were so close.

The lights came on, the documentary ended, and a bearded guide in a blue-and-white Civil War uniform stepped up front. "Thank y'all for coming. Any questions?"

With the lights on, Josie noticed a whiteboard on the right wall, divided into long rows and columns, with dates up top and numbers in each box. Simple words and abbreviations ran down the left-hand side: 'deer,' 'w. turkey,' 'otter.'

Josie raised her hand and pointed to the display. "What's that?"

The guide adjusted his stiff costume collar. "Nature society logs. That's just for staff use. I'm really here to answer questions about the film. Just over 7,600 casualties in the battle. You'll hear folks call it the Battle of Chaplin Hills or even the Battle of Kentucky—"

"But ..."

Josie kept her hand up, and now a camouflaged guy wearing a blue University of Kentucky cap turned in his seat to frown back at her.

"Sorry," Josie said, "what does the log mean? Are those the numbers of animals spotted here?"

The guide nodded, his face tight, trying to hide his irritation. "Right. Those are the numbers each year. *Now*, any of y'all have questions about the battle? It decided the Heartland Offensive, and after, folks raised money to preserve everything you see out there. Abraham Lincoln himself said he couldn't win the war without Kentucky. This was what decided it. First Confederate monument was dedicated in 1902 on the anniversary of the battle. Union monuments didn't go up 'till thirty years later."

An older woman asked, "Why did it happen here?"

Josie squinted to see the whiteboard. Starting at the top, a list of dates counted down to this year. A record of animals for the past fifteen years. And even from here, she could tell that all the numbers went down. 'Deer' started at '142,' before dropping to '82,' and then down to '30' this year. And for the other animals it was even worse.

"... Kentucky ain't really the South," the guide was saying. "More in-between. Below the Ohio, everything broke apart. Families went half one way, half the other. What do you call a place that isn't a place?"

*Strange thought.* People shifted impatiently on the benches.

"Have y'all heard of the time-traveling reb?" he asked. "No? It's a folk tale. And it ain't really about time travel, truth be told."

After reading the dropping animal numbers, Josie felt the room lurch a little, like she'd just stepped off a merry-go-round and lost her center of gravity. *It's not just the birds. The deer and snakes and otter—they're all going away. Disappearing.* Her heart pounded, and still this guy was droning on.

"So, the story goes that during the battle, a young Confederate soldier ran off and hid underground. The entrance to Mammoth Cave ain't far off, and those cavern systems run for hundreds of miles."

*Easy breath in, and then steady exhale. Should calm my pulse, but no dice. Why isn't it working?*

"U.S. geological survey says you can walk right under our feet here, down to Alabama, west to Arkansas and all the way up to New England, without ever seeing the sun. Crazy, I know. So guess where this Kentucky soldier shows up? Years later, he pops up in a cave near Boston, if you believe it. Right outside town. Half-blind, malnourished, he didn't know the war had ended. Wandered across the entire country underground. Was in all the papers."

"Is it true?" Josie asked and felt her face go deep red. *Shit, I said that out loud. I'm too tired for this.*

Everyone stared at her.

"Well no," the guide said. "Of course not. It's just a ..."

"But how do you know?" Josie asked. "How do you know it's not true?"

Clara squeezed Josie's hand and eased her up.

"Sorry," Clara said. "We have to ... it's been a long week." And back in the gift shop, Clara let out a nervous breath. "Josie, are you up for this?"

"You heard him," she said. "From here to Boston. Someone could have gone from Kentucky to New York—or the other way around."

"It's just a story, Josie."

"You don't know that. Someone could have traveled through the caves, all the way ..."

*Shit. Stop.* Behind the gift shop register, a round woman watched with one hand on her phone. Everyone else had backed away. *I was shouting.*

"Okay?" Clara asked softly.

"Sorry. Yes, I'm okay."

Josie grabbed a park map, then ducked outside to a monument at the edge of the parking lot. A metal soldier stood at attention on top. A plaque read, *'Lundsden's Battery.' I'm okay. Yes, of course I am.*

Resting the open map on the stone, Josie tried to make sense of it. Pale hills were marked off by numbers that coincided with a legend along the right-hand edge, all historic military what-have-yous. But at the top and upper left, an area was flooded by dark green trees, cut-through by a network of paths that snaked in looping zigzags. The creek. There: a slim line of blue in the forest. The bird in Mom's photo had water in the background.

Clara watched Josie, not the map. "Back there, you know that's not real."

"Yes, Jesus. I just said I was okay." Josie heard the quiver and bounce in her own voice. "Sorry, let's just go. We're almost there."

Clara pulled her close, and Josie pressed to her shoulder. *Tell me we made the right decision coming here.* She smelled Clara's deodorant and sweat.

"We're here now," Clara said. "Come on. Let's find some birds."

*Right. We took a risk. Time to see if it pays off—anything to lead us to Mom. Or—don't think it—Dad, dead or not.*

Josie straightened again, and they started onto a path that led into the park. Beside another blocky monument ahead, a small group gathered around an older tour guide.

"There aren't many headstones," the guide said. "After the battle, Bragg's army retreated into Tennessee. They didn't have time to bury the dead." The guide pointed to an overgrown, fenced-off area in a field of dandelions. "It's just over there. See that marker—to the confederate dead. A hundred men from the South buried over there. More graves all over the grounds. They reinterred the union troops after the war, carried them out of here."

The thought of people hauling off corpses on horse-drawn wagons didn't fit these quiet fields and trees. Come for the gore, stay for the Zen beauty? And it was silent AF. They continued on. In the dips between the hills below, white mist flowed through stands of trees and fence lines.

*Weird. It's hot out here, like sweaty-pits-and-dripping-forehead hot. So, where's that fog coming from?*

Josie checked the photo tag coordinates on her phone. It was 1.5 miles away, straight ahead. Around a bend at the next hill, she spotted six gray geese, with soft, pale bellies, hanging out around a shallow pond below. Continuing on the path along a high fence line and carefully maintained squares of trees, Josie opened her birding app. *Might as well.* She tagged a Kentucky Warbler, small and bright yellow, with brownish back feathers and a distinctive, mask-like face.

"Breeding season for them," Josie said.

Clara smiled. "For us, too."

Josie felt familiar heat in her cheeks. Clara was trying to help, normalize this. But it felt wrong. All of it. The sweeping hills and tall, green-leaf trees had a too-natural feel. Another park. When Josie first moved to New York City, Dad had led her into snowy Central Park to 'find' his tree. She had marveled at the wilderness. 'How is all this smack dab in the center of Manhattan?' she'd asked. Dense trees, boulders, hiking trails, and ponds, all framed by a backdrop of glass towers. Dad hadn't answered, until after he spotted the maple by the duck pond. 'There it is,' he'd said and drew his red Swiss Army Knife. He'd been totally oblivious to the runners, families, and other people in the park. The tree had been barren then, too. 'Want to know the secret?' He'd grinned. 'It's fake. The trees are real, but people designed the park to look this way. It's planned out, no different than the streets, bridges, and tunnels. It's not nature. It's pretend.'

The illusion of wild. These battlefield paths, sloping gulleys, and period fence lines all felt like that, too. A battlefield vista as a tourist depot. Atop another hill, Josie stopped at a plaque overlooking an expanse of purple, weedy flowers, with a low hedge in the distance. Farther off, she spotted a field of hay bales, a rundown house, and blue barn. No more birds, though.

Past drifting mist across the fields, their path led to a dense tree line, with a wooden visitor board out front. Bright laminated papers were stapled to the sides: *'Warning: Active Hunting Grounds.' 'Hikers advised to wear orange and signal.'*

"There." She pointed to an opening into the woods, marked with a red triangle, nailed to a tree trunk. Josie took a slow breath of pollen, dirt, and old leaves. "This has got to be it."

"How far?" Clara asked.

Josie checked the coordinates again: 0.6 miles. "Close."

Up ahead, beyond a log that had fallen across the path, a maple tree crowded the trail. Like Dad's tree in Central Park had been. Josie's stomach tightened again, and she watched the forest off the path. A breeze rustled through the woods in an invisible wave, swaying the branches overhead, nudging the thinner trunks back and forth. The tension felt like a cord around Josie's chest, squeezing every time she moved.

Off to the right, more steam rose out of a low ditch. Just like in the valley back there. Here, it looked like the ankle-deep mist of a fog machine from an old, scary movie, flowing over leaves and dead branches.

*That shouldn't be here. It's hot.*

"What's that?" Josie asked. "It was back at the battlefield, too."

"Steam?"

Josie slipped off the path and went to clear the dirt, where the mist rose. The earth was warm, *too* warm, as if it were being heated from underground.

"From the sewers or something?" Clara asked.

"Out here?" *Or caves. That's it, isn't it? The heat could be coming from the caves.*

Josie tapped her phone again: 0.25 miles to the location. But it wasn't directly on the trail. Holding the phone up like a compass, she led them through the brush. Only the wind and rustling of leaves overhead. No birdsong or even buzzing gnats and mosquitos. *It's basically summer. Where are the bugs?*

Dad's phone: 0.1 miles to the marker.

*It should be right here ...*

Josie stopped suddenly, and Clara bumped into her at the top of a limestone cliff, overlooking a shallow gorge and stream. The streambed was glittery gold in the sunlight, about fifteen meters below, packed with smooth white rocks. All along the embankment more rock shards were piled in heaps on larger flat boulders. A plastic bag and beer cans were caught in the current against tree roots a little farther up, and an old workman's boot had fallen into a crevice directly across from them.

*There.* Josie spotted a tree, sagging on the opposite bank across the creek, with words carved into it, too distant to make out. *But I know what it says.* She pointed, and Clara nodded.

"We came all this way," Josie said. "We should go down."

Josie clambered down the boulders, using tree branches to balance on the uneven stones. Closer to the bottom, the rocks were pockmarked with curly shapes, like snail shells and itty-bitty worm indentations, thin as angel hair pasta. *Fossils.*

"Jackpot." Clara lit up, running her hands along the bumps and twists like someone reading braille. "Look at this brachiopod. These guys were deep water, and here ... pentremites. Blastoids. These are Cincinnati—430, maybe 450 million years old ..."

Josie tried to step over the seashells and squiggles embedded in the rock.

"Cephalopods, like squids, grew to the size of school buses back then," Clara said. "And trilobites—oh look at that one! Amazing condition." She aimed her phone to take pictures. "Sea scorpions as big as people, larger even. All of these were alive 200 million years *before* dinosaurs."

Another cemetery without bodies, only markings left in the stone. Like the battlefield. No birds or fish, either, and still no bugs. They shouldn't stay here. Something was wrong.

Josie stepped to the edge of the creek. It wasn't deep, maybe one meter down in the middle, but it was louder here and fast-moving.

More fossils, too. The ground was thick with them. Above the creek, the sky was open and perfect blue.

"I've never seen this many in one place," Clara said, following Josie. "And the condition—they look like they were alive yesterday."

Finally, they splashed through the water, trying to find high steppingstones so their pants wouldn't be totally drenched. And there it was, the tress from the photo. The same writing—*my name ...*

Directly below her carved name, *'Josephina Elizabeth Morris,'* Mom's phone was centered in the grass, with the same blue-framed screen protector Josie remembered her buying at the NYU bookstore last month.

Slowly, Josie leaned in to pick it up—

"You should be in your room."

Josie spun: past Clara, a bleeding, skinless man—all exposed muscle and sinews—approached along the edge of the creek. Less than five meters away. His eye sockets were empty holes, but he had perfect white teeth. Small horns ringed the skinless man's skull and flesh throat. He left a trail of wet, bloody footprints in the grass. Three meters away, almost close enough to grab her.

*Run. Move.*

"Josie?" Clara came to examine Mom's phone in Josie's hand. Frowning, Clara tracked Josie's stare—looked right through the skinless man—then back again, confused at Josie's locked expression. "What's wrong? It's your mom's phone, right? Do you see something?"

"Yes," the skinless man said, his muscley jaw tugging a smile. Blood and fluid sluiced down his chin. "Tell us, Josie. What do you see?"

He stepped closer, right behind Clara, less than two meters away.

"Clara ..." Josie's hand jittered as she caught Clara's arm, fingers shaking down to tighten on Clara's hand. "I'll explain ... come with me ... we have to go."

"Josie, you should be in your room," the skinless man said. "No visitors today. Come on, let's get you back."

The skinless man raised both arms, and Josie pulled so hard that Clara shouted—"What the fuck!"—and they spun into a stumbling run. Josie slipped, almost fell, and yanked Clara on after her along the creekbank.

"Oh Josie," the skinless man said, disappointed, but when she looked back, he didn't follow. Just stood there. "The building exits are all locked for staff. Wherever you think you are right now, there's nowhere to go."

But she didn't stop.

# Chapter Nine

J osie led them along the creek, until the bank sloped up into a
gorge. It was a steep climb, but Clara followed Josie up boulders
and sharp, fossily rock beds, away from the water. *Away from the park
and our rental car. Where am I going?*

"Josie?" Clara asked, breathing hard behind her. Nevermind how
suddenly Josie had bolted, after the initial shock, Clara hadn't argued.
Now, though, as they climbed the embankment, careful but quick,
checking for loose rocks or slippery footholds, Clara asked again what
Josie saw. At the top, Josie leveraged her body onto a cliff with a
low-hanging branch, then reached back down, panting, to help Clara.
Josie's shirt was clingy with sweat. *What did I see?*

"I know it seems like I freaked out," Josie said.

"Hey." Clara made the top, and followed Josie into a wooded maze
of low, crunchy brush. "Don't apologize, just tell me what's going on."

"I did see something back there."

"Right, but what? Does it have to do with your mom's phone?"

"No, I don't know." There were no trail markers. Josie slowed, her
shirt sticky and jeans wet from the creek. The woods were still in every
direction. She scanned past broken-down logs, and walls of prickly,
sharp bushes. Nothing moved. A dead bird lay in the leaves, just ahead.
A beautiful little blackbird, with yellow stripes and its wings tucked

together, black eyes like beads. Josie couldn't think of the name of the species. *Don't look at it. This forest is a silent nothing, whatever is happening right now.*

"It was a man," Josie said. "No, that's not right—it was a horror movie demon."

"A horror movie demon," Clara repeated, as if waiting for the joke. "Where did you see it? Back in the woods?"

"No, he was right behind you. By the creek," Josie said. "You didn't see. I know you didn't, or you would've ..."

*I'm talking louder.* Josie's mouth tasted dry, and she stomped harder through the woods. *Slow down.* Clara caught up, fell into step beside her.

"Where are we going, Josie?"

"Out, I don't know. Away from that thing."

"Okay, stop." Clara touched her shoulder, and Josie did, pausing to meet her eyes. They were both sweat-streaked and dirty from the climb, but Clara's expression was even, almost calm. Not smiling anymore, though. "I believe you," Clara said. "I believe you saw that."

"But it wasn't there. You didn't see it."

"I know. But I see *that*." Clara gestured to Mom's phone. "I recognize Caitlyn's 'proud NYU college mom' phone protector."

"Someone wanted us to find it here."

Not 'someone.' The skinless demon back there. *My nightmare delusion. Clara didn't see. Dr. Laymon is right, after all. But I am not D ad.*

"Whatever you saw back there—the monster, whatever—it's okay," Clara said. "Really, Josie."

"I don't want to go back there."

She stowed Mom's phone in her bag with Dad's, checked her own satellite map again. *My parents' phone are lures, aren't they? Bread-*

*crumbs to make me wander off the path into a net. Then why didn't he chase me?*

"There's a road not far from here." Josie showed Clara their location in a splotch of green that bordered a gray curl, and just past that: another, much wider slice of water labeled: *'Chaplin River.'*

"That way?" Clara started off again, double-checking Josie's raised phone map. "We can follow the road back to our car. Maybe faster anyway. See? You found us a shortcut."

Josie glared at the empty woods behind them, then watched her phone and the blinking location dot, near the forest edge.

"I can't believe you didn't see him," Josie said.

"It doesn't matter," Clara said. "Or—it does, but we'll sort it out. Whatever you saw, you were right that someone brought Caitlyn's phone all the way to Kentucky and left it there for us. The bird photo and everything—none of that is imaginary. Someone *is* fucking with us."

*Us. Not me, 'us.'*

Josie stepped in to hold Clara's hand again, and Clara slapped a rock into Josie's palm. Her lucky fossil. "I want it back, when we're home," Clara said. "But for right now, you take it."

"Thank you."

Silly, of course, but holding this Clara talisman helped loosen the pull in Josie's chest. Still, Josie felt the after-rush of adrenaline from the run, but that was fading, too. *Just get out of the trees.* Josie slipped the fossil into her bag, so it could knock against Mom and Dad's phones and her wadded spare clothes.

"My dad saw things," Josie said, and when Clara started to protest, Josie continued, "No Clara, it's okay. I'm not like him. But at the museum, when I was talking to myself, thinking it was him, he—*I*, that Dad version of me—said that what if the reality of all this isn't the point. Because if I imagine my dead father, he can only say things that I already know."

"So you already knew that demon back there?"

"Or imagined him from something I saw or read. Like my dad's notebook."

Clara scrunched her face the way she used to do in Calculus class at the start of a new chapter, when their teacher, Mrs. Lineman wrote a problem on the board that they wouldn't be able to solve until the end of the chapter. A way of demonstrating how much they were about to learn by shocking them with an impossible puzzle that would feel straightforward weeks later.

"He's really gone, though, right?" Clara asked.

First time since their one fight way back when—Clara hadn't pressed about Dad's funeral since.

"He is. I read the obituary and everything. There's no way it's my dad doing this."

"Then it's someone else who knew him—your family," Clara said. "Because of the phones and the trees."

The phones and the trees: two of each. Dad's phone by his tree in Central Park; and Mom's phone here, near a tree Josie had never seen before in Kentucky. *With my name on it.* In all the places they'd lived, Dad cut one word, *Josie'* into the bark, not her full name. This was different.

"Josie, we don't have to talk about it, but can I ask how your dad …"

They stepped out of the woods. Across a short expanse of dying grass and a gravel road, a red-and-white steamboat docked at the lip of a bright, fast-moving river. *Just like with imaginary Dad four years ago.* No, this was real. That wasn't. *I'm not afraid.*

*If we don't have to talk about how Dad died, don't ask.*

Josie clipped faster over the crinkly grass, squinting in the harsh sun. Closer to the steamboat, words came into view over the door—'Captain's Quarters'—with a chalkboard posted on the wall, topped by: 'Today's Specials!'

"Is it a restaurant?" Josie asked.

"Hope so, I'm starving," Clara said.

*Good. Enough to stop the questions about Dad.* Josie couldn't let her thoughts settle on that the way she had four years ago when visions of him woke her in sweat-soaked sheets, tears still in her eyes from dreams she couldn't remember.

Up a short gangway, a hostess waved them onto the boat. "Howdy, y'all! Welcome aboard, you two!"

Inside, they entered a wood-paneled seafood restaurant, loud with conversation. The waitress led them to a table and left menus, as if this were the most ordinary thing in the world.

"Nice," Clara said. "Just the two of us."

Josie took a long drink of ice water, opened her menu. *Act as if this is okay, and it will be.* She held the edge of the menu tight, eased her breathing into a steady pace. The room smelled like fried fish, lemon, and white wine. Outside the windows at their table, Josie saw dark river water. Open blue here, but the sky faded pale gray over the opposite, wooded shore.

"I looked up your word," Clara said. "For the monsters, demons—whatever they are. On the plane, I looked it up: 'blacklegs.' It can be a kind of plant disease or a bacteria that kills cows, or ... in the 1800s, it meant 'strike breaker.' There's even an old song about fighting a 'blackleg miner' in an English coal mine."

*Fighting blacklegs underground, surrounded by coal. What if mine workers hurled the name as a slur at strike breakers, because it meant something else—or Dad did the reverse? Not important. Don't think about it now.*

Clara waited for a reaction, but Josie just concentrated on her menu, as if the seafood platter were deadly important.

"It also means a liar," Clara said. "Like a gambler or swindler."

"Great," Josie said, too loud again, but none of the overdressed people at the next table seemed to notice. "How does that help us? Sorry. I'm sorry, I'm just tired."

*The air feels coiled in here. Like a snake, ready to lunge.*

The waitress came, and they ordered drinks—two coffees.

Clara said, "It's okay, Josie. We'll fly back in the morning, or rent a car." Clara smiled and took Josie's hand. She lowered her voice, more serious. "Really, though, Josie. A big part of me—I mean this sincerely—was super tempted to insist we park in a deserted lot somewhere after the flight, so I could have my way with you. Skip this sleuthing entirely for a few minutes at least."

Josie felt a familiar rush of heat in her face. Excited embarrassment. "Seriously? You've got to tone it down in here."

"*Seriously,* I don't. Who is going to hear? Anyway, you like it, and Caitlyn is fine. Someone stole her phone, that's all. It's not normal, but it's going to turn out to be just a big mix up."

She didn't sound like she meant it. *Saying that to steady me. So I don't—what—relapse into hallucinations?*

"You just said it's not normal," Josie said.

They both smiled, and Clara leaned in for a slow kiss.

"That's one," Josie said, when Clara shifted back again. "Nine-thousand, nine-hundred, and ninety-nine to go."

"We made the right decision to come here," Clara said. "The bird photo was the only clue we had. This was the right thing. We tried."

The waiter brought more water, a pot of coffee, and rolls with butter. But still, something about this room felt wrong. What? Josie turned to watch everyone eating and chatting, oblivious. *It's my stress. That's what's wrong, not the restaurant.*

"Can we talk?" Josie focused on Clara again. "About what happens after the summer, I mean. You said you would."

Clara raised her coffee and sniffed the wafting white steam. "Okay. You're starting NYU. College is all about finding a job isn't it?"

Josie's guidance counselor talked about it that way and so did Mom. She had read the NYU course catalog using the words 'pre-law,' 'pre-med'—*pre, pre, pre.*

"I don't want to be pre-anything," Josie said. "Not right now. What I do isn't who I am."

In his fucked up way, Dad taught her that, didn't he? But it wasn't until she said it out loud that Josie realized she believed it.

"I think I got that in a fortune cookie once," Clara said, and when Josie started to argue, Clara touched her arm. "I'm kidding. I agree with you."

"Anyway, that's not what I meant. I meant *us.*"

"You're right. Okay. I'm in."

"I'm not trying to corner you."

"No," Clara said. "I'm in-*in* with you."

Josie's legs felt tingly. *I'm squeezing her fingers too hard.*

When Josie shifted, Clara held her hand and said, "I don't know why this is such a mystery. You're my girl, Josie. Not to go all Hallmark movie on you, but ever since I saw you out there, a drowned kitten by the river, I wanted to take you home."

"That's a different river outside."

"Doesn't matter."

"I noticed you at the protest back then, too," Josie said.

"Because we're supposed to be together," Clara said. "Happily ever after."

Josie watched for any sign she was about to laugh, maybe turn this into a punchline. Clara sipped the coffee and waited. *She means it. She's actually talking about it for real.*

"It makes no sense to stay with just one person," Clara said. "High school sweethearts never work out, you know? You're uber codependent and semi-crazy, but I don't care. It feels like we're already there. Like I can't ..." Clara set down her cup to rub her face, shielding her eyes. *Like she does to smooth out her emotions without me seeing. I tell her everything, try to. But she doesn't let me see her honest-to-God vulnerable.* Then Clara blinked up at Josie, grinning. "Without you, that Josie-sized hole ..." She shook her head. *Joking not to cry.* "I have no interest in knowing what that would be like, honestly."

"What if you get tired of me?" Josie asked. "You don't have to spend your gap year with me."

"Psh." Clara made a 'don't be dumb' face and leaned in, the air alive between them.

Josie felt warmth in her chest and between her legs, knew she was breathing faster. *Good-fast, this time.* When Clara kissed her again, Josie's phone buzzed, and she jumped, spilling her water all over the table and down her shirt and pants.

Josie answered her phone: the policewoman from New York. She apologized that they had no information about Josie's mom, but would Josie mind coming in to complete some paperwork?

"I can't," Josie said. "Not now. I'm actually in Kentucky."

"Kentucky?" the policewoman said, as if she didn't understand the word. "Can I ask why?"

"We found—my girlfriend and I found—a clue, a photo that we thought might explain where my mom went."

"A clue," the policewoman repeated.

Clara raised her eyebrows and rested her head on one fist, the way she did when Josie refused to hang up on telemarketers. *They're just doing their job.*

"I know I'm not explaining this right. My mom's cellphone," Josie said, "it's here, in Kentucky. She had it in New York, but we found it here, in the middle of a park."

"Then your mother's no longer missing?"

"No," Josie said. "I mean she is—I don't know where my mom is. I just have her phone."

"In Kentucky," the policewoman said again, as if it were a joke. "Well, we're not going to have any jurisdiction way down there. If you want to refile or get started with a new case ... you know what I'll do for you, let me give your contact information for local law enforcement, and you can stop in to see them."

New pep in the policewoman's voice, as she realized she could off-load this case to someone else halfway across the country. But Josie didn't' argue, just quickly answered questions: background information on herself and Mom.

"And your father?"

"He died four years ago," Josie said.

"Any other family?"

"I don't know," Josie said. "I'm sorry, I have to go. Thank you for helping."

She tapped off, before the policewoman could cut in. When her phone buzzed again with the New York police calling back, Josie watched it go to voicemail.

"Why didn't you tell her?" Clara asked.

"About what—my dad's mystery brother and mom? Just because he scribbled the name 'Don' in a notebook ..."

"The contacts in his phone, Josie." Clara stabbed a finger at Josie's bag, on the back of her chair.

And now the fun, animal energy Josie felt when Clara kissed her curdled into that familiar anxiety tug in Josie's guts.

"They're nothing," Josie said, but that sounded forced, even to her. "He just didn't delete their numbers and address after—whatever happened to them."

"Maybe," Clara said. "Maybe they are old, archival or whatever, but we don't know."

Josie got up. "I need to dry off."

"I'm sorry, Josie. I know your parents didn't talk about your dad's family. I'm not trying to pressure you."

"It's fine. I'm just going to towel off my shirt."

"Want some help?"

"Later. Behave."

"You behave. I'm caffeinating for *later*."

On her way to the restroom, Josie waited as servers brought a cake to a table of people in suits and formal dresses who were raising a toast. Some kind of milestone. Behind her, Josie heard women laughing and cooing over a baby.

In the black-and-silver granite restroom, Josie stared at herself in the mirror. She was a wreck. Her hair was matted the wrong way, like she'd fallen asleep in a sauna, and her clothes were still scuffed up with dirt stains from the woods. *Why did I run away from the table like that just now? Because I'm embarrassed. I should know about Dad's family—my family—but I thought his mom was dead. He never talked about a brother. Even if Dad was silent on it, why didn't Mom say anything? Mom should have told me.*

Josie dabbed at the wet lower half of her shirt with a towel. It helped but not much. What was the point? It was only water. And Clara didn't care. The future was happening. *Focus on that.* Clara wanted to stay together. They'd figure out the fall. And then college, an apartment somewhere, domesticity. God, maybe even kids someday. World travel and wherever else. It was all right there, almost real.

As Josie returned to their table, Clara watched her, taking quick, focused sips of coffee, like she wanted to finish the cup before Josie sat back down. Outside, the water was gray, dirty-looking. Foamy shapes churned around the boat-restaurant. Dead fish. Masses of them bobbed on the low waves like meaty-gray lily pads. The room smelled different at the table, too, the cooking smells fading under the thin, oily stench of rancid water. Runoff and garbage from outside, probably, and who knew what else.

It wasn't just the restaurant itself that was wrong. It was the context. *Something obvious I'm overlooking about this room.*

"I'll call," Josie said. "Dad's mystery mom and brother. When we're done here. Does something about this restaurant ..?

*That's it.*

"Where are the cars?" Josie asked.

Clara cradled her coffee in both hands. "What?"

"When we were coming in, there were no cars outside," Josie said. "How did all these people get here?"

Clara shrugged at the other tables. "What do you mean—did you see someone in the back? What people?"

*Fuck. She doesn't see ...*

A pigeon smacked into the window and dropped, leaving a bloody smear.

Josie jumped in her seat. "Jesus."

"What was that?"

Another bird fell out of the sky into the river, then another, and a second pigeon bounced onto the outside deck, stopped moving.

"What is happening?" Clara asked.

*No idea.*

Josie scanned the room. It was still loud with conversation. A skinny, disheveled man in a blue suit got up at the far end of the celebratory table. His jacket looked like maybe it fit him years ago, before he'd gone on a new starvation diet. Josie couldn't look away.

"You see the birds outside?" Josie asked, frozen.

"Of course," Clara said. "They're all just ..."

*All just dying. Now. In real-time.*

The disheveled man raised a hand to quiet his table, and a baby in a high-chair gurgled and clapped, drawing laughter. On the other side of the baby, a shampoo-ad beautiful blonde woman in Mom's red-and-blue blouse nibbled playfully on the baby's cheek. *Mom's red-and-blue blouse.*

"Thank you all for coming," the disheveled man said. His peppery beard didn't look intentional. When he raised one hand, Josie glimpsed brownish stains on his white shirt and tie. *He's so young.* He looked uncomfortable in the suit and with the attention, as everyone paused to listen. Other nearby tables quieted, too.

But it was him. It was *them.*

Mom and Dad.

"Josie?" Clara asked. "What's wrong?"

The river-sewer smell thickened. Across the room, the skinless man from the woods stepped in. *Not real. He's not there.*

"Thank you all for coming," Dad said. "We know it's a bit of a drive from Louisville, so thank you. But this neighborhood out here is pretty much all we can afford."

Supposed to be a joke, but no one laughed. People squirmed and murmured, looking away, as if embarrassed for him. But Dad didn't seem phased, his words slurring a little as he continued, "And our dear Josephina thanks you all, too. Give them a smile, sweetheart."

Mom rubbed the baby's back, and the people at the table relaxed again, focused on the infant.

*On me.*

The skinless man approached Mom and Dad's table. The thing had scabby tufts of pink flesh and muscle clinging to its smiling jaws. Long, sinewy lines of meat crisscrossed its ribcage and open pelvis in organic knots that clumped all the way down to the bare, yellow-ish bones of its legs and bare feet.

"You know, when we first moved back to Kentucky, some people thought we were nuts to pick a place like Perryville …" Dad's voice faded. He saw the skinless man, and his shoulders sagged, cheeks and nose swelling red. Other people at the table swiveled to see what Dad was staring at. They looked right at the skinless man—almost on them—and back again, oblivious. *Just like Clara.*

"I'm sorry," Dad said softly, but not to the table. He was talking to the skinless man. "Don't do this."

"Josie?"

Josie blinked back to Clara, her face pinched with concern.

"Did I lose you for a minute?" Clara asked.

"You don't see any of it, do you?" Josie asked, her voice too quiet. She gestured vaguely at the table, where the skinless man stopped, just behind a large, bearded guy in a brown suit and bowtie.

The skinless man motioned to Josie. "You should be taking your medications. Come with me right now."

"Don't," Dad said again, and when he started to circle the table, Mom stepped into his path, with practiced smiles for the table.

"Your family and friends are here," Mom said, half to Dad—reminding him why he couldn't run off—but loud enough for everyone else, so the group would pretend that Dad wasn't suddenly freaking out. *But he sees the skinless man. It's real.*

"Where do you think you are right now?" the skinless man asked Josie, then angled to face Dad again. He reached in to touch the bearded man's left elbow.

Frozen, Dad stared at the skinless man. "I'll fucking end you," he said. "All of you."

"Mark, stop," Mom said, still standing by him, a hand on his arm, trying to put Dad back in his chair. The baby leaned backwards to watch them, upside down.

"Listen to him," a thin, older woman said. "He can't last five minutes in public."

"Mark, we know," a younger, overweight man beside her said. "Let Caitlyn—"

"No!" Dad shouted and shook Mom off, pointing at the skinless man. "Do not touch him!"

Carefully, the skinless man slid one hand down to the bearded man's own hand, then guided the bearded man's fist closed around a steak knife. The skinless man eased it back up, turning it around to angle the blade so the bearded man was aiming at his own throat.

A small woman beside him straightened. "Bobby, what are you doing? Bobby?"

"I'll fucking kill you!" Dad screamed at the skinless man, and as he broke away from Mom, two things happened fast: the overweight man jumped to intercept Dad, and the skinless man dragged the bearded man's hand up and in, stabbing the steak knife into his throat, then around in a quick circle to encompass half of his throat—back to the other side to connect the slits in a deep gash that bled fast, matting his collar red and soaking the top of his shirt.

The bearded man choked and moaned. People screamed, rushing to him, but the skinless man didn't stop. He caught both of the bearded man's wrists—the knife fell away—and he planted the bearded man's hands tight on his own scalp. The skinless man manipulated the bearded man's fingers closed—shouting and crying from a small crowd around him, and the baby squealed in terror—and the skinless man yanked up, tearing the entire mass of skin off his head like a mask. Eyeballs bulged from the man's bare, red-muscled face.

Josie's tongue tasted like coins. Adrenaline. The room stank like soaking garbage. Her stomach swelled up. She looked away, folding both hands over her face. Stomach acid vomit taste in the back of her throat. They were still screaming, the bearded man—no face anymore—whimpering like a wounded dog. Dad's voice cursed and spat through the noise, his rage flowing into snarling noises.

"Fuck," Josie whispered.

*He tried to stop it. He saw, and he tried to stop it. It's real. Dad saw. The same way I do.*

Clara's voice sounded far away: "What is it, Josie?"

"I saw something over there. I still see something, hear it."

"What?"

"A murder. My parents a long time ago, and the thing from the woods killed someone."

"Josie, look at me."

Josie saw the fleshy dark of her fingers and slits of light between them. "I don't want to see it."

"I'm with you," Clara said, and Josie felt Clara rub her shoulder. "Okay? Whatever you see, I'm here with you."

Slowly, Josie lowered her hands, keeping the commotion across the restaurant in the corner of her vision. Frantic movement, and people shouted.

"What did you do, Mark!"

"Where's the Goddamn ambulance!"

"If we were closer to town ..."

Clara said, "Let's go. Right now, let's go. We don't have to stay here."

*Yes. Get off the fucking boat. Find the car, get out of here.*

Josie started to rise, and the skinless man, closer to her now—positioned between the two tables—pointed at the exit.

"Good," he said. "Thank you, Josie. Let's return to your room. Check on your medications."

Josie caught the table with both hands. Clara flagged down the waitress, a smiling woman who came to hear how they were so sorry but something urgent just came up, and they really had to leave—this very minute.

"No," Josie said.

The skinless man's arms dropped again, limp. "No?"

To Clara, Josie said, "No, that's what it wants me to do. It wants us to follow it off this boat. I don't know what this is, but we can't just go with it. Not yet."

A few paces in front of the skinless man, the waitress hesitated. "Y'all want some more coffee, while you decide?"

"You're sure?" Clara asked Josie.

*Fuck no.*

"Yes, I don't know." As Josie lowered to her seat again, the restaurant was suddenly empty behind the skinless man. No Dad, no Mom or baby Josie, none of it. The same tables were arranged differently, without place settings. They had the place entirely to themselves.

"What you're seeing can get worse," the skinless man said. "If you refuse treatment."

"I'll come back," the waitress said, and she started past the skinless man—he caught her arm to stop her.

Frowning, the waitress stumbled to a stop and tried to shake off the invisible pressure of the skinless man's hand on her arm.

Now Clara saw it, too, asked the waitress, "Is something wrong?"

"It's him. The thing from the woods," Josie said. "It's holding her."

"Do you really think your imaginary friends are afraid of a river?" the skinless man asked Josie. "Mark made up so many rules and explanations to explain his illness. It would be a shame to see that repeat."

"Ow." The waitress fussed and pulled, but the skinless man caught the back of her neck with his other hand, locking her in place. She shook her head, confused, and Clara rose, ready to help.

"Miss, are you okay? What can I do?" Back to Josie, Clara asked, "Where is it, Josie? What do you see?"

"Behind her."

"All right then," the skinless man said. "If that's the way it's going to be."

The fish man came in pushing a rolling kitchen cart. With bulbous eyes and gasping, purple lips, he walked the cart to the waitress, who stared, unmoving, as if for a big reveal to explain what she saw. Clara stopped, too, focused on the cart.

"You see that?" Josie asked.

"I see a metal cart," Clara said, her voice tremoring. "A cart that rolled out here by itself ..."

"It didn't."

The fish man circled the cart to the waitress and took her right hand. Just like in Josie's Brooklyn apartment, he had the bare, white-skinned chest of a man, blotchy with scars, naked, with a shriveled cock and too-thin limbs. He pressed the waitress's hand into the cart and brought out a tiny knife in her fist. *Just like the bearded man.*

A small crowd filed into the room in a semi-circle by the exit. Not people. The tallest was a woman-shaped larva, with rows of squirmy little arms all the way up her bare torso to a smiling, veiny head. She looked *melty*, like ice cream left out in the sun. Runny cheeks and droopy ears sagged, as she murmured to the top half of a man without eyes. His torso was mounted on a wheely wooden chair, and he held a chain in either hand that linked to the collars of two hairless cats that were missing their limbs and tails. There was a mole-man thing dressed in red religious robes, a pair of dark-skinned women with their faces pierced together, and others behind them that were a confusion of scaled arms, fur, and snake tails. All waiting on the skinless man.

"Do you see this?" Josie murmured. If she tried to get up, would her legs work? Her knees felt soft, feet numb and far away. *I have to do something. Don't sit here.* "Do you see them?"

But Clara still watched the waitress, as the fish man eased her hand up, so the knife was aimed at her pale blue shirt and stomach.

"Please," Clara said. "Put the knife down. Josie, what do we do?"

"Margaret Bishop," the fish man said. "What do I hear for the lullaby she sang to her niece after the car accident?"

"400!" someone called.

"425!"

"470!"

*An auction. Oh Jesus. It's a Goddamn auction.*

# Chapter Ten

*A* *song to a little girl. They're bidding on parts of her. For her.*

Josie just stared, while Clara's voice ratcheted up, more and more panicked.

"No!" Clara ran to stop her, and the fish man pivoted to punch Clara's throat, knocking her into a stunned, backward fall. Josie was around the table and to Clara before she realized she was moving.

Still down, Clara rubbed her throat, tears in her eyes. "What the fuck was that?"

Shaking and crying, the waitress stabbed through her shirt to cut a hole in her pale stomach. The skinless man still holding her, the fish man manipulated the waitress like a puppet. He reached into the wound—the waitress screamed and convulsed—to pluck a lump of glittery ore out, like a nugget of quartz, dripping blood. He tossed it back into the crowd to the larva woman who had won it.

"Call the police," Clara said. "An ambulance. We can't just ..."

The thought of uniformed cops and paramedics felt absurd, as if Clara had just suggested they phone the moon for help. But the world still existed beyond this room. Didn't it?

"We may have to cut today's event short," the fish man called, and the crowd grumbled in foreign, guttural languages.

Shaking, Josie's guts clenched as she pulled Clara up and away, toward the window. Josie grabbed her bag, found her phone. She tried to unlock it—fingers slipped, wouldn't hit the numbers.

Breathing hard, her face swollen with pain, the waitress saw them. "Help me," she said. "What is happening?"

The crowd shouted louder in overlapping cries, none of it English. Josie finally unlocked her phone, hit the emergency button.

"Don't worry," Clara told the waitress. "We're getting help."

On the phone: *"9-1-1, what is your emergency?"*

The glass-face man appeared at the door, and the room went quiet. Not dragging a chained woman this time, he stomped by the entrance on black hooves, curvy reflections shifting and blurring on his mask. Patterned insect wings flicked and stretched on his back.

Clara tensed, stumbling into the wall, looking right at the glass-face man.

"Do you see him?" Josie asked Clara.

On the phone: *"Ma'am, do you need help? Can you tell me your location?"*

"I'm near the park, Perryville, the battlefield."

*"Are you safe?"*

'Safe.'

*"Is someone hurt, ma'am?"*

"Yes," Josie said. "Send an ambulance, police ..."

The crowd parted around the glass-face man, whispering as he closed on Josie and Clara.

"What the fuck is that?" Clara asked. "Josie?"

"You see him—"

"Yes, I see him—what is it?"

The fish man flicked his head in Josie's direction. "She is not following the medication plan we discussed. This is a serious episode."

The glass-face man clomped closer, then paused, shivering.

"This is a mistake," the skinless man said. "The dosages are clearly not working."

The warped reflection of Josie and Clara swelled and blurred on the glass-face man's mask.

"Burn," he said.

"Burn," Clara repeated. "What the fuck—Josie, is this what you saw in New York?"

On the phone, the emergency responder asked questions, more frantic, but Josie caught Clara's hand and pushed away from the wall.

"Let her go," she told the fish man. "Don't hurt her aga—"

"Don't you wonder what color Clara's small intestines are?" the fish man asked. "How high will the bidding go?"

The glass-face man staggered back toward the crowd, then paused, as if waiting for Josie and Clara. He huffed and shook.

"You're not well, Josie," the skinless man said. "You know that, right?"

"It's a boat," Josie said into her phone. "Come to the steamboat restaurant. Perryville, Kentucky."

"Oh, don't be so negative," the fish man said. "We'll find the pit of Clara's dreams and womb. What will it taste like, I wonder?" He released the waitress, who jolted, dropping the knife.

The skinless man released her, too. "There," he said. "No need to go with him, Josie."

*The glass-face man. They don't want us following him.*

The waitress hunched, clutching the bloody tear of her shirt.

"Look at me," Josie told the waitress. "Walk over to us right now."

But the waitress shook her head, eyes on the glass-face man. "What's wrong with him? God, it fucking hurts ..."

"It's okay," Clara told her, but when she started toward the waitress, the fish man stepped in, too close. Josie yanked Clara back.

"Her night sweats and crystalline faith in humanity," the fish man said. "Oh, they smell lovely."

Josie kept herself in front to block the fish man, waving to the waitress. Still, she didn't move, holding her wound.

"Then her fingernails," the fish man said. "What noises will she make, as they come out?" He stepped in fast to reach around Josie. She swiveled to keep her body between them, backing away to the glass-face man.

"What is happening?" Clara asked. "Josie ..."

*We can't leave this woman, but we can't stay. Can't fight off all these things.*

"Please," Josie said to the waitress. "You have to come with us right now."

And when the waitress started to protest, Clara met her swollen eyes. "It'll be okay."

"Oh, no it won't," the fish man said. He hop-stepped after Josie, almost frog-like, and she pulled Clara back again.

The glass-face man limped toward the misshapen crowd. Already they parted to clear a path out.

"Josie, no!" Clara said and held out a hand to the waitress. "Come on, please!"

"*Please?*" the fish man said. He cocked his head from Clara to the waitress, then walked simply back to her, took her hand and plunged it into the cart—back out with a silver meat cleaver.

"No!" Clara shouted.

Josie started forward automatically, snapping her fingers for the fish man's attention, almost close enough to catch the waitress's arm—and the fish man spiked the cleaver into the waitress's throat. Behind Josie, the crowd groaned, disappointed. A mist of pumping blood and coppery taste locked Josie's legs—*Clara's hand still in my fingers*—and as the waitress slumped, blood spurted down her body, across the floor. Too much, almost comical.

"I'm so sorry," Josie said. Her shoes slipped, squeaking back from the bloody flow.

The waitress crumpled, stopped moving, with the cleaver still lodged in her throat. The fish man and skinless man both watched her now.

"I can't believe she did that," Clara said, too softly. "They *made* her do that."

"Didn't I ask you to leave with me?" the skinless man said. He stepped over the waitress's body, the fish man right beside him. "Didn't I express concern for your well-being—what you might *imagine*, if you stayed here?"

"Clara has pretty ears," the fish man said. "Lovely in a necklace."

Her fingers slipping out of Josie's hand, Clara swiped the tears in her eyes.

*We're not going to die here.*

"Clara, you see this thing—the thing wearing the glass mask—it can take us out. I think we can get out, if we follow him."

Clara shook her head at the waitress's body, where the skinless man and fish man carefully approached, positioning to the right and left, like hunters. "There are more back there?"

"Yes, the ones that did that to her," Josie said. "Trust me?"

Clara's eyes darted, as Josie tried to steady their vision together. She rested her forehead on Clara's.

"Okay," Clara said.

"We follow this thing out."

"The one in the mask," Clara said. "And outside ..."

"We fucking run."

"Running won't help," the skinless man said. "Really, Josie. We've talked about this. You can't outrun yourself—not when you have such an active mental universe."

The fish man muttered something ugly about hurting Clara, but Josie tried not to listen. Not to his threats or the skinless man's sensible, hospital language, tailored to make her feel like she was losing her mind. The words pulled, but she willed them not to register. *Just noise. Don't answer back.*

Keeping her eyes on the floor—no looking back or acknowledging the press of creatures around the exit—Josie followed the glass-face man, pulling Clara out and across the gangway, back to a rocky country road.

The glass-face man continued straight across to the tree line. *Where we just were.*

"No," Clara said and pointed up the road. "Let's follow this back. Let that thing—let him go."

The glass-face man stopped in the grass, waiting for them. Insectoid wings fluttered on his scarred back.

"Good," Josie said. "Okay."

They started along the edge of the road. From here, there was no sign of anyone in the steamboat restaurant, and the glass-face man didn't follow. A moment later, he was gone around a turn in the gravel. Dark lumps cluttered the path ahead. Smallish and fuzzy, they registered as Josie and Clara continued on: birds. Dead birds everywhere.

"Sorry, Josie. I know your birds are important." Clara shook both arms, as if trying to exorcise the tension in them. "What am I saying? What was that back there? Did that happen? You called the police?"

"We're in shock."

A nervous smile flashed across Clara's face. "That's your line in the movie adaptation of this, right? That scene back there ... I don't believe it. It happened, but I don't believe it."

"Why did you see him?"

Clara was right. It didn't feel real, couldn't be.

"You saw the waitress," Josie said, "and the glass-face man. That's all."

"That's all?" Clara said. "Don't tell me what else was there—not now. We know why they're after you, anyway."

"What?"

"You can see them. Whatever these things are, you see them, Josie, and other people don't."

*Like Dad. Just like Dad at the baby's birthday table. My birthday.*

The road wore on, until Clara checked her phone: nothing. It was the same for Josie. When she checked her phones—all three of them—no signal. No way to find their map location.

"It can't be far," Clara said.

Even without cell reception, Josie's phone still showed the time: 5:25 PM. How long had they been out here? Hours since they arrived at the battlefield visitor's center, a lifetime ago. This wasn't the same world.

"It is real, isn't it?" Josie asked.

"That back there? I don't ..." Clara swallowed, their footsteps crunching in the silence around another turn that brought a long view of empty, wooded road. No sign of the battlefield or any other marker. They were alone. "It might be," Clara said at last.

"My dad was committed, I think," Josie said. "He went to the hospital a few times when I was growing up. I used to think it was for the alcohol, but when I was really young, I think he was actually locked up for a little while. They never talked about it, except sideways, you know. Like he would say, 'I don't need to go back.' He wrote about that in his notebook, too. How he was locked up. I think it happened when I was a baby."

Beside Josie, Clara kicked a rock into the grass. "You think it was because he saw them, too?"

"Yeah," Josie said. "I think I may have just seen the moment that did it." She told Clara about the other people at the restaurant, the table with young Mom and Dad—and baby Josie. "And the same bleeding, demon man ... that same thing killed one of them."

"Like the waitress."

*No. He ripped his whole face off like a mask, while Dad raved and shouted obscenities.*

"Yes," Josie said. "Like the waitress."

They continued in silence for a long time, until the sky clouded and began to dim. Still, the road wound on between the quiet trees. Still, no service on their phones. 7:53 PM.

"I think it's possible," Clara said, "that this road does not, in fact, lead directly back to the Perryville battlefield."

"That does seem possible now, yes."

"You know what, though? I'm still glad I came."

Josie grabbed her and kissed Clara for a long moment of warmth that flooded out the exhaustion and lingering terror. Until Clara let go, grinning.

"You're glad, too, huh?"

"I love you so much," Josie said. "If you weren't here ..."

"I am here. And I'm completely wiped, but let's pick it up. We need to find cell signal or a phone or something, before it gets dark. Okay?"

They started at a slow jog that slapped a low dust cloud behind them up another hill. At the top, the trees on either side opened into fields looking over fenced pastures, with a distant farmhouse and barn set back on the right. A pick-up trick approached down the center of the road, its headlights already lit in the twilight.

"Jesus," Clara said. "Finally. Next time, maybe we follow the creepy monster into the forest."

"Or not."

"Right, or not. That's an option, too."

They both waved, blocking the road, until the pickup slowed to a stop on the slope down. A buzzcut man in a uniform leaned out the window. "Help you girls?"

"Yes!" Josie said. "Thank you. We really need a ride. We got lost, and our phones died."

"Hop on in, then," he said, and they did, Josie squeezing into the middle seat between Clara and the sinewy driver. He was dressed like a cop. The truck bed smelled like a wet dog and cigarettes.

"You're police?" Clara asked.

"I am indeed, young lady," he said and swiveled the wheel to turn them back around down the hill. "I can drop you at the Cadillac. They got a phone there, taxis—hell, they may even put you to work." He coughed a laugh, as if that were hilarious.

"Thank you," Josie said. "Is it far?"

"Two minutes."

"What is it?" Clara asked. "You said you're taking us to a car dealership?"

"The Cadillac *Club*," he said, shaking his head, as if they already knew and were toying with him. "I don't think they've ever had an honest-to-God caddy in their lot, like never.

"What's your name?" Josie asked.

"Nathan right now. But I'm Officer Peterson during the nine-to-five." He adjusted an old-fashioned radio dial, complete with an ancient console tape deck. Bigger and squatter than Mom's cassettes, even. What was this called, an 8-track player? It wasn't in bad shape, all of it probably retrofitted with new vintage parts. "Radio?"

He clicked the dial, and a broadcaster cut in about soaring energy prices and oil.

"Always something, isn't it?" Nathan swiveled the dial, and a Dad song—Creedence Clearwater Revival came on. "There *is* a bad moon rising all right."

A concrete and plaster strip mall appeared on the right, with red neon lighting around a black, windowless building: *'Cadillac Club.'*

"Really?" Clara asked.

"It's that or the cows," Nathan said. "I know most of the folks around here, and ain't nobody in twenty miles wanted to pay a phone bill for years."

Clara flashed Josie a 'what-the-fuck' look, but they didn't speak, as the pickup banked into the half-full parking lot.

"If no one's home, where'd all these cars come from?" Clara asked.

"You got an attitude, huh?" The pickup jerked to a stop. Nathan dialed the radio up loud, so he had to shout over the song, "You know, I've got a badge that lets me do just about whatever I want—especially here." He nodded to the dark building. To Josie, he said, "You want to keep your friend quiet, maybe."

Clara got out quickly, holding her door for Josie.

"Thank you for the ride," Josie said, and as she said it, slid across the seat to the door.

He caught her arm. "Hey, can you do me a favor, when you see him?"

Josie shrugged away, and he let go. She eased one foot outside. "When I see who?"

"When you see him," Nathan said again, more slowly, as if she hadn't understood under the music. "Can you tell him I was the one that brought you, okay?"

"Tell who?"

"He's inside." Nathan gestured to the dark Cadillac Club. "He'll let you make a call. You just remember that, right? Put in a good word for me. It was me that collected you. Nobody else."

*Collected us.*

Josie nodded and got out, slammed the door. The pickup peeled away in a sharp U-turn that rocked it back onto the road. They watched it disappear over the next rise.

"What the hell was that?" Clara asked. "Are we supposed to go in there?"

The sodium glow carved sharp shadows along the cars, the dark road and open fields loud with nighttime crickets behind them. They checked their phones again: no good.

"What do you think?" Clara asked.

"I think since we're here, we should check it out. Someone has to have a phone in there."

"But wasn't that fucking weird, just now? Very off, that guy."

"Come on." Josie started up the parking lot. "Yes, it was not normal. So that's more kisses you owe me. But we're also still probably wired from before. Not thinking clearly. Even the most boring person in the world might seem like somebody crazy to us right now."

"Yeah." But Clara didn't sound sure. "What is this place?"

Closer to the black door of the Cadillac Club—whatever it was—something thumped from inside: a beating, rhythmic noise. Bass, from a song. Josie knocked, and the door opened into a dark, glittery purple entry room, with *'Over 21'* and *'No Photography'* warning signs posted on the opposite wall. Nobody here, but the music got louder, as they approached another nondescript door. Even muffled out here, the beat was familiar. It was an old song, with slow, throbbing drums and synthetic-sounding guitars under loud vocals. She knew it but couldn't place it.

A Black woman in a white lingerie bikini-thing and knee-high boots opened the door. She was missing her left arm below the elbow and had a pangea of pale scars all over her neck and collar bone, as if a tiny grenade had gone off there. Her pupils and teeth were glowy white, and plants—*Jesus, stringy ferns and moss*—grew in her armpits, around her belly button, and on the insides of her thighs. Some kind of make-up, fucked up fetish paint. Had to be.

Behind the half-dressed plant woman, the room was a dark, cushiony strip club. A naked woman twirled on a pole on a main stage, while another danced on a second platform farther back. But no one else was there. No audience.

"And who do you belong to?" the plant woman asked Clara.

Clara caught Josie's arm. "Sorry, we're in the wrong place."

"You sure?" the plant woman asked.

"Do you have a phone?" Josie asked. "Our phones don't get signal here. We just want to call a taxi or an Uber."

The plant woman called back into the club, "Allie, we got lucid ones at the door!" Then, to Josie, "What's an 'Uber'?"

The dancer on the main stage had long black hair and was super pale, except for her back, which was twisted and bubbly brown from burns.

*Don't pay attention to this place. Just go back.*

"An Uber," Josie said quietly, and she backed away. "Like a car to pick us up."

A girl dressed all in leather, with open spots at her breasts and legs came around a bar on the side wall. Allie looked younger than the plant woman, but wearier, like even if she had been alive for less time, she'd been running faster.

"Are you lucid, honey?" Allie asked. "This ain't no place for you."

"We'll go," Clara said.

"Mm hm," Allie said. "You do that ..." She squinted at Josie. "Wait, now. You're familiar." Allie's expression had been distant at first. Now, it sharpened, confused. "How's that possible?"

"Can I go?" the plant woman asked Allie. "He's going to be mad, if I don't ..."

"All right, sugar," Allie told her, then pointed at Josie. The plant woman left. "You got the eyes of someone else," Allie said. "That's it. You remind me of a boy. Long time ago, he came in here, just as confused and scared as you. But that wasn't no brother of yours. No, that's too long ago. So why do I ... *oh*." Allie stepped back. "Oh. Damn, girl, what the hell are you doing here?"

*I'm not. This isn't real. I'm leaving.*

"We don't want to be here," Josie said. "We just need a phone ..."

"Come on, Josie," Clara said.

But Josie's legs didn't work. *What is this place?*

"You shouldn't be," Allie said. "I mean, you *really* shouldn't be within a thousand miles of him. And right now, you're on his doorstep. Do you know what he'll do if he catches you? Either into the stone or remade, like your daddy, or else he'll just gobble you up whole." She nodded to Clara. "She's cute."

"My girlfriend," Josie said.

"Is that right? You ain't going to find your daddy here. Mark's long gone."

Clara started to pull Josie back. *No. Wait.*

"You know his name," Josie said. "How do you know my dad's name? Is this real? Clara, do you see this?"

"I see it," Clara murmured. "Fucked up strip club. Let's go."

"Oh, I see—she's got no idea, does she?" Allie said. "Do you? Your daddy came here when he was just a little boy. You know that, don't you?"

The music changed to a cowboy song with a honky-tonk beat. The dancers switched out, and now the burned girl from the main stage passed behind Allie, pulling on a shiny red dress.

"Allie, who are you …" She stopped when she saw Josie. "Oh shit. She looks just like—"

"Yeah, she does," Allie said. "Wonder why."

"But she's too young, and I thought the sister was already—"

"She's the *daughter*," Allie said.

"Well, shit."

"You're famous. The stories I've heard about your family—brave or stupid, you tell me." Allie gestured deeper into the club. "Your daddy walked right over there, just past the bar. You see the door? That's where he went."

"You said 'Mark,'" Josie said. "My dad's name. You couldn't have guessed that."

"*Guessed?* Girl, your daddy made a few dumbass choices, but whose didn't, right? Mine sure did. Difference is, yours got himself swallowed up. Thought he could save them all. Nobody gets saved, not *his* daddy or sister …"

"The brother," the burned girl said. "Mark got him out, though."

"Sure did," Allie said and shook her head at both of them. "You look fucking confused, girls. Your daddy, Josephina—it's Josephina, right?—your daddy came to save *his* dad and brother, when he was little. And you know, one out of two ain't bad around here. Your eyes, same as his. I swear to God."

*Nonsense. These women aren't even much older than me. Couldn't have possibly known Dad as a kid.* This was a lie. A trick. Somehow ... but there was no 'somehow.' No way to put it together that made sense. Not waking life sense. This was something else.

"This is real, isn't it?" Josie asked quietly.

"Maybe, but doesn't really matter. Happening either way. So, are you coming in or ain't you?"

"No," Clara said. "Let's just walk away."

"Please," Josie said.

*"Please,"* Allie said, and the burned girl giggled, sauntering away. "That's a word we hear a lot of. Why are *you* here? I mean really: why? You don't belong. Look at you."

"We're looking for my mom," Josie said.

"Not your daddy, though?"

"No, my dad's dead."

Allie smiled sadly. "No honey, he ain't. Whoever told you that thought they were helping you, I'm sure. But Mark ain't dead. He should be, but he's not. Not sure I'd say he's alive, though."

"This is crazy," Clara said, breathing hard behind Josie. "Back outside, Josie, now."

Whatever chemical imbalance hallucination this was, Clara could see it. The club lights, shadows, and women made Josie's pulse loud, squeezing her thoughts into a stream-of-consciousness, dream-logic mush. Like if she stayed here, she wouldn't leave. Wouldn't *want* to or remember how.

"You can't really leave now, can you?" Allie said.

"Of course we can," Josie said, but she didn't turn away. "You said my dad came here to help *his* dad and brother. Why?"

"You want me to show you?" Allie asked, and when Clara started to object again, Allie crossed her arms, impatient. "What do you think this is? A titty bar? A country dive, like with poor working girls and cash registers and death dick bouncers? Let me say it again, real slow this time so I don't repeat myself: you got no idea where you are right now. If you walk out of that lot and turn around, you think we'll be here, waiting for you?" She gave them each a pointed look, as if that explained everything. The club would vanish if they stepped outside? "What year do you think it is in here?"

Now Clara stopped pulling away, as if stunned by the question. "What?"

"You think we even got a use for years and time the way you girls do?" Allie stepped aside to open a path. "Now. I'm offering to show you. The way down. The way your daddy went. Nobody else can do that. I probably shouldn't, but I don't think you want to go back outside right now."

As fucked as this was, the way Allie half-explained things helped. No whispered nonsense about Josie neglecting her medications or butchery vibes directed at Clara. At least there was a logic behind this. A strip club that existed out of time, somehow connected to Dad. At least Allie spoke like a friend.

"My dad came here ..."

"Come on," Allie said.

She walked them back to a black door, unlocked it. The room swam with the plastic-flower smell of strong, cheap perfume, with a charcoal undertow, like someone had barbequed earlier. Shapes of people were fused to the chairs and velvety booths, like melted plastic As Josie's eyes adjusted, she could make out corpses smeared into flesh, welded with the furniture.

Allie opened the black door to more stairs that led down to a passage of stone and harsh yellow light.

"What is this?" Clara asked, a frightened smile playing at her lips. "Josie, what are we doing?"

"The mistake you're making right now isn't being here," Allie said. "It's thinking you're ever going to understand all of it. You'll never know your daddy. Nobody does."

"But he went down there." Josie stepped in.

# Chapter Eleven

Still by the door at the top of the stairs, Josie asked, "Why did my dad come here? You said for his family, but why? What happened to them?"

Allie's eyes glossed empty again. "That's a question, ain't it. What's the worst thing out there? You have a midnight fear? For me, it was being tortured as a *thing* in a cage. That was my worst fear. And now that I live it, it's not so bad. What about you?"

"Stop it," Clara said. "Both of you. Does this lead out? What's down there?"

"Worst fear?" Allie asked again.

"I don't know," Josie said. "Loss, maybe. Losing people I care about."

"Oh honey." Allie shook her head and smiled, as if that were the stupidest thing she'd ever heard. "You're only saying that, because you've never had to bite through real pain. Serious body pain is always worse than your feelings. Your own body is what you should be afraid to lose, both of you." She slammed the door on them.

*Oh shit.* There was no doorknob.

"Allie?" Josie banged on the door. "Allie, what the fuck?"

"What are we doing here, Josie?" Clara asked. "My phone still doesn't work, and this place ..."

"I know, I'm sorry. This is my fault. She knew my dad's name."

"That's not a reason to ..." Clara stopped herself, face flushed and still breathing hard. "You know what, this is real, which means that, for real, at some point we will get out of here. This door will open, and we'll get out."

The walls were cut out of blotchy red and brown rock. Her eyes adjusted to the yellow tunnel lights hanging all the way down the stairs. Right beside the door, Josie could make out graffiti close to the ground: *'There is always an answer.'* Solitary confinement motivation from whoever Allie last tricked into this place.

Clara slammed her fists on the door. "Allie, open the door! Let us out!" The same cowboy song played from the other side. "Open the Goddamn door!" Clara pressed her palms to the door, testing to see if would budge. Nothing.

"I'm so sorry," Josie said again.

"I know. It's okay."

Josie's eyes and nostrils hurt. The air tingled and burned when she swallowed. A chemical smell, as if the air were drenched in bleach below.

"Goddamn it," Josie said. She wanted to scream, not words, just raging noise. At the bottom of the stone steps, the stairs ended at a bare landing and red door. *What do we do?* "Did you hear what she said," Josie said, "about this place not existing—or being somewhere without time ..?"

"I heard." Clara checked her phone again and shook her head. "What are we going to do?"

*Stone stairs into a cavern under the Cadillac Club. This is a real place. We aren't lost. There's music past this door.*

"There's light down there," Clara said. "The stairs ... we could at least check that door."

"No, we need to get out, not go further in." Josie banged on the door again. This was a trap. Panic swelled up from her gut. And they were caught in it—just like Elvis. What did Allie say? That Josie should be afraid of pain.

*Stop it. The door will open.*

The honky-tonk song ended, and in the sudden quiet, muffled voices and footsteps passed the door. They hammered their fists, both of them shouting and trying to shake the door. It didn't move. Another song started, this one with a disco-ish pulse.

"Damn it," Clara said.

"Someone will let us out," Josie said.

"We can't stay here, Josie."

"We shouldn't go down."

"I know that," Clara said. "But you're the one who wanted to see what brought your *'daddy'* here. Who knows, maybe he left something, or there's another exit? Maybe that's why she put us here, so we can sneak out, without people seeing us leave through the main entrance. What choice do we have, really?" And just like that, Clara headed down the stairs. "Josie, we can do this."

*No.* "Clara, please."

"Come on. If there's anything down here, we'll fuck up the oogly booglies. Dudes in masks don't scare me. Well, the one at the steamboat restaurant did, to be honest. But right now, I'm so tired and hungry that I just want to ..."

She went through the red door, and Josie ran after her ...

... and winced in sudden daylight, instinctively covering her eyes. White pain flashed in her left hand.

"Ow, what the hell?"

The world dilated into rapid focus. Josie stood outside a cavern entrance in the side of a woody, overgrown hill, ankle-deep in a fast-moving stream. Striated fossils glittered in the water—and there was Clara, slumped on the hillside, her shirt half-gone and the entire right side of her face misshapen and bloody, the eye swollen shut.

"What the fuck! Clara!" Josie's legs felt weak, as she ran to her, muscles aching, like she'd just run for hours. She still had her bag, but her arms and hands—all of her—was covered in wet grime and scabby wounds. "Clara?" Josie took her hand: warm and limp. She had a pulse, not strong, but yes, she was breathing. "Clara, what happened? Wake up."

When Josie tried to pull her up, Clara moaned a reflex noise. Pain. Too many bruises on her exposed belly and side. Their shoes and pants were torn, too, as if they'd crawled through sharp rocks.

"Okay," Josie said. "This is okay. We're together. We'll figure it out." She found her phone. All the phones and lucky fossil were still in her bag, but no water bottle. And where were her spare clothes?

Nothing had power. All three phones—Josie's, Mom's, and Dad's—were dead.

"Fuck." Josie turned in a slow circle. *Where am I?* Her mouth was parched, too dry to swallow, and she shouldn't—*dirty bacteria, whatever*—but she cupped a mouthful of stream water into her lips, then another, and forced herself to stop. Trees swelled on either side of the creek bed, but they weren't green like they should be. Swaying in the wind, their branches scraped, brown leaves cracking and falling like early autumn. It was late May, not autumn. *Think about that later.*

*The fossils.* This was the same creek from the Perryville battlefield, but why was there daylight? How long were they ... wherever they were?

*Again: file away. Focus. Clara is hurt. Get help. Get her up if you can. The car isn't far.*

*If it's still there.*

Josie leaned in to scoop Clara's arm over her shoulder, then slowly, wincing with the weight, guided her up. Clara's head lolled against Josie's shoulder, but at least one of her legs seemed to work, because the lift eased just a little.

"Josie ..." Clara murmured, eyes still closed.

"Yeah, stay with me. I'm not leaving you. Come on, just up this hill." Josie's legs dragged, everything heavier than it should be, as she strained, testing and retesting each step. "This ... fucking ... hill ..." To the top, where Josie held Clara up, trembling with fatigue. *If I stop, I won't be able to move. Keep going.* Josie didn't look at the barren, gray trees and bushes or the bodies of birds and squirls, all dead in the leaves. Somehow, miraculously, this was the right way.

The still, drained colors of the woods made the bright trail marker really pop, where it was still fixed to a tree far ahead. Any other time, with the world humming and in bloom the way it had been before, Josie might not have seen it.

*But it wasn't humming before either. Not really. The forest was quiet then, too.*

*Leave that thought. Come back for it.*

Only her footsteps and managing Clara's weight two-hundred and fifteen steps to the trail, and she stopped counting on the blessedly level dirt path, all the way back to the entrance and battlefield hills. The woods opened into a vista of fenced hills, monuments, and careful hedges, all washed out and dead-looking. Green grass looked burnt now, the bushes and trees soft black and brown. The whole thing like a shitty image manipulation or antique camera mistake, with unnatural steam still misting the ditches and gulleys.

Watching the ground again, Josie counted her pace in a slow drag, step-step. Every third step she rewarded herself with a moment to pant and blink sweat from her eyes. Clara didn't speak or make noise along the ridgeline, not even when the visitor's center and parking lot came into view, with their red rental car still there. *Still fucking there.*

Only two other cars in the lot, and as Josie staggered closer, an elderly couple came out of the visitor's center on canes.

"Look at that girl!" the woman said. "She needs help, Raymond. Go on. I'll tell them inside."

The old woman shuffled back into the visitor's center, while Raymond, a grim man in a military veteran's hat, approached at a too-fast limp on his cane. "She's hurt," Josie said, as he came close. The visitor's center documentary guide—still in his Civil War outfit—jogged across the lot, with the elderly woman right behind, shouting instructions.

"You got yourselves hurt out there?" the old man, Raymond, said. "Here now, I got you."

"Are you sure?" But Josie let him take Clara's other arm. "Thank you."

"Not half as feeble as I look," Raymond said, with a wink, and when the documentary guide arrived, he called, "Come on now, can't you see she can barely stand? Help her! Take that other arm."

Josie let the documentary guide and Raymond carry Clara into the lot and up to the visitor's center. *The rental car. I can drive her to a hospital. I can ...* But Josie followed them in, without arguing. They eased Clara down onto the carpet by the front windows, and Josie collapsed into a nearby chair. She heard the woman at the gift shop desk calling an ambulance, and while the elderly couple started talking over each other—"How long were you out there?" "Somebody attack you?" "Raymond, let the girl speak." "I'm only saying, those aren't hiking injuries. Not at all."—the documentary guide handed Josie a tall plastic cup of water.

"I remember you," he said. "Y'all were here last week, asking about the caves. Guess you found out for yourself, huh?"

Josie found a power outlet below the window and plugged in her phone. *Hurry up.* The screen brightened. *Thank God. Okay. Where is* ... Josie's home screen was cluttered with messages and missed calls, but the time didn't make sense.

The woman in the gift shop said an ambulance would be twenty minutes. The elderly couple were debating Clara's injuries, and the documentary guide just watcher Josie, as if she didn't fit.

*I don't.*

"What happened out there?" he asked. "You get lost?"

The time on Josie's phone read: 3:45 PM.

*No, that was hours ago, and* ...

*And the date.*

June 2nd.

"Yes," she said, voice hoarse. "I think so."

*One day left.*

# Chapter Twelve

"My phone is broken," Josie told the documentary guide. "It says June 2nd. Why does it say June 2nd?"

"Not sure I understand what you're asking," he said.

*Focus.* Josie tapped the message icons. Texts, mostly from numbers she didn't recognize, all dated from between late May and today, June 2nd. The phone announcements ratchetted up and up *and up*, all with the same urgent theme: *Where are you?* There were voicemails and unopened emails. *Throw it out the window. The phone is crazy.*

She stared at the unread notes and calls. Missed calls from the Louisville police department, messages and calls from Clara's foster parents, and a couple from other friends from school, and then an official note suggesting there was a reward for information leading to Josie's safe return.

*They thought I was kidnapped for days. This isn't possible.*

*Maybe I was.*

Josie looked up at the documentary guide and elderly couple, who quieted, as if eager to hear her speak. "I don't remember what happened. I don't know where we were or how we got here. That's my rental car outside, but we left. We walked away from here to a ..." A trap in the stone basement of a strip club. Josie sank bank in her chair, and her stomach growled, suddenly hungry. "I think I need to eat and ... more water, please."

"Turkey sandwiches are four-fifty," the woman in the gift shop said. "Water is a dollar."

"Laura, you give her whatever she wants," the documentary guide said and went to gather a make-shift meal. "We are judged by our decisions in moments of crisis." Grabbing a sandwich, ice cream cup, chips, and water, he gave Laura a serious look on his way by the cash register. "Not when it's easy, when it's hard. That's what makes a man."

Laura rolled her eyes and rang up the items. "Well, I'm not a man, and that's from your boring TV show in there."

"It's an award-winning film," he said. "Laura, we got two hurt girls in there. What if they were your family?"

"They're not."

As they argued, the old woman came to Josie's side. "Is there anyone you can call, dear?"

Josie watched the battery icon blink on her phone, as it slowly charged. *Anyone I can call.* Clara's foster parents, yes, but they would be difficult, maybe even blame Josie at first. Better to let the police or hospital reach them. Josie tapped to bring up recent contacts: police, Mom, Clara, Dr. Laymon ...

Dr. Laymon knew. Or, at least he knew more than he told her, if he'd been seeing Dad.

*The woman at the strip club, Allie, said Dad is still alive.*

The words hadn't registered when she said that. Josie looked right past, as if her mind were filtering toxins, cancer-causing syllables. But no, that wasn't quite right either, was it? She didn't say Dad was alive. She said he wasn't dead—and stressed the distinction.

*What about Dad's phone? Charge it up and call 'Don,' the same number Dad labelled 'Mom'? Dr. Laymon should know them, too. My mom is still gone, so I have to call them, just like Clara said. But who are they?*

She dialed Dr. Laymon's office, and a man answered, "Hello, yes?"

"Hi, I'm calling for Dr. Laymon. I'm sort of one of his patients ..."

"Visitation is at Solomon's, noon to four tomorrow."

The words didn't register. Wrong number?

"My name is Josephina Morris." Josie paused to accept a plastic bag of food and water from the documentary guide. He gave her a 'thumbs up' to signal that he didn't want to disturb her call.

The elderly woman stage whispered, "Make your calls, dear. Come on now, Raymond."

"But that girl, your friend," Raymond told Josie, "she was clearly attacked."

"I know," Josie said and missed something on the phone. Back on the call, she said, "I'm sorry, can you please ask Dr. Laymon to call me back?" Silence on the line. "I need his advice about my dad's family. Anything he can tell me that I should know ..."

"Let me stop you," the guy said. "Dr. Laymon passed away. Sorry. Visitation will be at the Solomon Funeral Home. Do you have the address?"

The elderly couple left for their car outside, and the documentary guide went to over-explain something to Laura in the gift shop with big hand gestures.

"I don't understand," Josie said on the phone.

"He died," the guy said. "Right in his own place. These things used to make the newspaper, but with everything ... well, there it is."

Dr. Laymon wasn't dead. Josie just saw him. "That's got to be a mistake."

The guy gave a short, ugly laugh. "I wish. I am sorry, believe me. You want to leave your number for a referral? We're sorting that next week."

"Why did you say he died in his apartment?" Saying it out loud made Josie's eyes sting with surprised tears. She wiped them away. *No warning.*

"People think they're safe at home, I guess," the guy said. "But those animals break in and ..."

She ended the call.

*No. Don't listen. With everything, don't. Call someone else.*

She did. After trying to wake Clara enough for a sip of water—no good—Josie finally called Clara's foster parents, then a few friends from school. But didn't give them any real explanations. *Because what can I say? I don't know where we were. I don't know what happened. We were there, and now Clara is hurt. We're together and maybe not safe-safe, but alive and together.*

When an ambulance arrived, paramedics loaded Clara onto a stretcher in the back. Did Josie feel well enough to follow in her own car? She wasn't family, and strictly speaking, they shouldn't let her ride along.

Too weak to argue, Josie downed another water and ate a dry turkey sandwich fast, as she followed the ambulance onto I-65 north, back to Louisville. *Good. Out of this place, whatever it is. Closer to the airport home.* No flashing lights or sirens from the ambulance on the interstate, except when slow-moving cars blocked the lane. Josie stayed too close behind all the way through the suburbs and outskirts of the city.

Finally, off the highway, they followed a main street lined with mansions and newer glass apartments, ringed with balconies and satellite dishes. None of this was familiar, as the ambulance sped past more mixed neighborhoods and through a network of office buildings. In the near distance, a highway overpass rose along a wide, gray riverbank. Maybe a mile away, but even from here, it looked the same as it did the day she met Clara. When she saw Dad's ghost for the first time.

They arrived at a hospital that was bigger than Josie expected, a new-looking, white brick building with two floors of wraparound glass that towered over the front drive. Inside, a nurse took Josie back through an ER admission area to a partitioned exam room. Still unconscious, Clara already had oxygen tubes in her nose, an IV in her right arm. At first, the hospital staff tried to persuade Josie to leave—"Much easier, if we can see you individually"—but when she refused, the nurses finally took blood and examined Josie right beside Clara.

"Stop worrying about me," Josie told a young doctor, when he ducked in. "Why won't she wake up? What's wrong with her?"

"Obvious head trauma. We are prepping for a scan and more tests," the doctor said. "I'm sorry, but you really can't tag along for all that. Don't worry, we'll take good care of her."

In a chair beside Clara's table, Josie took Clara's hand. "I can't leave her."

"I understand." He met Josie's eye, as if he really and truly did. "But it's policy. Not our decision to make."

"They might be looking for her, like that *thing* said on the steamboat," Josie said. "If they show up, you won't see them." A quiet part of Josie said, *'Stop. Listen to your words. You're going to scare the nice doctor.'*

*I have to calm down. Somehow, I need to be rational.*

The doctor stiffened, watching her differently, almost suspicious. "Our treatment areas are very safe, I promise," he said. "Whoever did this to her, that's for the police. No one can come in."

"They can," Josie murmured.

But he was already on his way out. A new nurse appeared, ready to guide Josie away.

"Wait." Josie got up close to Clara, still holding her hand. "You don't know if she can hear me, do you?"

The nurse frowned. "We don't know anything yet, dear."

"Clara, I'm right here." Josie stroked the hair from her broken face. One entire side of her jaw, cheek, and forehead were out of place and bulging, like bruised fruit.

Clara's good eye fluttered open, bloodshot. "Caitlyn ..." Clara whispered.

"I don't know," Josie said. "She's not here."

"Caitlyn. Is not ..."

"No," Josie said again. "She's not here, Clara. I'll find her. I love you. I'll find whoever did this to you. That's next."

Clara sagged, quiet again.

"Fuck." Josie straightened, let go of Clara's hand.

"She'll be fine," the nurse said and touched Josie's arm to turn her away and out.

*This is too much.* Out of the emergency room, the nurse walked Josie to an elevator, then along an emptier hall to another exam room, with American flag decals and anatomical posters covering the walls. *What if I can't find Mom?* The nurse left, promised they'd check back in "two shakes." *What if I have to stop looking, and Clara never wakes up?*

Josie remembered the gray, cold light in her bedroom in Connecticut, before she met Clara. Most days, Josie played puzzle games on her phone, while half-watching reality shows on her computer. When Mom and Dad knocked to check in, Josie had shrugged. Things were fine, boring. And it was mostly true. The kids at school weren't cold like in Boston. Here, they just didn't care. They sensed she was a visitor passing through.

They were right. So, Josie had crowded her mind with bright shapes, social media, and inane, dating reality competitions, until the urge to scream and cry dissipated. Each night, Mom cooked, while Dad prowled the house with papers and a drink in-hand, talking about his latest electrical job or how no one else at the jobsite could drill a proper hole in concrete. Hartford only lasted a year and a half anyway, before Dad loaded a moving truck for New York City. *Could I do that again? Start again someplace new?*

A tired-looking police officer knocked and came in to interview her, and Josie apologized, said she had no memory.

"But I really have been gone?"

"You really have been," he said, a big guy, built like a human re-frigerator in a stiff uniform, with the *'Notes'* app up on his phone. "And now, we've got to huddle up to find your mom." Mom *was* still missing. "I'm sure she's fine, though, Josie. You'll probably hear from her soon."

*Just like the police in New York.*

"But I might have been drugged," Josie said. "I saw things at the restaurant, Captain's Quarters."

He paused in his notetaking. "You mean the market at fisherman's wharf, downtown?"

"What? No, 'Captain's Quarters' was the name of the steamboat restaurant. It was in Perryville, near the Civil War battlefield.""Okay," he said, "sure thing." And tapped something on his phone. He said it like he was humoring her, knew the right answer, but didn't want to start an argument.

"That's not the name?"

"The restaurant probably isn't important, Josie. It's what happened after—"

"What's the name of the steamboat restaurant?"

He stiffened. "There's no steamboat restaurant that I know of. Unless it's brand-brand new."

"What about the Cadillac Club?"

He lowered his phone. "You mean from the fire? That spot is out a ways, by Perryville. But I don't think there's a restaurant there now."

"What fire?"

"Back awhile a lot of building codes had to change, because of it. Liquor licenses, too. We still cite the Cadillac Club law sometimes, if folks ignore the fire marshal."

"I don't understand," Josie said. *"What fire?"*

"The Cadillac Club fire. Isn't that what you're talking about? It burned down a long time ago, lots of people died. Then they demolished it. Kind of a national scandal. I guess the place had too many bad wires and not enough exits. An officer died in that fire, too. A buddy of mine's uncle."

"Nathan Peterson," Josie said automatically. "His uniform was different and that truck was much older ..."

The policeman stared at her. "That was him, yes. You must have looked it up online? Long time ago, but maybe it was in the news stories about the fire up in Chicago yesterday?"

The room felt far away, the policeman's voice echoey and distant. *Don't ask.*

"Chicago?"

"I guess it was a school event?" he said. "High school prom in a nice neighborhood on the northside, but the same thing happened—bad wiring. Sprinklers never started."

That quiet part of her said to stop. Lincoln Park was on the north-side of Chicago. Her old neighborhood. *Get up and leave.* Bile pinched at the back of her nostrils. Her stomach might come up.

"When?" Josie asked.

"Couple days ago," he said. "I thought you heard. That's why you mentioned it. Horrible damn thing. Bunch of kids died."

*They'll start with your family.*

Josie swiveled her feet off the exam table. *Dad and Mom. Now Dr. Laymon, and high school kids in Chicago ... Not kids. You know it was them. They wrote you back.*

"I was in the Cadillac Club," Josie said.

"No," he said. "I told you, that was all torn down."

"Well, I was. And Captain's Quarters, too. A restaurant on a steamboat. Look it up. I bet it was shut down, after a man killed himself. Tore off his own ..."

He was quiet, as she closed her mouth, swallowed slowly. *What am I doing?*

"Josie, want me to call that doctor back in here?"

"He said I could go."

"I know. But is that the right play?"

Josie slouched against the table, staring at a color-coded picture of the inner ear that was posted above a metal sink across from her. Probably not. But she wasn't going to hide in here. Maybe he was right. Mom was fine. Josie just didn't know where.

"What's wrong with the plants outside?" she asked.

He shuffled awkwardly. "Nobody talked to you about that? A 'ten-thousand year drought,' they're calling it. More than a drought, if you ask me. Plants don't just die like this out of nowhere. You haven't seen a grocery store in a minute, have you? The Kroger down a ways, we had to shut it down. It's only open a couple hours a day, with a line around the block."

"Why?"

"Because there wouldn't be enough otherwise." He watched her, frowning again, as if this should be obvious. "Grocery store usually means you have food. Still, not as bad as other places. Those big cities are in a bind. Honestly, I feel for those folks."

"The food is running out?" Josie asked. "How is that possible?"

"I wouldn't worry," he said. "It'll come back. Just going to be a little lean for a bit. Another buddy of mine grew up in Havana, and he told me that after the Soviet Union broke up the Cubans never had enough, not ever. People got shorter, lost weight—for *years*. You know what they called that? The 'special period.'" He burst out laughing, slapping his leg with his phone, and Josie smiled. Not even a little funny, but his laughter was contagious. "So, we have ourselves a *special period*, too. The whole world's special period."

First birds, now this. Like Clara's fossils. 'Special' wasn't the right word.

"Can I ask you," Josie said, "after I talked to the police in New York about my mom, they said they'd send my information, all of that, here."

"Right on." He wagged his phone like a winning lottery ticket. "These new systems they've got us on, it's all right here. Almost like the movies, if it weren't for all the damn updates they make us download."

"My dad," Josie said. "Do you have information about him?"

The policeman started nodding and tapping faster on his phone, suddenly more animated. "That we do. Nine times out of ten, you get a missing person, you knock on the ex's door, and—bam! No more missing person. Let's see, your dad ..." His face fell. "That's right, I saw this earlier. I'm sorry, you know this already. Deceased four years ago, 'commercial accident.'"

Suicide. 'Commercial accident' might have been Mom's lawyer talk to manage the life insurance coverage and who knew how many other issues.

"Was he ever in prison?" Josie asked.

"Your dad? Let me see." The policeman adjusted his phone for a long time, then brightened, when he found it. "Here it goes. Mark Morris. Misdemeanor disturbing the peace, seventeen years ago, and charged with kidnapping, whole slew of other things, nineteen years ago. Those charges were dropped, though. Nothing on here about him being locked up."

"Does it really say 'kidnapping'?" Josie asked. "My dad wouldn't …"

"Yes indeed," he said. "Kidnapping … Ms. Caitlyn Fisher. Wait." He looked up, half-smiling. "That's her, isn't it?"

Before they were married. Before I was born—right before I was born. *What the fuck?*

"I tell you, if he wasn't out of the picture, we'd have a great prime suspect," the policeman said.

"You mean if my dad wasn't dead, you'd be happy, because you could arrest him for my mom's disappearance?"

The policeman shuffled back, as the words registered. "That came out wrong," he said. "You know what I mean. Anyway, I got to push on. You hear anything at all, you give us a shout."

Josie watched him leave. If Dad wasn't dead, he'd be in a cell some-where, was that it?

When she was alone, Josie let out a shaky breath, then rooted through her bag to find Dad's old phone. She tethered it to a wall socket and waited for the screen to light up.

"Who were you, Dad? I need to stop asking, right? It's a waste of time. You kidnapped Mom." Vocalizing the words didn't make it sound less absurd. "Why?" she asked the empty room. "The disturbance on the boat—fine, I get that. I saw it, too." She watched the hospital room, listening to her own pulse. "Now. Now you could come back. Not in the middle of my high school graduation, how about right now? If you exist, like Allie said, where are you?"

Nothing. *Screw it.*

Talking to herself didn't help. Nothing felt clearer.

Dad's phone came on, and she found his contacts. There it was: 'Don.' *My long-lost uncle.*

*Am I doing this?*

*He won't be there. It's an old number and leads nowhere. This is just a box to check, to say I did everything I could.*

She pressed a green phone symbol to call. *Here goes.* The line rang, and then a slow voice said, "Hello?"

"This is Josephina. Everybody calls me Josie. I think you're my uncle."

"You're. All right!"

He spoke with a halting, deliberate cadence, some kind of speech impediment. Josie's math teacher in Chicago had a stutter, but not this bad. Why was Uncle Don so happy to hear from her?

"Yeah, I'm fine. My mom told me you lived in Louisville, and I just thought—"

"Do you want. To talk to her?"

*The fuck?*

"My mom is with you?"

He called away from the phone, "Caitlyn! Your daughter. It's Josie."

The line ruffled, and Mom's asked, "Josie, are you there? Where are you?"

"Mom? Where are *you*—here in Kentucky?"

"Yes, I'm so sorry, sweetheart. I came to see your uncle. You're safe? Are you hurt?"

Frantic thoughts swam and fused in her mind. Mom left in Brooklyn in the middle of a storm. No car. And she came here, to see relatives Josie didn't know existed before? Was this real?

"I don't understand," Josie said.

"Do you have the address?" Mom asked, and she gave Josie the same 'Tyler Lane' house address in Dad's contacts. "Can you make it here?"

"What happened, Mom?"

"It's been crazy," Mom said. "I'm so sorry, Josie. Please, just come here, and I'll explain." Mom sounded like she was about to cry.

"I'll be there." Josie plugged the new address into her phone's mapping app. It was only ten minutes away, farther from downtown in a neighborhood called 'The Highlands.' No problem.

"Clara is in the hospital, Mom. She's hurt."

"What happened?"

"I don't know. I don't remember. Nothing."

"We'll figure it out. Don't worry."

Josie closed her eyes. *See, it's okay. Mom is there. She'll know what to do.* And something else nagged Josie, like a high pitch playing in the background that she'd been tuning out. But now, when she focused on it, the non-sound unsettled her guts. Why did Mom come here? How did she get here?

Josie pushed out of the exam room and followed the hall to a desk staffed by two nurses near the elevator. She asked Mom to wait one sec, then asked about Clara.

"We'll call you as soon as we know, honey," the first nurse said.

"Can I see her before I go?"

They said 'no,' and after another back-and-forth, Josie gave up. Too tired, she took the elevator down, then found the rental car outside. More wiry, dead trees around the hospital. No birds, and not many other cars on the road either.

"They all flew away, didn't they?" Josie asked, still on the phone with Mom.

"Who did?" Mom asked.

Josie hesitated. *Who do you think?* "The birds, Mom. Like from the birding app Dad got me. That's what the birders used to say."

"Oh yes. They did."

But Mom's voice hung for a moment, like she wasn't sure what Josie meant. *You know what I'm talking about. Stop it.* "Why did you come here, Mom? I found your phone in a park an hour and a half from here. What happened?"

"Just be safe, and I'll see you soon," Mom said. "And call this number, if anything happens on the drive."

The line clicked off. *What the hell? Mom isn't herself. Maybe she resurfaced after I was gone. Maybe she has been going out of her mind with stress, searching for us.*

Josie guided the rental car out and found the highway. As she merged onto empty lanes, she tapped to hide the old messages on her phone. *I'm found. Not lost anymore.* And as more notes minimized, another notification blinked at her: *'Save new recording?'*

*I didn't record anything.* Josie saw the date: June 1st. *Holy shit. A video was saved on here yesterday in the amnesia gap, when I was gone.* Slowly, Josie eased the car onto the shoulder and coasted to a stop. A car whipped past. Josie tapped the 'Play' arrow icon, and a fuzzy image popped onscreen and came to life. She was looking at a dark hallway lined with big black wall panels, like sound-proofing pads in a recording studio. Yellow light shivered at the far end. Someone was breathing heavily close to the phone, and at the edge of the frame, Josie could barely see the arm of whoever was holding it.

A frantic whisper behind the image.

"Oh Jesus, I can't see them. Why can't I see them, Josie?" Clara's voice.

*Okay, Clara had been filming.*

Onscreen, the other person, backlit and dark, said, "I'm here. Stay close. I think we're almost there."

*My voice.*

She felt an involuntary shiver. *None of this happened—except it did, even if I can't remember. My phone proves it.*

The image swung up, looking back and forth down the hall-way—yellow light at one end, darkness the other way. And what was that muffled breathing sound? Josie squinted. Behind the black wall panels, the surface wasn't dark. It was red and oily pink in the gaps. And it was *moving*.

*No, it's a trick of the light or glitch in the recording.* The video was shaky, borderline pixelated, as it focused on shadow-Josie again. The face was too dark to see, but now Josie heard her own voice, scratchy and no-nonsense, "They said there's water this way."

"You're joking," video-Clara answered back. "There's no light down there."

"They're right behind us. Look at me. We're okay."

"I'm recording this."

"You'll waste the battery," shadow-Josie said. "We need the light, not the video."

Then she scrambled off screen. The video just showed the empty hallway and distant yellow light. The walls *were* moving, throbbing behind the black panels, with the breathing sound.

A soft voice called, "Are they going to the Salt Lake?"

It sounded like a little girl. A shape hopped into view onscreen, the size of a large stork or heron. That was how it moved, too, bird-like. And as it continued closer, the perspective rose, backing away. Shadow-Josie murmured something.

Video-Clara said, "Shit, Josie, is something there?"

The shape in the hallway trotted closer on chicken legs, with webbed, pointed toes. *Except not a stork or any kind of bird.* The top half was the skinny bare chest and arms of a child, and it was wearing a girl's face. *Wearing,* because the face was dangling sideways and split down one side, exposing a sliver of red flesh underneath. The little girl's mouth was cut off above the jaw, and the thing's narrow animal jaw—taut and aggressive like a lizard's—was smeared and streaked red. In one of its human hands, it held a short knife.

From the hall behind the girl-bird-thing, another voice called, "They can't go there with their faces."

"They can't, no," the girl-bird-thing said, and the top half of the girl's face smiled, as it drew back its jaws. Josie glimpsed rows of tiny teeth. *Oh God, this isn't real.*

"We can help!" it shouted down the hall. "Don't run. We can show you the way, if you play with us."

Another small shadow hopped out behind the first, and shadow-Josie's voice said, "Clara ... come on—"

The screen froze. That was it.

# Chapter Thirteen

J osie stared at the silent phone for a long moment. She reached to press the screen, but her hand slipped, and the phone dropped, bounced onto the floor of the car. *I'm not going to bug out, because it isn't real. A strange, hollow feeling in my belly. Not hunger exactly, but like I'm missing a piece, and there's a stringy cord running right up into my abdomen, between my lungs, so all those fleshy organs tug too tightly when I breathe. And I feel the shape of that anxiety hole.*

*What is that video?*

*Fuck if I know. I'm scared and not thinking like I should. I just want to close my eyes and wake up at home with Mom and Clara, all this an anxiety delusion. Because it is.*

The video was real. It was right there, saved on the phone. Monsters underground. *Where Allie trapped us. I really should have tossed the phone out the window when I had the chance.*

Josie picked up the phone and looked out past the mostly empty highway at rust-colored grass and naked foliage. She switched on the car stereo and synced it with the phone, so she could stream music over the speakers. *Not much farther to 'Tyler Lane,' but I need to hear something that isn't demon noises right now.* Josie and Clara kept an always-updating playlist, just like the Clara-Mom playlist, this one nicknamed, 'J and C Against the World.' There were close to 500 songs on it. *Super fitting now.*

Josie swiped, and the speakers gave a reassuring electronic sigh. She opened the audio program—and stopped. There was a new file. Not a song on the playlist, an unknown audio snippet that was seven minutes and six second long. Recorded on May 31st.

Another lunatic clue from when she was gone. *A Goddamn microphone recording someone made on my phone during the missing week.*

*Don't,* a part of Josie said. *Leave it alone.*

Josie's finger hesitated over the play tab. *Ease your fingertip down, just a little to touch the screen. Listen to the recording.*

*No.*

Josie scrolled past that to find the 'J and C Against the World' playlist and skipped past the first two songs, until Elvis Presley's voice came on over the stereo, backed by guitar and drums.

*See? Nothing wrong with the world at all.*

On her phone, with music still playing, Josie looked at the audio file again. Seven minutes and six seconds.

She started driving again, and it took about that long to reach the exit off-ramp for Uncle Don's house. She passed through a quiet neighborhood of strip malls, schools, and churches—all with cars in the lots, but no people. Like an artificial town created for a movie or to test a bomb. Down a suburban street crowded with big, unnaturally leafless trees, Josie checked the houses. As the car slowed to bounce over a speed bump, she noticed pink and red ropes splayed out in curling loops on the front lawn of a house on the right, like a multi-colored garden hose. What was that? And there were more in front of two houses on the left, in the shape of concentric, overlapping circles. The ropes wound together on the brownish grass, up the front porch steps, and into both houses.

*Weird.* No one out, and there was Uncle Don's address, just ahead, a one-story brick ranch. The house was dark and quiet, with all the window shades drawn and a black sedan in the driveway. *How did Mom get here?*

Josie pulled in and stepped out into the quiet. As she crossed to the porch, the grass crumbled under her shoes, leaving gray-white footprints.

*Get back in the car. Go somewhere else.*

Josie called, "Mom? Uncle Don?"

Silence, and she ascended the porch.

*They know I'm coming. They should be watching for me.*

"Mom?" Josie called again and knocked.

The front door wasn't closed. It creaked open. Inside, the entryway was still, with a mail-piled side table and a dead potted fern back in a corner under a wooden crucifix. But Josie didn't step in yet.

"Mom!"

A crunch of tires behind her sent a panicked rush up her spine, and she spun to watch a delivery van pass. It accelerated down the street and was gone. Josie checked the front address again. This *was* Uncle Don's house. So, where were they?

*Don't go in.*

Stopped in the front doorway, Josie found Dad's phone and tapped Uncle Don's contact. Inside, a phone rang. An old-fashioned electronic trill. *A landline, really?* She pushed the door all the way open. Left of the entryway, a carpeted living room with a worn couch, flatscreen TV, and more crucifixes flowed back into a kitchen Josie couldn't quite see. That was where the phone was ringing. Another doorway led off the entryway into a dark hall on the right. Probably bedrooms.

Josie approached through the living room. Photos, dead plants, and dog-shaped figurines—all black Labrador retrievers—lined a display case under ornate, crystal-studded crucifixes, and a hand-colored image of Jesus, with one hand raised in some kind of blessing. One photo was of two boys sitting on the front steps of this house, the taller boy grinning and giving a thumbs-up, while the smaller, skinny boy squinted into the sun, looking confused.

*Dad and Uncle Don? If Uncle Don is older, that must be him.* He looked confident, cocky in that stance. The next, larger picture showed the whole family, but younger and posed on a red-and-green Christmas set with artificial snowflakes dangling behind them. A handsome, narrow-jawed man was smiling, with a thin, dark-haired girl on his knee. Beside them, a young woman with bright, sharp eyes posed behind two younger boys. A boy who was maybe five or six years old hammed it up for the camera next to a toddler, with bunched up cheeks, about to cry. That was Dad, too, just like the younger, squinty kid in the other photo.

The father in this shot must have been her grandfather, but who was the girl?

"Josie?"

She turned: Mom crossed the living room, her eyes bright with tears. They collapsed together. Josie buried her face against Mom's chest. A slow breath of her smell from her blue-patterned blouse … and something else. An undercurrent of leaves and fresh dirt, like Mom had gone for a hike and forgotten to wash. Maybe she had. Maybe in all this time, she hadn't paused to care for herself. Mom stroked Josie's hair, her other arm stiff behind Josie's shoulder and back, almost too hard.

"Thank God," Mom said.

A heavy-set man with friendly green eyes rounded the entryway corner behind Mom. Josie had seen him before—*where?* Uncle Don offered Josie a hand. No thumbs. Jesus, he had scarred stumps on both hands where his thumbs should have been. "It's wonderful. To see you. Josie."

She shook his hand fast, let go. *The steamboat. He was at the baby Josie birthday table. He jumped up and tried to stop Dad from losing his shit, when the skinless man appeared.*

"I am sorry," Uncle Don said. "We didn't hear you. Come in."

Mom squeezed Josie's arm too hard, like she'd forgotten how soft Josie was. "Ow, Mom."

"I'm just so happy to see you," Mom said. "You have no idea how worried I've been. I never should have left like I did."

"You think?" Josie asked. "We were freaked, Mom. Where did you go? I called your work, and they said you didn't come in. How did you even get here? You just left, in the middle of that storm. Oh, you should know, I bought two plane tickets with your credit card. I panicked, didn't know what else—and the money ..." As she spoke, Josie kept waiting for Mom to jump in, say it was okay, they would figure it out, and of course, it was normal to worry. But no, she just stared with a 'uh, what's money' look. *What is wrong with her?*

Uncle Don nodded to the photo display beside Josie. "You probably haven't. Seen these before. Have you?"

"No," Josie said. *Why isn't Mom answering me? Why does she just smile and stare? Did something happen to her?* Josie tapped the little girl in the Christmas picture. "Who's that?"

"Abby," Uncle Don said. "She was. My—our—older sister."

"She would be your aunt," Mom said.

"*Would* be?"

"She died," Uncle Don said.

"When did she die?" Josie asked.

"We don't need to talk about that now, do we?" Mom said. "Josie, she died as a child."

*As a child?*

"Not a nice. Story," Uncle Don said.

Mom stepped away, toward a glass backdoor that looked out on a rear patio and wooded yard.

"Kidnapped," Uncle Don said. "Killed."

"Why didn't you ever tell me?" Josie asked Mom. "Seriously—I know we're just back together, but I have so many questions, Mom. About my uncle ... and do I have a grandmother, too?"

"Sleeping." Uncle Don nodded. "She's not well. I haven't. Woken her to. Surprise her. With this visit."

"Why did you hide this?" Josie asked Mom again, but Mom just stood there, facing away out the back glass. *What is wrong with her?*

"Your father, Mark," Uncle Don said. "Never got to say. Goodbye. He never saw. Abby again, after."

"Jesus, really—"

"She went missing," Uncle Don said. "For years. Then, they found. Her. But the casket. Was closed. Mark—"

"But I didn't even know you existed!" Josie said, voice spiking and raw.

Mom  sighed. "Before something like that happens, it's unimaginable, Josie. After? It becomes an emptiness that doesn't fill. A wound you carry around. Mark was damaged long before you were born."

Mom almost never used Dad's first name, always said 'your father' or 'dad.'

"We all were damaged," Uncle Don said, with a weak smile. "You must be. Hungry?" Past Mom, he opened kitchen cabinets to find plates and a knife, then checked the fridge, arranging plastic-wrapped sandwiches and mayonnaise on the counter. *Health food central, huh?*

"Was there ever a birthday party for me," Josie asked, "on a steamboat—a steamboat restaurant?"

Uncle Don froze, palms flat by the plate. He flashed a worried look at Mom, who didn't react, just continued to zone out, watching the backyard.

"Why?" Uncle Don asked softly.

"There was, wasn't there?" Josie came around between them. "I don't want to ask all these questions, but I feel like I need to know that I'm not losing my mind."

"Who told you?" Uncle Don asked.

"A cop," Josie said. Not true, but close enough. "He visited me at the hospital ..." Mom should have interjected, derailed Josie's explanation with a sharp, concerned cross-examination about her injuries and Clara. But no. She didn't even react. *What happened to her? Don't push her. I'll find out. We'll make this better.*

"Mark was ..." Uncle Don rubbed his eyes, then forced an uncomfortable smile and started arranging sandwiches to slice on the plates. "That was. A bad time."

"He saw things," Josie said. "Didn't he? My dad always saw things no one else did."

"No." Uncle Don offered her a plate loaded with white bread bologna and cheese sandwiches.

"No?"

Seeing the food made Josie's gut rumble. She grabbed half a sandwich, eating in rapid, giant bites that made her cough and choke. She barely tasted the squishy bread and salt of the sandwich. It was already gone, and she started on the second half.

"Well, he did," Uncle Don said. "But I saw them. Too. Not real. Of course. We inherited. *Our* father's debt."

*Debt.* Where did she hear that? Someone else used that word, like this whole thing were an unpaid loan, swelling with more ugly interest every year. With each generation.

"Other people didn't," Uncle Don said. "But Abby saw them. Too."

"All of you see them?" Josie asked, trembling from the rush of calories and sugar—and answers. Order to this mash-up nightmare. Uncle Don and Dad saw them, too—and their dead sister, Abby. That meant ... what?

"Mental illness is. Heritable."

"No," Josie said. "They're real."

"You don't know that," Mom said quietly.

*Now she talks? To tell me I'm nuts? To question this?*

"Mom ..."

"No," Uncle Don said. "Caitlyn is right. It's not real. We know that. Now. We didn't as. Kids. But Mark never stopped. Being a child. In some ways."

"Did you see them when you got older?" Josie asked. "Do you see them now? I have my dad's notebook in my bag in the car. I can show you—he wrote it all down."

"Oh yes," Uncle Don said. He watched her, as if he were impressed and disappointed at the same time. "You remind me. So much of him. Mark had. It all figured out. Do you want to. See?"

From across the room, a woman said, "See what?"

They all stopped to watch a skeletal woman enter the kitchen on a plastic-steel walker. Her face was drawn, like a museum mummy, her head wrapped in an elaborate silk scarf.

She frowned at Josie. "What do you want to show her?"

She was a shrunken, whittled-down version of the lady in the family Christmas photo. *My grandmother.*

"Mom," Uncle Don said. "Josie and Caitlyn—"

"Answer me," Grandma said. "You let her in. After all these years, she shows up, and you just let her back into our lives."

That felt like a slap. Josie glanced at Mom—still distracted by the oh-so-interesting backyard—and set the sandwich plate back down. *This is why you didn't tell me? So I wouldn't walk into this? This angry, defensive woman, but why aren't you sticking up for me, Mom? I have to get to the hospital. I have to be the adult here, with all of them.*

"Yeah, he did," Josie said, staring down Grandma. "It's nice to meet you."

"We've met before," she snapped. "You don't remember. You were tiny, but ..."

"When my dad lost it at my birthday party, did you have him committed?" Josie asked. "Even though he didn't touch the man who killed himself? That guy with a beard, who cut off his own face in the middle of a restaurant—don't ask me how, but I know about that."

Uncle Don backed away, and Grandma blinked, like she hadn't seen Josie in focus before: 'who was this new girl?'

"I know what happened," Josie said. "And later, he kidnapped my mom ..."

"Mark wasn't well," Mom murmured.

"He didn't," Uncle Don said. "The kidnapping wasn't ..."

Grandma pointed a shaky finger at Josie. "You're on vacation from your high-priced college to stir all this up? I can't count how many years and thousands of dollars I've spent keeping this house together without Mark's old nonsense."

"I want to know," Josie said. "Please, I'm not a kid. I know we don't know each other, but I can handle it."

"Oh can you? Your uncle *handled* it. Lost his tongue, but he handled it," Grandma said. "Why do you think he talks like that? That's from the transplant."

*Lost his tongue? How is that possible?*

"Mom," Uncle Don said. "Please don't."

"Your father, though. He *didn't* handle it," she told Josie. "Too much like *his* father. All about excuses. Mark barely knew his sister. He was so young. But he always acted like it hurt him worse than anyone."

"That's not true," Uncle Don said.

"Oh, don't stick up for him. Mark made it his mission to fix things. He couldn't accept that she was gone, the same as his father. Those funeral directors only care about money. Why? So they can pump dead people full of chemicals, slap on some makeup—all so people can *say goodbye.*" She huffed. "But maybe I should have listened for Abby. I couldn't do it for the boys' father either."

Josie swallowed, her mouth sticky-sour from the sandwich. *Dad's sister, Abby, died when he was young. And Dad's dad, my grandfather, too. What happened to them? No wonder you were you, Dad. Uncle Don's tongue—what kind of trauma would have to stack up to cause all this?*

"I couldn't let the boys see Abby or their father, after they died," Grandma said.

*Why not?*

But Josie didn't press. Uncle Don went in to rub Grandma's back, murmured to her, and she relaxed. Not crying, but her jaw was tense. She stared past Josie at Mom, like she was thinking about something else entirely. Not her dead child and husband. *God, what is wrong with me? Maybe she's right, and I shouldn't have come here. Mom and Dad hid this for a reason.*

"He was sick, yes," Grandma said, "but maybe you understand now, Josephina, how your father got to be so over-protective of you. He lost his mind, just like *his* father. Monsters coming in the night, and no whiskey lamp to protect you."

Josie felt a chill. "What did you say?"

Grandma waved that away, slouching on her walker. "Nothing. It's nice to see you again, young lady, but I'm tired."

Josie glanced at Mom. *Why doesn't she say something? I'm running out of time. Only a few hours left. And then what?*

"Thank you, Grandma and Uncle Don. For the sandwiches, and it's nice to finally meet you. Thank you for helping, but we can't stay here. I want to get back to the hospital to check on Clara, while there's still time."

Grandma crossed her arms. "Still time?"

*Dad's countdown.*

"It may be in my head," Josie said. "But my dad told me—no, I *imagined* he said there is a countdown. Time's up today."

Uncle Don tensed. "How did. Your friend get. Hurt?"

"My girlfriend," Josie said. "We were underground somewhere. I can't remember."

"You can't remember," Grandma said, as if she were pleased to find a flaw in Josie's reasoning. "Then how do you know you were underground?"

*Fine, screw it.* Josie whipped out her cellphone, dialed up the volume, and flipped it around to play the creepy bird-child-murder-cave video clip for them. Uncle Don leaned close, Mom squinted, silent but like she couldn't quite see. Grandma watched for a moment, then went to glare out the front window, like she was pissed Josie had blocked them in with the rental car.

When the video ended in a frozen crush of yellow dimness, Uncle Don let out a slow breath. He was trembling. "Jesus."

"What are we looking at?" Mom asked.

"I don't know what it is," Josie said.

"You're in the recording," Grandma said. "It's just you and the girl holding the phone."

"Well, yes. And the other things."

"Other things?"

"Maybe they're wearing costumes or something, but they're right there on the video. Those monsters, whatever they are ..."

Grandma sighed and mumbled to herself, then smirked at her own joke.

"She can't see," Uncle Don said. "I can. But my mother. Never could."

*What does that mean?* Without asking, Josie found a kitchen glass and filled it with warm tap water. She downed it fast, then a second.

Behind her, Uncle Don said, "I don't. Want to see them. But I do. Just like you."

*And Dad.* Josie glanced at Mom, who was shaking her head, as if apologizing. *She doesn't see it either, does she?*

Uncle Don asked, "Is there. More?"

*The audio. Yes, there's more.* Josie let her phone screen go black. *They know something, don't they? Does he recognize those things on the video?*

"Don't start with that," Grandma told Uncle Don. "Next thing, you'll have her marching off into a snowstorm."

*What?*

But that triggered something, and Uncle Don motioned to Josie. "Follow me."

Uncle Don led Josie and Mom through the entryway to a carpeted hall. Two bedrooms were across from each other, a bathroom past that on the left, and another closed door at the far end. The room on the right was a cluttered guest bedroom with wooden beads dangling over a window that looked out on the front lawn. Across the hall, the second bedroom was organized around a treadmill, an old fan-wheel stationary bike, and a long rack of dumbbell weights. It smelled like the evergreen tree pine-fresh air freshener hanging from the ceiling fan—and something else. A specific Old Spice deodorant musk. *Dad.* The odor was thin, but that was him. A swell of blood made Josie's vision spot. *Not since the old apartment, I haven't felt him like this.*

Discolorations in the raggedy carpet meant there had probably been a bed in here once, up against the back wall under the window, and maybe a dresser on the right wall by the closet.

"Mark hasn't. Live here in. Years," Uncle Don said, as she followed him in.

*But this is where Dad grew up.*

Uncle Don went to the closet. Inside, built-in shelves were stacked with books, papers, yellowed notebooks, and newspaper-wrapped jars. Retro action figures stood guard on the shelf ledges, an old-school Darth Vader and other muscular warriors Josie didn't recognize from back when boys' toys were one-hundred percent machismo. Jars were lined up on a low shelf. Carefully propping up one from the bottom, Josie raised it to get a better look at the cloudy yellow liquid and muddy shapes inside.

*Got to be kidding me. Now this is a Kentucky Creepshow—seriously? Why did he bring me in here?*

Uncle Don watched beside her. "Careful. It's precarious."

On the bottom of the jar, Josie noticed a handwritten label. 'Bardstown, Kentucky, 1956.' *A jillion years ago.*

"I think my. Grandpa. Your great-grandfather. Collected these," Uncle Don said.

Josie turned the jar for a better look. A pale, segmented shape was attached to a brownish lump. Some kind of insects, both preserved and skeletal in the jar goop. A caterpillar with a wasp perched on its back. *Not great.* Josie put the jar back and the inky shapes drifted like big worms in cloudy tequila. Definitely dead, but the wasp stayed planted on the caterpillar, attached.

"All this belonged to my dad?" Josie pulled three notebooks off the shelf: red, blue, and yellow. They smelled like mildew. The red one was crammed with Dad's sideways cursive writing and loopy, manic sections of what looked like a maze. Page after page of it. Bits of the hand-drawn maps were marked with numbers that lined up with Dad scribbles, like an amateur atlas. On the first page:

*'(5) salt forest ... (32) broken steps – manmade(?) ...'*

And many, many numbers simply labeled *'torch.'*

"Mammoth Cave," Uncle Don said. "And Mark explored. The caves near here. I tried to. Stop him."

Josie flipped the pages faster, the old ink already staining the backs of her hands and fingertips. At least thirty or forty pages of the red notebook were covered in it—and then it just ended. When Dad stopped writing.

Carefully setting the red notebook aside, she checked the blue one: dense pages of almost-illegible cursive, all organized around more numbers. At the start:

*'(page 10) A reference to creatures that sing, but nothing too specific or
     obviously useful. Not sure it's the same.*
*'(pages 24-25) Here, he's talking about 'monsters' and one in particular
     who sounds like my friends, the fish and muscle man, but still he's*

*writing like the 18^{th} century asshole he was. Give me more information, please! Why can't this be organized for my impatient 20^{th} century brain? Come on, man!'*

And on and on like that. Some kind of stream-of-consciousness research notes, jotted in conversation with whoever the author was. *'Fish and muscle man.'* Dad was trying to understand these things. He was mapping the caves and searching for anybody else who saw them—even hundreds of years ago. Because if we see them, if they're here for us, maybe some were around before, invisible or not.

*It makes sense.*

Josie felt a chill, as she finished flipping quickly through the blue notebook, then arranged it on the red one. All of it started to fit. 'Sense' wasn't the right word, but 'shared delusions, an inherited, genetic hallucination' didn't have the same ring. *Uncle Don sees those things on my phone, even if Grandma and Mom don't. The same way Clara couldn't see any of them—except the glass-face man. Why?* Still no explanation for that. What made that creature somehow more real than the others, if the others could grab the waitress's hand and force her to cut her own throat? *Pretty fucking real.*

*The fish man and the muscle man. The fish man and the skinless man.* They were right there in Dad's notebook.

"I kept these," Uncle Don said. "For years I. Kept these. Because he cared. So much."

Josie checked the yellow notebook, and the air seemed to buzz suddenly—maybe the wires in the walls or appliances and electronics around the house. Everything frizzy and charged.

Nothing on the first pages, but when she rustled through it quickly, writing stopped her in the middle of the notebook. Uncle Don stepped close behind her, cleared his throat. It was a list. A neat, organized checklist, with items crossed off. All the script much more ordered and careful than Dad's other writing. The lettered curves and dashes looked the same, though. The list began:

*-30 gallons diesel*
*-length of hose and tubing, 250-300 feet*
*-shovel*
*-styrofoam (polytyrene) plates (10)*
*-engine oil, qty TBD*

"What is this?" Josie asked.

"The last thing. Mark wrote."

The list continued:

*-two knives*
*-concentrated orange juice*
*-barrels (10-15)*
*-miscellaneous wiring, 200-400 feet*
*-duct tape*

It continued for two pages like that.

Josie closed the yellow notebook, fingernails digging into the cardboard-plastic front and back. "Did he buy all this ... before ..?"

Grandma came into the bedroom doorway. "*This* is garbage," she said. "You are a guest in this house, Josephina. You shouldn't be, but you are. You dragged her in here, Don. Are you going to tell her what happened the first time? Go ahead."

Don shook his head, covering his mouth.

Grandma licked stained yellow teeth. "If he won't talk about it, I will. I told you, Don lost his tongue, both of his thumbs. The police picked the boys up in the parking lot outside a condemned brothel. Along with their father."

Josie felt a chill and tasted warm nausea in the back of her throat, fucking bologna sandwich trying to come up.

Mom still wasn't reacting.

"The Cadillac Club?" Josie asked.

Uncle Don's cheeks went bright red, his hands clenching, releasing again. He looked like he wanted to dash outside. "What did you say?"

*No stutter that time.*

"Was that the name?" Josie asked.

Grandma started to answer, and Uncle Don said, "Yes. You saw it?"

"I went to a place that was ..." Josie shook her head, trying to replay the sequence from the steamboat to that club. "The police told me later that it burned down, but there was a woman there—Allie—she said she met my dad. That dad went there when he was a kid to help you and your father. Is that possible?"

Uncle Don ducked, not meeting her eyes. "Absolutely not."

*What happened to him? It's wrong to be standing in this closet.* These shelves, layers of crap, felt like wreckage. Like the debris from an exploded airplane or the remains of a smoldering building. *He's holding onto Dad's stuff, because he doesn't know what else to do. But maybe they shouldn't keep it. Maybe this is my last chance to just walk away. Mom is right there. She's shaken, not acting right—not making sense—but she's here. We can just go.*

Josie said, "If you know about it—"

"No. Move on."

"I heard you. Let me finish." Josie swallowed, steadied her voice. "You're scared. Fine. I'm not." Not true, but right now frustration cut through the anxiety coil in her belly. *Screw hiding in this house.* "I want to know what's going on. Uncle Don, you recognized those things on my video, didn't you?"

"This is crazy," Grandma said. "She sounds just like Mark."

"Stop," Uncle Don told Grandma, and to Josie, "Yes. I've been there. No, we're not. Going to. Talk about it."

*Bologna and more baloney.*

"Before he left, what do you think Mark talked about?" Grandma looked past Josie at the closet, as if she were embarrassed by it. *She is.* "This. All this."

*She's right. Of course, she is. Waking dreams, drugs, mind tricks, costumes—there are explanations for that phone video and the rest. There have to be.*

But Josie said, "I can't just pretend it didn't happen."

Uncle Don nodded. "Sure, you can."

*Just walk away. Take Mom and Clara back to New York and shut this all off.*

"There's something else." Josie adjusted her phone again and opened the audio player. *Now, before I lose my nerve.* "There's an audio recording. I haven't listened to it yet. No video. It's from when I was gone."

Grandma started to say, "Who ..." and the phone crackled.

On the weak little speaker, Josie heard rustling sounds, with the same pulse-y breathing noise from the video, then a soft voice: "... stone isn't quiet ..."

*My voice. I recorded this, just like the video.*

# Chapter Fourteen

"He says the stone is alive. Like people."

They all watched a small tracking line on the phone screen, as the audio played. *Like maybe if we stare at the progress bar long enough, it will explain what the hell this means.*

"He slept under rock piles taller than skyscrapers," the recording-Josie continued.

Josie hit 'Pause.' "I don't know what this is." She looked from Mom to Uncle Don and Grandma. "I don't think we should listen to this."

"I do," Uncle Don said. "Maybe. Play it."

When Mom didn't answer, Josie tapped to play.

"... he has been alive since the spongy water people sang in the oceans, with tendril bodies like jellyfish, wrapping the world in music ..."

In the recording, it sounded like Josie was crying. *Who am I talking about? 'Water people'—what does that mean? Where was I?*

"... the water people sang and created for generations ..."

A long pause. Seconds ticked past on the recording. Grandma cleared her throat, like she was about to tell them to stop, then the recording-Josie continued: "... and then they died. All of them. And everything else ..."

*I don't want to hear any more of this.*

"... the oceans changed," the recording-Josie said. "And when the last water person died, he was there. Surrounded by shells and carcasses, the last water person asked what he was. A god? No. He ate her alive, then dropped back into the stone ..."

Josie stopped it again. "I can't listen to this." And when Uncle Don started to argue, she said, *"No.* That isn't you on the recording—it's me. What is this? How could I have recorded this and not remember?"

Grandma was holding her forehead, sagging in the doorway beside Mom, who still just stood there, watching the phone.

Uncle Don wiped his eyes. *Is he crying? For real?*

"Talk to me," Josie said. "Somebody say something."

"That's *him,*" Uncle Don said, his voice low and detached. "That's. The dragon."

"No, that's my voice," Josie said. *Throw away the phone. That's not a monster. That's me.*

"You are talking. About him," Uncle Don said. "You were there. Deep underground. With the monster ... We should. Listen to the rest."

"Should we?" Josie asked. Still no reaction from Mom, and Grandma's breathing was unsteady, as if she were wincing through pain. "I don't talk like that."

"It was you," Uncle Don said. "Play the rest. Please."

Josie looked at Mom, and Mom nodded. "We should hear it."

*Now Mom is on Team Crazy Pants?*

"Really?" Josie asked her.

"It's better to know."

*Better to know. Unless knowing wrecks everything. I don't remember any of this.* The recording was like a car hydroplaning around a sharp curve, skidding toward the rail. Total loss of control. What if it got worse? None of this was in her head. She shouldn't have opened the audio file. Shouldn't have done any of this.

"I'm going to delete it," Josie said.

"No!" Uncle Don reached for the phone, and Josie jerked it out of his reach.

"It's evidence," Grandma said softly. Eyes closed, she was holding her head with one hand, as if her neck were too weak to hold up alone. "Nonsense, yes. But it's evidence from your missing days." She hesitated, took an unsteady breath. "If someone hurt you and your girlfriend, we should know."

"Fine," Josie said, "but after ..."

She hit 'Play,' and the recording-Josie continued: "...the oceans and land bloomed again. But eventually, the sky rotted a second time, and so again, he rose to hunt..."

*Turn it off. This damn lunatic recording.* But Uncle Don and Mom were both leaning in to watch the phone, as if they could see Josie speaking and not just the scroll of a thin line on the app.

"You're talking about. Extinctions," Uncle Don said quietly. "Mass extinction events."

The recording: "...it was a purposeless itch. He just *was.* Then, it happened again—a third time, a fourth, and by the fifth dying, that's all he was. Teeth and tricks, with hunger. There was nothing else ... until he held the last dinosaur child ..."

"Okay," Josie said, "a *dinosaur* ..."

Uncle Don shushed her, edging closer to the phone, an arm's reach away.

"... it was sickly and gave a dumb horsey moan when he broke its legs. It bleated and begged. It asked, 'Are you the only one ...'"

Uncle Don nodded and started pacing in a tight loop between the treadmill and the exercise bike, his eyes never leaving the phone screen.

"... he left the dinosaur child on a beach of charred plants and sank back into the stone. And in stone pockets close to the warm center of the world, he found them. Others, like him. All different, all hungry. And he told me that the next time the waters began to cloud, and human death streaks filled the air, they joined him. The hungry ones, blacklegs ..."

The recording ended.

*The things on the steamboat and the demon bird-children on the video, they're all part of this, aren't they? A dragon found them at the center of the Earth, and now they're here.*

Josie leaned on the closet shelves. Her arms and legs felt strangely numb. She imagined knocking the phone onto the floor and stomping it, before they could stop her. This was only real, as long as those recordings existed.

"I'll call the police," Grandma said.

An off-kilter laugh bubbled up in Josie's chest, but she clamped it down. Grandma was serious. That was her takeaway from this. *Evidence for the cops to find whoever drugged me.*

"I told you, I already talked to them," Josie said.

"Did they hear that recording?"

"They've got it covered." *So freakin' covered. And why didn't Mom call the police to let them know she's okay?* Josie pointed at Uncle Don. "So? You understood some of that. What was I talking about?"

He slowed in his pacing but didn't stop, tapping a fist against his side, as if he were keeping time with a song they couldn't hear.

"There's something living. Under this town. Since we were kids," he said. "It's why. The grass smokes, and the. Snow melts. It lives. In the caves. In the mines. That's him. The dragon."

From Clara's obsession with fossils, Josie knew that there had been five mass extinction events in Earth's history, when almost all life ended. The Cincinnati Series fossils Clara loved so much were all from before the very first extinction, hundreds of millions of years ago. *The dragon was here for that, too? And now?*

"I almost get it," Josie said.

Maybe. Sort of. All the coral, fish, insects, and birds disappearing in real-time—they're all part of the sixth mass extinction in Earth's history. They flew away.

Grandma shook her head again.

"Now she says she *understands* this. No." She squinted at Josie. "You're never going to understand, because you can't. It's not a puzzle, just trash. And you know where that comes from? Not from some monster in a cave. It's *you*. Your brain and your blood, they're both broken, the same as Mark. We're finally going to get rid of all this. That garbage your father kept in this room."

"No, we aren't," Uncle Don said. "It belongs to ..."

Grandma snorted. "*Belongs to Mark.* He's gone. I'm sorry, but he is."

"He had another. Notebook," Uncle Don said. "I saw it once. He kept. Descriptions of the. *Things*. In letters to Caitlyn."

Josie nodded to Mom, and Grandma frowned, checking Josie's stare, as if to be sure they weren't signally something private. "That notebook is in my bag in the car. The one he wrote to you," Josie said, nodding to Mom. She started into the hall.

Behind her, Grandma called, "Wrote to who?"

Josie continued through the entryway and then out, off the porch to where the bag was still safely stowed in the backseat of the rental car. *Wrote to my mom. Who else?*

Adjusting the bag, she started back in, already digging one hand in, past the cellphones for the edge of the notebook. She lifted Clara's fossil out of the way and ...

... Dad's ghost sat on the front porch.

# Chapter Fifteen

A half-remembered dream, Dad smiled and folded his hands. He still wore the same white shirt and dirty black pants from the graduation.

"How are you doing?" he asked.

*How am I doing?*

Josie stopped on the lawn, the lucky fossil still tight in one hand, her bag in the other. No sign of anyone inside yet. "Are you real this time?" she asked.

"This time?" Dad gestured her over. "Come see for yourself."

She did. Josie went to touch the coarse fabric of his shoulder sleeve. Not imaginary or a ghost phantom. He felt solid.

"If I'm a hallucination, I'm pretty convincing at least, right?" Dad said.

"I feel like I'm going insane. No—not 'feel like.' I *am* going insane, right?"

Dad leaned back to stretch his shoulders, rolling his neck with that crinkly, half-smile he always got when he stretched. "Sanity is relative, but who says your *relatives* are sane?"

"Why are you here, Dad?"

"Should I not be?"

"Just answer me." Josie checked the front hall through the entry door past his shoulder. Still no one came after her. *What are they doing? I bolted out here. Why isn't Mom, at least, checking on me?*

"I think we should be past the whole 'real-not real' discussion by now, Josie. That's not the most important part of this conversation."

"No? Then what is?"

He stood slowly, windmilling both arms to limber up. "That I love you."

A gut punch. Hot tears already started behind Josie's eyes, so she closed them, stepped away, feet shaky on the grass. *Shit.*

"You ..."

"I am sorry. I really am. For disappearing on you and your mother like that. But you're starting to see, I didn't have a choice. Or at least I felt like I didn't."

Josie kept her focus on the front porch, when she opened her eyes again, and wiped them fast. "I'm not going to hug you ... because you're not here. But if this is just me doing this again—talking to myself—tell me what I know but don't know."

"You're out of time," Dad said. "I told you, ten days."

"I know, ten days, and I ran out the clock under-ground-I-don't-know-where ..."

"They took you to *him*," Dad said. "That's what the blacklegs want to do, Josie. He wants you. He wants my brother—our whole family."

"How did I get out with Clara?"

"You got lucky? Or you had help, I suppose," Dad said and shrugged. "Don't count on that happening again. The next time, you have to kill him."

"The next time? Dad, I'm done. I'm not ..."

The world stuttered into shadow. The light blobbed blotchy orange, with low, dark clouds overhead that swelled into little up-

side-down pyramids in the distance. Funnel clouds. Tornadoes form-
ing over the rooftops and bare trees. Parts of the sky mottled from gray
to bruise-colored purple and green.

*I'm not thinking clearly. I'm not processing this like I should.*

The rest of the neighborhood was different, too. A tree in the next
yard had collapsed onto the road, the roots ripped up in a maw of
exposed soil. And there were sticks with shapes on top—one by the
rental car and others along the road. Not heads. Masks of skin were
mounted on the poles, just like the bearded man from the steamboat.
Everywhere, smoke curled around the brown grass, wafting over the
road.

"Why are you doing this?" Josie asked.

"*Me?* Josie, pay attention." Dad's voice tightened, with that familiar, usually alcohol-smelling impatience. "A long time ago, he took my
sister. My father tried to protect Don and me, keep it from us, but he
couldn't. Not forever. It's a debt to the dragon. Our family carries it.
An obligation, and these things, these blacklegs, can smell it. Do you
know what happened to him, my father? Moody, brilliant man. He
died in a very bad way, worse than me even. Come here. You should
see this."

She followed Dad across the lawn toward a lumpy patch at the edge
of the yard. The turf sagged in unnatural waves, as if it had been rooted
up by a pack of giant voles. A froth of white steam poured out of
a sinkhole around another upturned tree ahead, and as they crossed
onto the next lawn, a bigger tree caught her eye. All the leaves were
gone, but its thin branches were decorated with ornaments. That was
what it looked like, *ornaments*. The shapes were small, attached to the
pointy ends of branches and covering the trunk.

"I got close to stopping him. I really did," Dad said. "And it's mostly still there, my preparations. They cut the wires, but you can reseal them. Get some electrical tape."

Josie stopped. No closer to that fucking tree, whatever those ornaments were.

"It's just on the other side," Dad said and nodded past the ornament tree. "A little further."

"A woman told me you're not really dead,' Josie said. "Is that true?"

"Didn't she say I'm also not really alive either?" Dad asked, with a faux-innocent smile. He shrugged, as if he were hamming for a camera. "What are you going to do?"

"But you died."

"Yes. I set myself on fire at a gas station in rural Kentucky. 'Commercial accident' it was called, as if the gas pump just turned itself on to drench me. The whole front seat of the car filled to my shins." Still smiling, he waved her closer. "Josie, please. I need to show you this."

"Why, Dad?"

"Why did I do that?" His smile slackened, as if he were confused. "You don't know yet?"

"Please. Just tell me."

"Do you think maybe that wasn't supposed to happen? Maybe I wasn't meant to die like that? Burnt to death in the front seat of a blue Ford Taurus? Melted into the seat cushions."

Josie's ears clicked, smoke catching in her nose. She tried to sniff it away, no good. "Stop, Dad." Her voice cracked.

*I sound like a kid again. What did I say in there—that I can handle this?* She followed him closer to the ornament tree. On the other side, a smoking tear came into view, with curled up, muddy edges, like something had pushed up, birthing from underground. Voices in the hole. *Don't.* Josie stopped, a tingle of heat already warming her cheeks from the hole.

"You asked why I'm here. What's the common denominator?" Dad asked, and when she shook her head, he raised both hands, palms up, as if the answer were obvious. "Why *now*? You've seen me like this how many times? Three. What was the same each time?"

"I don't know," Josie said. "I'm stressed. People are hurt. I'm losing my shit …"

"No. You're thinking about it wrong. What did the nice woman at the club tell you?"

*Allie? The girl who knew Dad as a kid?*

From the hole in the lawn, a patient man's voice rose, followed by a woman shouting back, and then more low, easy reassurances. Dad stepped to the edge of the hole and met her stare. His forehead and cheeks beaded with sweat, face lit in a yellowish glow from below.

"She said you visited as a kid," Josie said. "And she warned me about … about worrying about psychological things—she said I should worry about pain."

He snapped his fingers, pointing at her. "And? What's physical? What's the same each time you've seen me?"

Josie stabbed one hand back at him with the lucky fossil. "I don't …" *The fucking rock.* "Jesus."

Dad nodded. "It's possible, isn't it? If that stone can preserve four-hundred million years of animal memories, isn't it possible that I found a way to imprint a version of myself on it? Or someone else did?"

Josie adjusted her bag and turned the lucky fossil over in both hands to inspect the familiar, ancient curls of a sea mollusk shell. Usually, she barely looked at it. The fossil was important, because it mattered to

Clara. *But, he's right. I found it on the riverbank, where I saw you, Dad. And I had it at the graduation. Now, here.*

"I can speak to you through this fossil," Josie said slowly. "I don't understand how this is possible."

"Look around, Josie-bear. We're past the word 'possible.' But you've got to be realistic about this, too. There are other possibilities."

"Like?"

"Like maybe some version of me was preserved in a fossil by the Ohio River …" He hesitated. "… but not for you. Maybe I had another reason, too. After all, I wrote down locations of all the fires underground. I called them 'torches' in my notebook, remember?"

The man's voice in the hole rose just loud enough for the sounds to separate into snatches of conversation: "… therapy is a two-way process … working through it together …"

And then the woman again: "Stop it. This isn't real. I don't believe in you."

The man: "… people who love you … worried about you … want to help you get well … Josie …"

Josie's stomach clenched up, but she held it down. "What is that?"

"Well, I guess that's the other possibility, isn't it?" Dad said.

Swatting sweat from her eyes again, the ornament tree came into focus. Not ornaments, those were birds on the branches, with nails sticking out of them at disjointed angles. All missing their faces. Pigeons and ducks, a big white swan impaled on the end of a low branch, with a thin crane behind it, and nails in the crane's breast and both wings so they stretched out to either side like an avian Jesus. A mockery of Grandma's crosses inside, with skinned bird heads, and bare beaks.

Josie couldn't move. The tree was too big, too many birds up the trunk, all the way to the highest perch. She covered her face and felt sobs rolling through her. Uncontrollable. Josie tried to hold the tears in, but no good. She shook, tasted stomach acid.

*That's me in the hole.* The voices continued back-and-forth. The patient, skinless man. *The creature following me, eager to convince me to give up. That this isn't real. And me.*

"This is what they do, sweetheart," Dad said.

Josie looked back at him, and he returned from the hole, still totally calm. Just like the museum and the riverbank.

"Your brain is either rotten, or they *really* want you to believe that it is," Dad said. "They did it to me, too. And to my father, my brother, all of us."

Josie squeezed her fists so tight on the lucky fossil her fingers hurt. "They're monsters."

"No, just animals," he said simply. Dad took a slow, uneasy breath. "I am sorry you have to see this, Josie. I really am. I am sorry I have to tell you these things. None of this is fair."

"I'm either crazy or this is real, and end-of-the-world *animals* that no one else can see are waking up to murder us all, before we go extinct."

"To *help us* go extinct," Dad said, nodding. "Yes. And you know our mutual therapist hates that word. But screw Dr. Laymon, right? Imaginary or not, they got him, too."

"What do I do?"

"Kill the dragon. Don will help you. You can trust him."

Behind Josie, the wind was picking up. Tree branches rattled, scraping with an uneven chortling underneath, like wind-chime bird-song. She didn't look back, kept her eyes on Dad.

"But *how*, Dad?" Josie asked. "Even if I believe in this ..." She waited, with him staring back, patient again the way he was at the kitchen table in Indiana when she was memorizing the multiplication tables.

*Waiting for me to realize I already know the answer.* "You had a plan," she said.

"I mapped the tunnels, didn't I? I bought supplies. It's all still there, Josie. Just needs to be repaired. It can work. You can kill the dragon. Prevent this."

"Tell me specifically: do I go back to the phantom strip club or the cave? Extinction wakes these things up, I get that. This—all this—is what will happen if I give up. Angry, prehistoric evil. But what did you prepare, Dad? Those supplies were survivalist bomb-making materi-als, right?"

He studied her for a long moment, then threw up his hands and stepped by, headed back to the house.

"You already have what you need," he said. "Except for tape. You'll want to buy electrical tape, remember—that's always useful."

A running joke, Mom always bought him a roll of electrical tape for Christmas. Every year. Not funny now, though. Josie felt a swell of adrenaline. Already shaking, she wanted to run or fight. *Slap this stupid, imaginary-fossil version of Dad. Just make this stop.* The ground felt like a tilt-a-whirl that was spinning, spinning, spinning, gears and sockets in the soil shuddering from the speed. She closed her eyes for a long moment, waiting for the world to steady, her heart to slow. Didn't work. *Dad is gone and not coming back.* But even in her mind that sounded flat now, like a memorized line she'd been taught to recite.

As the wind's birdsong amped up again, Josie stomped after Dad, back to the porch.

"If you want me to save the world, I need more, Dad."

"Killing the dragon won't 'save the world,' Josie," Dad said. He stopped at the base of the front steps. Still, no Mom, Uncle Don, or Grandma inside. *Because this is a fever dream nightmare. None of it actually actual.*

*Stop it.* None of that rationalizing helped anymore. Her old mental routines to explain away Dad's ghost felt suddenly juvenile. Reverse Santa Claus. *Of course he's real, has been all along.* It was childish repression to pretend otherwise.

*This is happening. Dad isn't wrong.*

"And you didn't ..." Josie's voice softened, died. *No. Fucking say it.* "It wasn't your fault, was it? At the gas station?"

Dad watched the quiet house, until Josie stepped close, their reflections fuzzy in the front glass. Like the swirly monster's glass-face mask.

"No," he said. "I didn't do that."

"They did. They killed you. You didn't ..."

Dad turned to her, his face twisted with a weak smile. That disappointed, sad expression she remembered from Lake Shore Drive. Back then, his eyes had been glassy with bourbon. Not now, though. Now, he just looked like he was trying to hide his broken, true self. *Protect me from it, maybe. But failing.*

"Fire matters to them," he said. "You've seen that yourself, haven't you? What's the opposite of belief?"

"What? I don't know, Dad. Loss, nihilism ..?"

"They believe, Josie. The blacklegs believe that this world belongs to them now. That *we* are a glitch in the fossil record, just like all the others before us."

Josie rubbed the lucky fossil. *Let him speak.*

"It's your job to erase their belief," Dad said. "We aren't *food*. People matter, even if we are just animals killing the world. So what? Send the blacklegs back into the dark. Break their god."

He was breathing hard, eyes wider and frantic, just like a hundred other times from her childhood.

"Their god," Josie repeated. "The 'dragon.' That's why he's so important?"

"Yes. Bingo. He's a cancer metastasizing in the rocks. He woke them up. His fires are beacons showing them the way up. Kill him, and it all stops, Josie."

Josie watched the jittery shake in Dad's jaw, the way his right arm fluttered and dropped again and again. *He's right here. My dad is here with me.*

"How?" she asked. "I don't exactly have a sword, Dad. How do I kill a dragon?"

"You'll figure it out. You're every bit as smart as I am."

She gave him a look. *Really the time for a self-serving compliment, Dad?*

"Smarter," he said. "There, I said it. You always have been. Braver, too. I was too arrogant, watching you grow up. Always moving. Sharing your name with the magnolias and oaks. I thought I could protect you from how hollow and hungry the world is. You turned out to be a good person, Josie. Not like me at all. You're not poisonous. I am. Always have been. The moment I stopped fighting that, I found the answer. Your weapon."

"*My* weapon? What ..."

He was gone. Just like that, the daylight flicker-flashed back—the neighborhood pre-apocalyptic whole again—and the half-lit silhouettes of Mom, Grandma, and Uncle Don approached out onto the porch.

"Did you. Find it?" Uncle Don asked and spotted the lucky fossil in her hand. "What's that?"

"Nothing." Adjusting her bag, Josie swapped it in for Dad's demon-letter notebook. Climbing the porch steps, she showed the scribbly pages to Mom. "Dad wrote all this to you, didn't he?"

Still in the open front door, Grandma said, "There she goes again. To who?"

*Why is she pushing me like this? Grandma's constant shoving to make me justify every word—fucking annoying. Not what I need now.*

"My mom," Josie said and flapped the notebook at Mom, where she stood between them.

"If you're tired," Uncle Don told Grandma. "I can help you. Back to your ..."

"No," Grandma said. She gave Uncle Don a hard look. "You know what she's talking about, don't you?"

Shaking her head, Mom stepped past, off the porch. "Come on, Josie. Sounds like we've worn out our welcome."

"No," Uncle Don said. "Don't go. Please, you only just. Got here." *Something is wrong.*

Mom paused at the bottom of the steps, waiting for Josie. "Ready?"

Josie looked from Uncle Don to Grandma, whose eyes flicked up and down Josie, as if to be certain she wasn't about to change into someone else. The same expression Grandma had a moment ago, inside, when Josie said something to Mom. Suspicious. Like Grandma didn't ...

Josie's stomach clenched. Air sucked up and out of her lungs and mouth, until she coughed, eyes tearing.

"Okay?" Uncle Don asked.

*No.*

"Come on, Josie," Moms said, smiling. "Let's leave them in peace."

Josie forced herself to turn back to Grandma. *It's not possible, is it? Oh God.*

"Grandma," Josie said quietly.

"Josie," Mom said, "come with me."

"Grandma, you see my mom, don't you?"

Grandma blinked, then made a sour face and licked her stained teeth. "Come in the house. Both of you."

*Both of us. Two, not three.*

Uncle Don shook his head, confused. "Josie? What are you ..."

"That." Josie swung her hand up to gesture at Mom. Her arm quivered in the air. "That isn't ..." She met Mom's too-vacant eyes. "You're not my mother," Josie said. "Are you?"

# Chapter Sixteen

---

"Almost. You almost had me," Josie said, voice weak. Breathing faster, her vision pinned on Mom—*no, not Mom, a predator in Mom's skin.*

"Are you feeling okay?" Not-Mom asked. "Josie?" Then to Uncle Don, "What is she talking about?"

But Uncle Don took Josie's arm, backing them into the house. "Mom," Uncle Don said to Grandma, "do you see Caitlyn?"

"Do I *see* Caitlyn?" Grandma repeated, as if it were code. She hobbled back on her walker to clear the doorway.

Not-Mom started back up to the porch, shaking her head. "I don't believe this. I'm standing right here. Josie, whatever they're trying to convince you of ..."

"No," Uncle Don said and slammed the door—Not-Mom caught it with her forearm to hold it open. She pressed inside. "Do you," Uncle Don said to Grandma, still pulling them away, into the living room, closer to the back kitchen. "See her. Right there?"

"Is my mother here with us in this room right now?" Josie asked Grandma.

Grandma slipped, and Uncle Don propped her up on the walker again. She looked weak, ready to slump back to the couch. Not preparing to dash out, whatever they had to do.

Not-Mom padded closer, both hands up, as if this were a playful hostage situation. *As if we're insane.*

"Don," she said, "I don't know why you're trying to trick my daughter into thinking ..."

"Back away," he told Josie. "Come on. We can go. Out the back."

"The back?" Not-Mom said, with a thin smile, as if he were a child. "Don, you want to take my daughter—and do what? Run out into the backyard? Then what?" She rolled her eyes and stretched a hand out to Josie, almost in reach.

Grandma's walker dragged too slowly, her feet slipping sideways with each step, before she planted them solidly on the carpet again. Even with Uncle Don's help, she could barely move. Hunched on the walker, Grandma's thin frame trembled from the exertion of coming back in.

"No," Grandma said.

"Josie," Not-Mom said and stepped close, reaching for Josie's hand.

Josie pulled away, knocking into the side display. Black Labrador figurines and framed photos rattled behind her.

"I don't see anyone," Grandma said and looked up at them, her head heavy on her thin, straining neck. "Both of you ... just like Mark and his father ..."

Watching Not-Mom, Uncle Don kept his body between them. He waved at Josie. "You go. I'll help her."

"Come on, Josie." Not-Mom sighed, smiling at Josie. "I've seen enough. You're not well, and this isn't helping."

"You're not my mother," Josie said again. *Run out the back, like Don said? No. I can't just leave them here, with whatever this is.* "How did you make yourself look and sound like her ..?"

"Stop it," Not-Mom said. "Josie, I'm serious." She moved between Josie and Uncle Don, with Grandma still shaking on her walker. No way Grandma would make it out to the backyard. They needed another plan. "We'll go check on Clara," Not-Mom told Josie. "Whatever you want. But I'm done with this game."

"And what music should we play for her?" Josie asked. "In the hospital, Mom. When we get there, what should we play?"

"Josie, stop it."

"Tell me the music, and I'll come with you."

"Whatever you want—"

"No," Josie said, voice rising. She pushed forward, hiding Dad's notebook in her bag again, zipped tight on her back to free both hands. She balled her fists, and Not-Mom straightened with a surprised smile.

"Are you going to *hit* me, Josie? What is this?"

Behind Not-Mom, Grandma murmured, "I need to rest. Let go."

But Uncle Don kept her up, focus tight on Josie, watching to see if he needed to jump in. Manage this somehow.

"Elvis," Josie said. "Clara would want to hear Elvis."

*You would know that, if you were my mother.*

"I've had a long few days," Not-Mom said. "You're going to feel very silly about this later, I promise, Josie. So I'm too tired to remember her music—so sue me."

"Who do you think you're talking to?" Grandma asked Josie. She struggled to pivot her walker to face them. "Is it Caitlyn? Is Caitlyn right there? Both of you see her?"

"Yes," Uncle Don said.

Josie nodded, started to answer, but Not-Mom turned away, glanced back at Grandma with her arms crossed. Uncle Don stepped up to block her, one arm out protectively. His hands and fingers shivered, as Not-Mom came closer.

"Is that shake from the whiskey or ..." Not-Mom swiped a hand, as if flicking him away. Like he was a fly, irritating her. "Why are you standing like that, Don? Are you afraid I'm going to do something to her? Don, your mother is old. She can barely see *you*, and you two live together—which is odd, by the way. A little stunted." At the last word, she nodded to the dull end on his raised hand, where a thumb should be. She smiled again. "Please, let me talk to her. I'll prove that she can see me, okay? Then we can all stop this nonsense and get Josie the help she needs."

*The help I need. Talking like that other thing, the skinless man. Mom's voice, sure, but those are his words.*

"Don't," Josie said. "Uncle Don, don't let her ..."

Not-Mom leaned in to wave in Grandma's face. "Hey there. I'm standing right here. You see me, right? Let's tell these two sillies that I'm not some scary monster ..." Not-Mom lowered her left hand to Grandma's walker.

"No," Uncle Don said. He pressed Not-Mom's shoulder, but she didn't budge.

Her face closer to Grandma, Not-Mom smiled wider. "There. You see me, don't you?"

Grandma huffed, breathing hard. She stared straight through Not-Mom. "I'm tired," she told Uncle Don. "Too much excitement ..."

"Oh, she is stubborn," Not-Mom said and tugged the walker forward. Grandma slipped, surprised by the sudden movement. She tightened both hands on it.

Uncle Don shoved harder, but Not-Mom didn't react. "Josie!"

Josie came in behind Not-Mom to grab her left arm with both hands to try to pry her off the walker. Not-Mom's sleeve fabric tightened in Josie's fingers. The arm was warm, but inflexible as a block of marble.

"Don't pretend," Not-Mom said and guided Grandma's walker forward again, so Grandma staggered, gasping.

"Don, what's happening?" Grandma said.

Josie strained on Not-Mom's arm, and not Uncle Don checked his body against Not-Mom's shoulder. She barely shook.

"This is so frustrating." Not-Mom smiled in Grandma's face, then raised her right hand with two fingers out, her left hand still on the walker. "But if you're going to pretend you don't see ... well."

"Stop!" Josie shouted. "Grandma—"

Not-Mom yanked the walker hard, and the momentum pulled Grandma forward—Not-Mom's fingers went into her eyes. In one movement, Not-Mom drove them deep, crumpling Grandma back onto the couch. The walker collapse sideways. Uncle Don shouted, punching Not-Mom's face, Josie still pulling helplessly on her left arm. Blood pulsed out of Grandma's eyes over Not-Mom's hand. Grandma's arms flailed, slapping at Not-Mom, her thin legs spasming.

She gurgled, and something cracked in Grandma's head. Not-Mom's fingers sank in to the knuckles. A low murmur from Grandma, and Uncle Don caught her hand, tears in his eyes.

"Fuck you," he murmured at Not-Mom. "Why ..?"

Josie's hands hurt, and she let go, staggering back into the center of the room. She couldn't feel her fingers, numb from squeezing uselessly on Not-Mom's arm. *Run. Whatever this is, I have to get out of here.*

Grandma's head dipped forward, and her arms slacked. Her legs stopped moving. Not-Mom slid her bloody-wet fingers out of Grandma's mashed eye sockets, spilling gore down her cheeks.

Uncle Don still held one of Grandma's hands, his weight shifting back and forth, face dark red. "Kill you," he said. "I will."

Carefully, Not-Mom straightened again, wiped her bloody hand on the end of her shirt, then turned to Josie. "You're having an episode," she said, voice warm and full of concern. But that wasn't Mom's voice anymore. It was a man, a calm man.

*The skinless man wearing Mom.*

"Is she alive?" Josie asked. "My real mother, is she alive somewhere?"

Not-Mom stepped in, and Uncle Don rushed around to stand beside Josie. "No!" he shouted at Not-Mom. "We're weak? Maybe. But you don't. Touch her."

"It's okay," Not-Mom told Josie, totally oblivious to Uncle Don. "None of what you see right now is real. Come with me. Let's get you back in your room, until it's time for visitors. Wouldn't it be better to know that this isn't real, Josie? That's the truth."

"Josie ..." Uncle Don said. "Don't listen. It's a trick. They play."

"I know." She took his hand. "The car," Josie said. "Run."

Josie banged out the front door and almost slammed into a friendly woman coming up the stairs. Pale and familiar somehow, the woman smiled when she saw Josie and Uncle Don. Dressed in a starched blue dress, Josie knew her. But something was wrong with her eyes.

*"The lion is alone,"* the woman sang, her hands raised, as if she expected Josie and Uncle Don to join in. *"alone, alone ... sleep little darlin', alone ..."*

*Her eyes.* The woman's pupils were fuzzy, tiny worms glistening in them. No, they were *made* of rice-sized worms. Maggots.

*I know her.*

"Josie," Uncle Don said. "Keep going."

From the living room, Not-Mom called, "Go where? Josie, this is the world now. Your psychosis has advanced ..."

The sweet-faced woman came closer. *"The rabbit is at work ... at work, at work ... sleep little darlin', at work ..."*

Josie slipped past her, taking the porch steps fast. A long red rope stretched out of the woman's back, slinking across the front lawn and away down the road. Wet and wrinkled with purple veins, the rope flexed and pulsed.

Not-Mom approached in the hall, fixing her hair with one hand. Red stains on her fingers. "The next time we see each other, I can't promise I'll be as patient, Josie ..."

The singing woman reached for Josie, and Josie dodged across the lawn, careful not to touch the red-rope thingy. "Uncle Don!"

"I know," he said and hefted a ceramic flowerpot up from the porch—then winged it into the hall like a bowling ball. It smashed across Not-Mom's face in an explosion of gray pottery smoke. She staggered back, face coated in chalky shards. A long strip of skin hung loose from her left forehead, cheek, and chin to expose shiny meat. No blood, just wet muscle.

"You see!" Uncle Don shouted. "Not her!" And he hustled down the steps, ducking by the singing woman.

*The waitress.* It was the waitress from the steamboat restaurant.

*"The walrus is at sea ... at sea, at sea ..."* she sang.

Moving fast, Josie got in the rental car, unlocked the passenger door, so Uncle Don could climb in beside her, and she backed out, bouncing hard onto the road.

*"Sleep little darlin', at sea ..."*

*The lullaby she sang to her niece after the car accident. That's what they were bidding on, wasn't it?*

Across the street, an identical version of the waitress, with the same organic rope stretching out of her back, climbed the steps of another house to knock on the front door. *Don't watch. One thing at a time.* Josie glanced in the rearview: Not-Mom descended the porch steps—not her anymore. The skin of her face and the top part of her neck hung down over Not-Mom's chest like a flesh hoodie flipped around backwards. Even in the tiny mirror reflection, Josie recognized the meat-muscle face of the skinless man. Approaching the street, he was tearing his clothing and skin down from his torso, as if it itched him.

Across the street, a front door opened to a polo-shirt man, holding the newspaper. He greeted the identical waitress, as she sang to him.

"What are they?" Josie asked. "What is this?"

Driving to the end of the block, Josie counted more meat ropes flowing onto all the nearby lawns from the street. She slowed at a stop sign, swiveling to look out the back window.

"What. Are you doing?"

Trees on another front lawn blocked her view of the skinless man from here. The meat ropes tracked together in the street, rebounding in splayed lines that linked to a knobby, short-armed figure that crawled down the center of the street, less than sixty meters away. Like a melted sculpture of a person—the larva woman-thing from the steamboat. Dozens of ropes stretched out of her in different directions through the neighborhood. Josie glimpsed another waitress copy between the houses on the sidewalk one block over. It wasn't her, not exactly, a near-perfect imitation with maggot eyes. But close enough to get people to open their doors.

*We're out of time.*

Josie looked at Uncle Don. "Do you know what this is?"

"No," he said. "Demons? Prehistoric monsters?" He shook his head at the shapes behind them. Not-Mom was already across the lawn onto the street. Moving calmly, like she wasn't in a rush. And she wasn't.

*Because she isn't going to stop. That thing will keep following me forever. This is what Dad was afraid of.*

"My dad knew." Josie spun her bag off her back and onto Uncle Don's lap. "I'll drive. His notebook is in there. See what he said." Josie took out her phone, tapping to call Clara, stomping the accelerator. The car surged faster.

"If you. Want me to drive ..."

"No," Josie said.

The call went to voicemail, and Josie swiveled the phone on the wheel in front of her to type a text: *'Coming to get you now. Love u.'*

"Where are we. Going?"

"The hospital," Josie said. "I'm getting Clara, and we'll ... I don't know. We'll find somewhere safe. But I have to get her first."

They rolled by the stop sign and over speedbumps toward a larger intersection. The passing houses were bigger and brickier, as they neared a main street of gas stations and shopping centers that crowded around churches and a stone high school complex. Everywhere, trees shrouded the streets in a spindly canopy that should've been dense and green.

"This notebook entry is dated. May 20th. Four years ago," Uncle Don said, flipping open Dad's legal pad. "One of the. Blacklegs looks. Like a fish ..."

"I read that one already," Josie said. "And the next page, too. Skip ahead. Is there anything ... I don't know, any *explanation?*"

"Mark didn't ..." Uncle Don paged through the notebook. This pause wasn't a difficulty with his speech. He didn't know what to say.

*Join the fucking club.*

They passed a deserted shopping center, with a billboard above it: *'Welcome to the Highlands! Keep Louisville Weird!'* White smoke rose from a coffee shop, with red points bristling on the rooftop. *Like claws. The burning building is growing claws.*

"Mark didn't explain things," Uncle Don said. "He hated. That. This page?" He showed Josie a dense mat of Dad cursive, full of doodles, cross-outs, and unreadable margin citations.

"Sure," Josie said. "How much more is there?"

"Just one. After this," Uncle Don said. "But it's long."

"Is there anything about this—what's happening right now."

*What is happening right now?*

They passed a Kroger grocery store, with a black-and-red shell growing around it. In gaps along the bottom, Josie glimpsed cars half-sunken into the parking lot concrete, like the ground had gone oozy, then hardened again. Someone's arm was sticking out, too, the rest of the body trapped underground.

"The blacklegs," Uncle Don said. "Are reaching. The surface."

"I thought we had more time." But this wasn't a Goddamn Google calendar notification. This was tides, gravity, and monsters and magic, and who knew what else—just like Dad said. *Time's up.*

Almost to the highway, Uncle Don pointed to a massive Wal-Mart parking lot ahead on the right. "We need to. Make a stop. For supplies."

*Supplies.*

Josie started to say that no, they needed to keep moving and what if—but maybe he was right. Cars and a few moving trucks ringed the lot. She pulled in, guided them to the front, where Uncle Don hopped out. "I'll be one. Minute," he said.

"Get electrical tape," she said, and before he could argue, added, "Seriously, Uncle Don. It's important."

She watched him go in, silently ticking numbers down from sixty. He would be longer than that, of course he would. Uncle Don disappeared past the checkout registers and clothing displays by the front of the store. When she counted to zero, Josie started again. No one in the parking lot or on the road. Another minute passed, then another. *Where is he? It shouldn't take this long, should it? I shouldn't have let him go in like that, without a plan if he didn't come back. Go in after him or just continue on?*

*Fuck, I can't leave him.*

The store doors opened, and Uncle Don hurried back to the car, with two big plastic bags. He showed her energy bars, chips, water bottles, and a roll of black electrical tape.

"That was more than a minute," she said. "And all you got was junk food?"

He smiled and passed her a *Doritos* bag and the tape. "Calories."

Josie shoved the tape in her bag and pulled away. Back on the road, she ate the chips and downed two water bottles. Uncle Don paged through Dad's old notebook again.

"No date," Uncle Don said. "He probably. Wrote this at the same. Time as the rest."

Josie banked toward an empty highway onramp, merging to head toward downtown and the hospital. Empty cars were stopped along both shoulders, nobody in the lanes but them. "Where is everyone?" Josie asked.

Uncle Don didn't answer, frowning at Dad's notebook. "He talks. About you."

"Read it," she said. "Please. Can you read it out loud?"

A pickup truck was on fire in the road ahead, a charred ring of shrapnel around it. Josie drove past without slowing.

Uncle Don started reading, but in Josie's mind, staring at the ruined, gray highway, she didn't hear his voice. She heard Dad, as if he were perched in the back, a travel bourbon bottle in one palm.

*'Caitlyn, you want to know why I'm writing this? Not so you can save me. Don't try. And don't bring our daughter back to Kentucky. If she sets foot on the limestone, he'll hear. I'm alone. That's why I'm writing. Because it's lonely, with Mr. Evan Williams as my only companion. 'But I think a lot about failure. A lot. No, don't tell me that I'm a success, "if I can only be there for our little girl and create a family." I hear you saying that's a victory. It isn't. Not when they rise. I know you don't want to hear about this, but I've identified thirty-four different blacklegs territories. Call them "species," if you like. Doesn't matter. They're more like fiefdoms, with their own cultures and needs. '"Konos the Farmer," do you know what he does? A 19<sup>th</sup>-century opium addict met him—no, really, he did—in the South Pacific. Konos harvests laughter. He grows animals that can laugh, feeds on it. "Vatial the Breeder": a long time ago in Greece she bought part of a woman and multiplied her into a hundred oracles, like puppet-people on flesh strings. "Skalen the Trader," I met him myself, I think. In a cemetery, he offered me ... I don't want to talk about that, sorry. I'm doing this for Josie. After I'm done, if this works, I'll be locked up. If it doesn't work, who knows? I'll probably be dead, I guess. Remember her name protects her. Always has. Now, it's time to use it.'*

Josie pulled off the interstate, back into the familiar, mixed neighborhood leading to the hospital.

"There's only. One more entry," Uncle Don said.

They drove through empty streets of discount stores and apartments. Overcast, but light glared off the windows of a burger chain on the corner ahead. Josie blinked, but the too-bright glint didn't clear or change as they got closer. The light spread, smudging out the windows and exterior walls of the fast food building. A trick of light on tinted glass, had to be.

"Do you see that?" Josie asked.

"Yes. Well, I *can't*. See," Uncle Don said. "There's something ..."

Josie turned away from it, speeding around the next corner: the hospital came into view at the end of the block. Unchanged, with a mercifully full lot of cars outside. But no people.

They turned in, and this time, Josie drove straight to the *'Emergency Vehicles Only'* curb entrance. She hit the hazard lights. No movement inside the automatic entry doors, just an ordinary hospital hall decorated with photos of smiling patients and some kind of children's hand-paint collage.

"Do you want to stay with the car?" Josie asked. "I can get my girlfriend and come right back."

He stuffed Dad's notebook back in the bag, handed it across. Josie zipped up, then stretched an arm trough the straps.

"It won't. Be that simple," he said.

"It might," Josie said, but even saying that out loud brought a grim smile. "No, probably not. How do we kill these things?"

"We don't."

"Then how do we fight them at least?"

Josie switched off the car and got out. Uncle Don followed. They stood on either side, too still in the sudden silence. The air tasted like faint charcoal, summertime humid and thick in Josie's lungs. She started to slam her door—stopped, as Uncle Don carefully eased his shut. *So they don't hear? Who is 'they'? Maybe it's a normal hospital.*

Uncle Don circled to her, as Josie quietly clicked her door closed. She led him in. The emergency doors *whooshed* wide automatically, and they followed a hall past a vacant waiting room. *Wait.* Someone slumped at the reception desk, only their shoulders and short, dark hair visible.

"Hello?" Josie called.

Beside her, Uncle Don shook his head, whispered, "We should be—"

"No. If there are people alive in here ..."

From the desk: "Help me."

A man's voice, but the person didn't move.

"Hello?" Josie said again and crept closer. When Uncle Don touched her shoulder, she flinched away. *I'm not here to let people die. And where is she? Clara could be in any part of this hospital now.*

Halfway there, blood came into view on the desk and back carpet, a deep crimson crust, with patches of shiny wet.

"Hello? Are you okay?" Josie asked. *Stupid fucking question. Are you okay? No. Clearly not. Stop stalling. Clara: think about Clara.*

Josie walked to the desk, started to reach over, and froze. One hand up, an inch above the face-down man. *Body. Face-down body.* The arms were separated at the shoulders but still attached with wires in the broken joints, leaving small gaps. The head, too. It was propped on with a wire, and all the way down the back of the man's torso, as far as Josie could see in his chair, the body had been divided into neat sections, then reattached.

"Help me," the body said. "Please."

*Walk away.* Cold spiked up Josie's back, through her neck, and the sides of her scalp. Slowly, she lowered her hand to the man's shoulder. Warm. It moved.

*Fuck.*

This person was alive. Impossible, but he was still alive. Josie couldn't see his face or anything below the chopped-up shape of his blue outfit and white, sliced up skin and exposed wounds. Nevermind Uncle Don's hissed warning behind her, Josie touched the head to guide it back up, so the whole body leaned to sit up in the chair.

A man's frantic, decapitated face came into view. His neck was joined by a metal cord that left at least two inches between the ends of broken bone and ragged viscera on his torso. He'd been hacked apart, but impossibly, his chest trembled with breathing, blood still spurting around the open sections.

"Help me," he said. "I don't want to die."

"Don't. Touch him," Uncle Don said.

*Too late.*

Josie pulled her hand away, and the man's head dipped forward, ready to slam on the desk again—she caught it, holding him up. His blue, bloodshot eyes widened. Dried blood coated his teeth, when his mouth moved. This close, the stench of raw meat swelled up. And something else. A sewer water smell, the same as the steamboat.

"Where is everyone?" Josie asked.

"They took them to the basement," he said. "The ones who are alive."

"The basement," Josie repeated.

"They dug a hole," he said, eyes snapping back and forth to read her expression. "I'm dreaming? This is a dream. I want to wake up. I can't die here. Help me."

"We can't," Uncle Don said, still a few paces back, by the hall. "Josie ..."

"I know," she said. *But I don't. I don't know how to process this, what to do. A thing that isn't my mother murdered a grandmother I didn't even know existed until today. And now?* Still holding the man's head up, she looked back at Uncle Don. "We can't just leave him."

Uncle Don drew a pistol out of the back of his pants—"What the fuck?" Josie shouted—and he aimed. "Get out. Of the way."

She let go and stumbled back. "You have a fucking gun?"

The gun cracked, exploding the back of the man's head on the wall and floor behind him. He stopped moving. Josie's legs felt weak, and she was already backing around the edge of the waiting room, away from him and the metallic smell of the gunshot.

"Josie?" Uncle Don held up the pistol, fingers loose on it. "You asked. How we hurt them."

"And you said we don't. When did you get a gun?"

"This is Kentucky," he said, with a half-smile, then eased the gun into the back of his pants again, adjusting his shirt to hide it. "I grabbed it. At the store."

"You should have told me."

He turned away, the blocky bulge of the weapon obvious now that she knew where it was. He gestured to the empty hall. "Find the basement?"

"Yeah."

They followed the hall in silence to the elevators and an empty nurse's station, leading to the main partitioned emergency room. People hung in three neat rows, strung up, with their arms tied behind their backs with wire. Patients in loose hospital gowns, nurses, and a few doctors in full-on lab coats had all been hanged on metal nooses. *How many were there?* The metal cords were fastened into the ceiling somehow, and Josie scanned the three rows quickly, trying to blink away their blue-red discolored cheeks and swollen tongues, as soon as she saw them. Three rows of nine. Twenty-seven people, but not Clara. *She's not here.*

Josie's phone chimed in her pocket. *What the fuck?*

Turning away from the bodies, she checked. A message from Clara: *'I am below. Come down.'*

Goosebumps on Josie's arms, and she realized she was holding her breath. The hot rush of her pulse muted the sound of Uncle Don's nervous pacing.

"What. Is it?"

*It's a thing using my girlfriend's phone. Clara would never type that. 'I am'? Never.*

Josie showed him the phone, and Uncle Don's eyes narrowed. "I know you. May think—"

"It's not her," Josie said. "But they have her." Her voice sounded flat, borderline defeated. *Fuck. Am I doing this? Down into a hole under the hospital? If it comes to it, yes.* "Uncle Don, you don't have to ..."

"Stop it," he said. "We're family."

"Family who never talked, didn't even—*I* didn't know you existed before."

Uncle Don went to kick open the door to the stairwell, waited for her to join him. He led the way down utilitarian concrete steps, with exposed pipes and *'Warning: Authorized Staff Only'* signs along the walls.

"You don't want to take out your gun for this?" she asked.

"Not yet," he said, as if he had a plan. The perfect, surprise moment to ambush the monsters with a pistol. Still, it *was* a fucking pistol. Maybe it would ... "Mark loved you," Uncle Don said. "That's why. He kept you away. You heard. What he wrote."

"He was afraid of this place, Kentucky."

"Yes. Afraid for you."

*Afraid for me, and now I'm here, marching down to Hell. Or to the basement of Norton Hospital anyway.*

"He wouldn't have approved of this," Josie said, as they passed a landing marked *'B-1,'* and continued.

"No," Uncle Don said. "Mark would have. Killed me. For letting you—"

"You're not *letting me* do anything. I'm doing this," Josie said, and when he slowed with the kind of weak smile middle age people reserve for know-it-all youth, Josie continued, "Anyway, *you're* tagging along. Not the other way around." She swallowed. "Thank you."

"Almost there." Below the *'B-2'* landing, they could see that the steps ended two flights down: *'B-3.'* "Last chance," he said.

*What's on the other side of that door?*

At the bottom of the steps, a deep part of her shouted and twisted her muscles, struggling to make her stop. *Get away. Go back up.*

*No.*

Holding Uncle Don's hand, Josie opened the door and went in.

# Chapter Seventeen

The door closed behind them. A rush of hot, chemical air made Josie's eyes water, and she blinked, willing her vision to adjust to the dark. *Same smell. From the stone basement under the strip club.*

What should have been the bottom of a hospital had been replaced by a round, sloping passage of rock, with reddish brown walls that flexed and pulsed—*breathing, like the video*—down and out of sight. *How is this possible?*

*It isn't. None of it, but we're here.*

"You see this?" Josie asked, and when Uncle Don nodded, she said, "Just thought I'd ..." *What—check to see if we're shaking a delusion?* They dug a hole. They created a different reality, a living tunnel where there should be maintenance rooms or boilers or a morgue, whatever normal hospitals keep at the very bottom.

White neon lightbulbs were strung up at regular intervals along the ceiling on either side, and rectangular stone slabs centered the floor. Not quite stairs, more like steppingstones over the fleshy ground.

*What if I forget again? I don't want to take two steps and wake up at the riverfront a week from now.*

"Clara!" Josie called.

Her voice echoed, then silence. No answer.

"We should go back, right?" Josie asked. "This is a trick. An obvious trap."

"Yes," Uncle Don said, still holding open the door to the stairwell, as if worried they might get locked in. "But that. Doesn't mean she. Isn't here."

Still, Josie didn't move deeper into the passage. "If they lured us down here, where are they?"

"They're afraid. Of us," Uncle Don said.

"Yeah, they should be." But Josie's tongue tasted of sour copper. She couldn't slow her breathing. "This is fucked. All of those people up there ... why aren't the blacklegs attacking us?"

"They want you. To give up," he said. "Like Mark. Like me. We frighten them."

*Because we see them?*

"Still, this feels dumb," Josie said. "But if we go back ..?"

Uncle Don checked the empty steps out, shaking his head. "I don't know. The man. At the desk. He was telling. The truth, I think. If she's alive ..."

*She's here. Either accept that Clara is dead or go in.* "Fuck."

"I know," he said, but he followed Josie onto the floor stones. She started forward, unthinking. *Don't think. Find her and get out.* The pale bulbs cast long shadows and the acrid air got clingy and damp, as they descended. The corridor turned to the right, deeper underground.

Footsteps below hustled up toward them. No place to go, no side passages and barely an arm's length on either side.

The footsteps stopped.

Josie heard their overlapping breathing, watched the steady pulse of the walls and floor. *This is fucked, every part of it.*

Nothing happened.

"Okay," Uncle Don murmured.

*Okay?*

They crept down again. No one there.

The passage ended at a red door. As they got nearer, tiny black writing came into focus on it: loops and cross-trails of intricate symbols and foreign words. Just like the last time.

"I've seen this before," Josie said. "Scribbles on a red door."

"I've seen. It, too," he said.

"The last time, going through this door made everything disappear, and days passed ..." Josie took his hand again. "We'll do this together. Maybe that makes a difference."

He rubbed sweat from his face. "When I saw this door. I was younger than you. There were things. Things that took *these*." He slapped his hands together over the scars where his thumbs should have been, then opened his mouth to pull on his chalk-colored tongue. "And *this*." Uncle Don lowered his hands again. "This isn't *my* tongue. They cut me."

*Almost no stutter at all when he said that.*

"We'll be quick," Josie said.

Josie opened the door to a low, rock passage with two paths: left or right. There were narrow train tracks on the hallway floor and more white bulbs at the ceiling. The floor pitched down to the right, leading deeper underground. The walls here were granite gray, cut-through with slats of white and lumpy black coal-looking pockets.

The corridor levelled off at an open doorway. No red door this time, and the space beyond was bigger, darker. Josie paused. What were they walking into? A steady *plonk* of water dripped inside. She heard a murmur of voices, under another, crinkly beating sound. Insect wings, like the glass-face man.

"I hear them, too," Uncle Don murmured.

*Yeah, hear what, though?*

Josie raised her cellphone and hit the light button. In the hazy light, the cavern was a vast, shallow pool. The floor bulged with dark, curving formations that multiplied like oversized veins. As she moved into the ankle-deep water, Josie tracked the growths all the way to a stone wall, where they snaked up too far to see. Roots. The roots of trees that somehow grew through the stone. Not a cave exactly, the walls were smooth and round, and the floor under the roots was perfectly level. She raised her light, and shapes darted overhead. Too high to see, but something flickered past. She heard whispering and wings. Thin, crooked legs flashed overhead, like giant wasps.

There was another doorway on the far wall.

"There," Josie said.

They splashed along the edge of the room, using the light from Josie's phone to pick over the roots and slippery stone. When she swung the light into the center of the room it lit the outline of a man with a baby on his shoulder. The man's eyes were too wide and shiny white in the phone glare. The bottom half of this mouth and jaw were missing in a jagged tear that exposed a pointy anteater-like snout. *Not his face. He's wearing someone else's.* The baby burbled, flexing a pudgy hand in the air.

"You are awake," the man said.

"Don't stop," Uncle Don said.

*Steady, don't lose it now.*

"Right," Josie murmured. "The doorway—almost there."

Laughter rippled above them, and a cascade of quiet voices mimicked her. *"Almost there. Almost there…"* Josie's hand slid to Uncle Don's sleeve, tightened.

"You're not well," the anteater man said. He didn't follow, and as they circled him, a long horn came into view in his lowered arm. Some kind of trumpet, except knobby and pale, like bone.

"Josie ..." Uncle Don said.

"Keep walking."

More laughter above. *"Keep walking. Keep walking ..."*

"You're safe here," the anteater man called.

Almost to the doorway, Josie hustled faster, Uncle Don splashing to keep up.

"Where do you think you are right now?" the anteater man asked.

*Don't look back. Keep moving. The doorway is right there.*

A low bleat of noise.

Uncle Don spun, his eyes wide. "We have to run. That sound ..."

Laughter. *"That sound. That sound ..."*

In the dripping blackness, the anteater man held the horn to his snout, like a musician warming up. The baby on his shoulder waved.

*'Where do you think you are right now?' I heard that before. The fish man in our New York kitchen, and the skinless man—they all repeat some version of that.*

The horn sounded in a slow, rising treble. The fluttering quickened overhead. Josie guided Uncle Don in a stumbling dash toward the doorway. The horn echoed, then droned up with a one-two pulse, like an announcement or an alarm.

Something small hit Josie's back, then her shoulder, like rolled-up balls of paper, then a metal bottle cap opener, a black sock, and an old wallet—she caught it with her free hand. A leather fold-out, Josie opened the wallet. A New York driver's license was in the clear plastic window inside. And rows of expired credit cards, with little wedges of paper stuffed behind them, scribbly with notes and phone numbers. Even in the shadowy phone glow, she could read the license and cards.

Dad's. There was cash in it, too, a layer of singles and twenties, backed by neatly folded receipts. *He had this with him. After he left. Just like the bottle opener and sock.*

Now here.

"What is that?" Uncle Don asked.

Josie pulled Uncle Don on. The wings still beat overhead, and more debris rained on them. A heavy belt that grazed Josie's elbow, plunked into the water. All Dad's.

*No way this is real.*

Laughter chattered above them again, as a car key hit the back of Josie's head. She dropped the wallet. *No.* She tried to grab it. No use, it was lost in the dark.

They reached the doorway, where a rusted barrel propped just inside. Even sealed, it smelled oily, like the mechanic's garage in Boston—the last time Mom and Dad owned a car.  More objects pattered off the roots behind them, hit the water. A ring, a glittery cloud of quarters and dimes, a Swiss Army Knife, small plastic liquor bottles. Josie traced a line of wires fixed to the top of the barrel up the wall. The wires were duct taped to tree roots in the wall, snaking back over the doorway, into the room, and up toward the dark ceiling.

"Electrical wire," Uncle Don said, as if Josie had asked didn't understand what they were looking at.

*I don't. Did Dad rig this here?*

This passage was dry stone. It smelled like dirt, without the coiled moisture of that tree-root cavern. The anteater man and baby weren't visible anymore, but the air above still moved and laughed behind them.

*How did they have his things?* "Did my dad do this?" Josie asked, banging a hand on the barrel with a sloshing clang. Her palm smeared black.

The whiney high-pitched horn echoed, reverberating, then went quiet.

"Uncle Don, do you have any idea?"

"No," he said. "Except in his. Notebook ..."

"I know," Josie said. "In his notebook, he made a list." Josie stepped away from the barrel, and the fluttering, wet room. "Is this some kind of bomb?"

"It might be." Uncle Don shuffled further down the hall.

Ahead in the passage, words were smeared on the rock: *'Visitors must wear identification at all times. Absolutely no residents beyond this point.'*

"What is that?" Josie asked quietly.

"They're messing with you," Uncle Don said. "That's for you."

*Where do you think you are right now?* Josie kept her phone light aimed at the rock hallway ahead. The passage widened. The floor dipped in stumbling stabs and indentations. *Not people. People didn't make this. Not with dynamite and pickaxes anyway.* This looked crude, almost like an oversized animal den. *So, what's with the graffiti?*

"What do you mean 'for me'?" Josie asked.

"They want. To keep you here," he said.

Josie watched her footing, slipping sideways on a rock-step. It was silent, except for their breathing and uneven footsteps. Ahead, more messy letters arced across the stone: *'Cell phone use by residents prohibited.'*

"I don't understand," Josie said. "Why write words like that?"

"Don't read it," Uncle Don said, behind her.

"That barrel back there," Josie said. "That was my dad. Has to be."

"Maybe."

The ground dropped in a series of cascading ledges. Numbers were smeared on both walls, lined up with each ledge: *'103,' '105,' '107'* on the left; *'104,' '106,' '108'* on the right.

"The first time," Uncle Don said. "When I was young. I came to save. My father."

"Small world."

*Except Dad is long gone.*

The ceiling got lower, and as they picked their way down the first ledge, Josie heard more water dripping below. She eased herself to the second ledge, helped Uncle Don, then the third ledge, and Uncle Don slipped. Josie caught him.

*If one of us sprains an ankle, what happens? We'll be trapped. No room for anything to go wrong here, is there? Not even a little.*

"But I couldn't," he continued. "They trapped us. Mark saved me. Couldn't save our dad."

*Just like Allie said. It's true.*

After one more ledge, the hall levelled off again into a small passage. No more wall numbers. Too cramped for them to stand, they sidestepped through irregular gaps until the tunnel opened into a circular chamber, with white, sparkly stalactites overhead and bulbs of reflective crystal rocks on the walls. Blackened bones were piled against one wall inside a circle of stones, rags heaped beside them. There were scratches on the rock above the bones, like angry claw marks, and more words, smaller than the last ones: *'Resident Check-In. Please refrain from loud conversations or sudden movements in the common areas.'*

"Mark came back," Uncle Don said. "Years later. He came back. Before you were. Born. That time, I think. He lost it."

"I think we've all *lost it*, Uncle Don. Look around. Look at this fucking place. 'Resident Check-in'?"

*Like a mental hospital. I'm not really here, am I? Not underground in a surreal cave populated by face-stealing monsters. I'm like Dad. He got anxious on his bad days? Ranted about things that weren't there. I'm his daughter, so that's in me too. Just like Grandma said, and Mom always worried about. There was no Not-Mom or glass-face man or skinless man. All of that, completely absurd.*

*What if Uncle Don isn't Uncle Don? What if he's an orderly walking me through an institution right now? I can't see what's really happening, because I've lost my mind, just like Dad. He believed in this shit.* She was breathing fast, her vision narrowing, shrinking around the middle. *'Lost it' indeed, Crazyballs-Josie.*

"If Mark did …" Uncle Don hesitated. "The barrel. And the wires. If that was him. It didn't work."

*Because they killed him first. At the gas station.*

"Was it really suicide?" Josie asked. "At the house, when I went outside to get my bag, I thought I saw him—my dad. I talked to his ghost again, and he said …"

"The staff saw it happen," he said quietly. "There was a camera. Terrible camera."

*They saw him die on black-and-white security footage, by himself in a rented Ford. Gasoline all over the interior, until Dad flicked a light or a match.*

She tried to slow her breathing, walking Uncle Don toward the next tunnel. "But they wouldn't have seen the blacklegs. Uncle Don, did you watch it?"

"We shouldn't. Talk about …"

"Yes, we should," Josie said. "Did you watch it?"

"No. But everyone said …"

His explanations shoved in the background, behind Josie's pulse. *Everyone said it was a suicide, because they watched it happen on tape. Because the eye witnesses swore there was no one else.*

"... called a 'commercial accident,'" Uncle Don was saying, "because the pump. It should have. Switched off. He shouldn't have been able to ..."

"They did it to him," Josie said, voice rising. "They held Dad's hand on the fucking pump—you know that, even if you never watched the recording."

"It doesn't—"

"Don't say it doesn't matter."

Ahead, the passage grew. Color drained from the rock walls, until they were walking through a muted white cavern, with ripples of gray and stark black.

"It *does* matter," Josie said. "Because he prepared. He was ready to stop this. Dad had a plan—he rigged a fucking barrel to the tree roots back there, Uncle Don."

"Mark wasn't well," Uncle Don said. No stutter at all. "There *are* animals down here, yes. Your father wasn't 'crazy.' But he wasn't well, Josie."

Pale dust swam in the light, and the cavern opened up. Not a hall or path anymore, this was a cave. They entered an expanse too vast to see the top or walls, but now the phone lit swirls of falling snow. *What the hell?* White flakes drifted around them, and they were leaving quiet footprints in the powder. Josie held out a hand, watched the snowflakes collect on her fingers. Not cold enough for snow, of course. So, what was it then? She sniffed: a familiar, kitchen scent. Stupid, but she licked her finger.

"What is that," Uncle Don asked.

"Salt," she said. "It's snowing salt."

Josie checked for other prints, then jerked to a stop, almost slammed into a person. No, a white sculpture, with a woman's gaping, blank skin mask laid on top. The body's shoulders and crooked arms were carved out of glittery white. A salt pillar person, with a real face. Josie had the urge to yank it off. Maybe a kind of statue, but that face was human skin, with dark hair—*real.* A flat circle of stone was mounted on the chest of the salt-pillar person, like a breast plate. No … it was a fossil. Josie inspected the tiny grooves and knotty bumps on the stone circle. A fossil and a human face.

"*This* is what they're doing?" Josie whispered. "Why?"

*What did Dad say about Clara's lucky fossil?* It channeled him for her, preserved his ghost, so Josie could …

She fished the lucky fossil out of her bag and held it up, as they continued into a maze of more low, white pillars. More people. Wiping the salt from her eyes, Josie tried to process it. A forest of salt people, all with cut-off faces. Too many, dozens, hundreds, maybe more, all with fossils on their chests. Like a fucking human server farm.

"Dad, can you hear me?" Josie said, waving the lucky fossil in a circle. Uncle Don stepped behind her, unspeaking. "Dad? You said I could speak to you with this. Where are you? Help us understand what this is …"

A low wind whipped the falling salt into concentric curls, and when it stilled again, a fish man was watching. Dressed in red, he wore a limp flag banner out of his back and held an iron poker, like a fire iron.

"Are you confused?" His voice was scratchy, almost a croak.

*Not the one from New York or the steamboat, it's a different voice. Different fish man.*

Uncle Don squeezed her arm. "Josie …"

But Josie said, "I know where I am."

No Dad. She slipped the lucky fossil back in her bag. Whatever it was, the fossil talisman couldn't summon him on demand. Of course not.

The fish man didn't move. "You're a resident, preparing to check out. Do you understand that?"

"Stay away from her," Uncle Don called to the fish man.

Josie backed away, keeping Uncle Don right beside her.

"It's okay," she murmured.

*No, it isn't. Not even a little.*

"I heard the alarm a moment ago," the fish man said. "I hope that didn't frighten you."

Josie kept the light on him. *If I swivel it away, what will he do?* The fish man closed his eyes and straightened, gills rippling in his neck.

"Which way?" she asked Uncle Don. "What do we do?"

The wind kicked up a whirly column of salt again, under the fish man's whistling. When it stopped, he relaxed.

"I hear water," Uncle Don said.

"You go by 'Josie,' don't you?" the fish man said. "You don't have to be afraid, Josie. You're in a safe place now."

Josie swung her phone light in a frantic circle to look past the salt statues, then back on him. The fish man was still planted there. Something shuffled behind her—another fish man, with a droopy, bulgier face and the same little flag post on his back.

"Your family are coming to see you," the first fish man said.

Uncle Don's fingers clenched on Josie's arm.

"It's okay to be nervous, Josie. You feel better, don't you?"

Josie's mouth was dry. Backing away, she heard more movement, and swung the light around quickly. Past the second fish man, she spotted a third, and another beside him, and a fifth one. They stood in a tight circle, each with different tools: one had a warped, shovel-ish thing, another a jagged little knife and a three-pronged rake, and the last one was holding a meat cleaver. *An actual Goddamn meat cleaver, like the steamboat. Is it the same weapon?*

Josie felt a frantic tingling in her chest, down both arms.

"Can you tell me where you are right now, Josie?" the first one asked.

"Sedatives," the cleaver one said. *Same voice. He murdered the waitress, threatened Clara.*

"No," the first one snapped at him, and then to her, "Josie, can you describe where you are?"

Uncle Don squeezed harder. "Don't listen to them. Don't answer. I hear water."

The salt forest ended at the edge of a flat, blue-white expanse. It rippled in a long line against the salty ground, extending back into blackness. A lake, some kind of underground reservoir. The fish men were all still here, gathered in a semi-circle, backing her up to the shore.

"Are you still underground somewhere?" the first fish man asked. "Is that where you think you are?"

*Ignore them.* Josie tasted the salt, smelled it, felt it coating her mouth. *This is real. My phone is waterproof, at least—not that there's anyone to call with a skyscraper of rock on top of us.*

"There it is," Uncle Don said, and he splashed into the water. "Josie, come on."

"Monsters and the end of the world," another fish man grumbled. "She thinks we murdered her therapist. Burned her Chicago friends alive. And her father."

The first fish man chortled at him, then to her. "Is that what you believe, Josie? That monsters followed you to Dr. Laymon's office?"

They knew his name. *Somehow that's exactly what happened.* Behind the fish men, another round, white shape hovered in the dark: the glass-face man. Josie could only see the vague outline of his body.

The glass-face man ambled past the line of fish men. They approached Josie in tandem, like a synchronized dance. She backed away. Her shoes slipped into the water, and she stumbled in up to her shins. *They're fish. Where am I going to go?*

"We have to jump in," Josie murmured. "Uncle Don?"

"Turn and swim," he said.

"Yes. It's the only way."

Uncle Don held her hand. "Are you. Sure?"

*No.*

The glass-face man approached, almost in reach. No way out. He rasped, "Burn."

*That same fucking word.*

Josie shoved Uncle Don into the lake and dove in.

# Chapter Eighteen

The black water numbed the world. Josie's hands and feet were freezing, and her limbs and torso stretched like putty. From somewhere far away, she heard muffled voices. The glass-face man and fish men above the surface or some other new horror. No air. Josie twisted in the water, stroking down. The muscle memory of steady, powerful swimming came back, even in this darkness. No clean, chlorine-drenched pool, though. This was totally fucking black.

Voices called again from the surface. *No. Stay under. Get away. Uncle Don is somewhere in this water, too.*

She released a stream of bubbles from her mouth, felt a familiar burn in her chest. *Air. Surface and breathe. Go up.* But Josie swam farther, reaching out with each stroke, away from the salt shore. The empty pain in Josie's lungs swelled, bleeding into her thoughts. *Swim up now. Just for a second.*

She needed air. Without even deciding to, Josie let her arms slacken and straightened her back to glide up, felt the buoyant rush and then broke through—into daylight.

She sat up in bed. Not her bed, it was a thin, almost-cot up against a wall, facing window shades that glowed with daylight in a simple, dorm-looking room. A closet, dresser, and a wall painting of rolling, fenced farmland that glowed with color: neon yellow and red flowers, like an explosion in the bright green grass, where horses grazed.

Josie heard her heartbeat, smelled rank sweat. *Me. That's me.* She pulled herself up, her back to the wall. Dressed in a blue shirt and sweatpants under slimy bedsheets. They stank of her.

A knock at the door, and Josie froze, as a thin man in a checkerboard sweater and khakis stepped in. He carried a legal pad and phone in one hand.

"Wide awake?" he asked. "I heard a rumor you might be back among the living."

The skinless man's voice. *Why does he have the same calm, reassuring voice? He's wearing someone new. Not Mom anymore, another person they murdered.*

*Or it's not him, because I passed out in the water, didn't make the surface, and this is my brain losing oxygen.*

He stopped in the doorway. "Josie? How do you feel?"

"Okay."

*No, not okay. But stay calm.*

"You're safe now, Josie. You understand?"

She nodded. Same cadence in his voice as when he stalked her at the battlefield creek. And the steamboat.

"I'm a little confused," she said.

"Do you remember our conversation yesterday? This is a big day. Visitors and checking out, if we all agree. Moving on, do you remember that?"

*Sure, why not?*

She nodded again, and he said that he would step out so she could get dressed. Josie found her bag, already packed in the closet. No phones in it, though. Dad's notebook and the lucky fossil were gone, too. Her mind went blurry. She dug out a fresh shirt, jeans, underwear, then slouched out of her soiled clothes and into the new ones. She found her sneakers and dragged the bag to the door. No mirrors, not even in the little adjoining bathroom. *Just as well.*

"Perfect," he said, when she came out, and they started down a quiet hall, part hotel, part hospital. They passed *'108,' '106'* on the left, and odd numbered rooms on the right. *The cavern. Reverse sides, because I was coming in before.* And there, at the end of the hall, a sign beside a simple white door: *'Resident Check-In. Please refrain from loud conversations or sudden movements in the common areas.'*

*The Goddamn cavern. Either there is here, or I'm still in it.*

Josie paused, and he said, "You can do this."

*Why not?*

They went out. Another hall, with bright windows on the wall overlooked a suburban parking area and wooded lot across the road. The trees all had healthy green leaves, and the grass was high and wild. In the sunlight, Josie's reflection looked too pale, with shadowed eyes. *Like I have scurvy or something. But the plants are all back.* A line of birds, crows or ravens, glided down to disappear into the foliage. *Thank you. Whoever you are, whoever did this—thank you.*

"They fixed it," she murmured.

On the opposite wall, another sign: *'Cell phone use by residents prohibited.'*

He gestured down the hall. "You can do this, Josie."

*Do what? Walk this hall, with the world alive again? With another chance? Of course, I can do this. I can do anything. Maybe more time passed. I blacked out in the cavern, and it's a week or a month later?*

She couldn't stop smiling. Josie pinched her forearm and twisted with her fingernails until it hurt. *Real pain. That other dead world isn't a thing, probably never was.*

At the end of the hall, another sign beside double doors—*'Visitors must wear identification at all times. Absolutely no residents beyond this point.'*—that opened to a wood-paneled cafeteria room, where Mom and Clara were waiting. When Josie came in, Clara grabbed her in a tight hug, even as the thin man told them in the skinless man's voice to be careful, no excitement. Clara turned Josie's face to her with both hands and kissed her full on the mouth. Josie closed her eyes, the familiar warmth of Clara's tongue and breath. Nothing else but that blood rush to her head and in her belly and groin.

"This shouldn't take long," the thin man said.

Josie blinked to look, and Clara nodded their foreheads together, her eyes glassy with tears. "Hey, you."

"Hi," Josie said.

"Don't do that again, okay?"

*Do what?*

Josie nodded, and they joined Mom at the table. Mom opened one arm to fold Josie against her, as if she were a kid again. Like an infant chick under her mother's wing. Mom kissed Josie's forehead, smoothing back her hair. "My baby is back."

The thin man arranged a set of papers on the table, with letterhead that read: *'Greater Stamford Mental Health Center.'* A psychiatric hospital in Connecticut—this was where Dad came. When he tried to get well and failed. Where Dr. Laymon wanted to send me—no, *did* send me. He never died. Of course, he didn't.

"I promise you," he told Mom, "if she sticks with the recommended treatment plan and medications we discussed, the risk of relapse is low."

Mom argued that they needed more assurances, until Josie said, "It's okay."

*I've been seeing things that aren't real. Living in a terror haze of chemical imbalances. Maybe it should be scary to know that unpredictable me is hiding in my brain, but it isn't. Not one little bit, because screw the blacklegs and Not-Mom and Kentucky caverns with a dragon who needs slaying for Dad's ghost. That's a tangle of frayed wires under my scalp. Not real. Can't believe I bought into it.*

When they were headed home in a red rental car, Josie tried to make sense of the residential streets, saw a sign for I-95. All of it back. Cars, people, and an airplane that left parallel cloud trails in the clear sky. They were less than an hour from Brooklyn.

"What's today?" Josie asked.

"Tuesday," Mom said.

"No, I mean ..."

Mom and Clara exchanged a quick look in the rearview. *They're worried, probably hoped I wouldn't start with time traveler-esque questions. 'No, what year is it?' Keep that to a minimum. Find out other ways, don't make them freak.*

"The 25th, I think," Mom said.

*Still May or is it late June already?*

"Where's my phone?" Josie asked.

"At home. They said—they suggested easing you back in, not overloading you all at once."

Clara rubbed Josie's shoulder. "You missed nothing, promise."

*But when did it start? When did the real world crap out? Don't ask. Just wait and find out on your own. Pretend to understand.*

After they stopped to pick up Josie's new prescriptions, it didn't take long to drive back into city, and Mom made dinner while Josie and Clara sat in the TV room. No moldy Dad boxes on the floor, none of it. Out the window, house sparrows, hopped and chirped on a ledge over the back alley. *Should confide in Clara, should-should-should ... but no. Not yet. The only thing I want to do is hold her hand and listen to birds. All of it restored and alive, because it was never gone.*

"How are you feeling?" Clara asked.

*Like I don't know who I am. Should remember more.* "I'm ... how bad was I? Shouting-lunatic-on-the-street bad?"

Clara's stare wavered, then steadied again on Josie, as if she were trying to gauge how much to reveal.

"I mean ..." Clara said. "Yeah. It was bad."

"Thank you," Josie said. "For ... I don't know—I honestly don't remember much."

"They said that might happen. Give it some time, okay?" Clara handed Josie her phone. "Here."

Josie stared at the date: May 25th.

May? Three days after graduation, the day before they caught the flight to Louisville. No Mom disappearance during the storm, no blacklegs to worry about or long-lost Dad relatives, none of it. Josie tapped an icon on the phone to open a news feed: political scandals, a rundown of stock market updates, and summer fashion.

*The world before. There was no collapse, all in my mind. Of course, it was. The world can't die overnight. It's all still here.*

*Tell her. Talk to Clara.* But no, Josie told herself to shove it down. *Plenty of time to run through it later.*

*But still.*

She turned off the phone screen. "How long was I there?"

"Three days."

"And before that?"

"You really don't remember?" Clara asked. "It was ... it happened fast. You started talking to people who weren't there at the graduation ceremony."

Josie tried to work through it. "There was a storm during our graduation."

"Right. That's when it started. Do you remember telling off your dad to the whole world?" She smiled. "You made a kerfuffle and then …"

*When I saw Dad's ghost—that's when reality clicked off, isn't it?*

"What happened after that?" Josie asked.

"We had to take you to the hospital." Clara hesitated. "Ready to let it go?"

*No.* But Josie did, all summer, until that fall, when Clara and Josie were together in Josie's NYU dorm room, and Clara got news that she'd been admitted to Columbia—actual Columbia University in Morningside Heights. Josie's roommate was out at a performance art set, and so Josie and Clara drank too much vanilla-flavored vodka and tried to memorize the words to Columbia's school song. They mangled it, then collapsed, laughing and goofy in Josie's bed. Josie had sworn off alcohol after she woke from the fake, dead world months ago. It wasn't good to mix with the happy pills, but so what? This was her first *drink*-drink. Besides, avoiding booze completely made it *too* important, right? Better to be merry to prove that vodka wasn't cursed like Dad's bourbon.

"We should remember to ask about housing first thing," Josie said. "Here. I'll write that down."

"Think we'll remember I need a place to live without writing it down."

"*We* need a place to live," Josie said.

"Josephina Elizabeth Morris!" Clara rolled onto Josie, while she leaned off the bed to root through the floor debris for paper and a pen. "Are you suggesting we *cohabitate* out of wedlock?"

"Are you proposing to me?" Josie asked. "Wedlock is a funny word, like we're locked together. Click-click."

But that wasn't funny. It should've been. Why wasn't it? Josie found a notebook and blue pen, but now the room was spinning from the booze, and she imagined chains linking her wrist with Clara. *Weird.*

She wrote: *'Do you love me?' 'Yes' 'No' 'Maybe'* and shoved the paper at Clara, who just rolled away on the bed, covering her face. "No quizzes right now! Too much vodka for quizzes."

Josie laughed. "Quizzes or kisses?"

"Perfect amount for that."

And it was, but the next morning, Josie's skull felt like a squished bicycle tire. While Clara slept, Josie vomited in the common bathroom, then stumbled back in. No movement from the bed. Still early, though, not even 9:00 AM yet. Maybe brunch would help, but *Mike's Place* on the corner would have a stupid-long wait by the time they got there, and the *Nine and Five Diner* on 4th Street was too expensive. *But good, maybe worth it today.* Josie was careful with money, from her part-time gig at the campus bookstore, three blocks east of Washington Square Park.

She stopped. The notebook was on her side of the bed, right where she'd been sleeping. *Forgot to put it away. But I didn't. No way I slept holding that notebook like a blanket.* But there it was.

Josie got back in bed, started to toss it away—the question was answered: *'Do you love me?'* with a dark box drawn around *'Yes.'* And below that, a pigeon scrawl: *'you were my ... tried to teach ... the miserable open nothing ... heat death ... I failed ... they took you ... I am so sorry ... find the river.'*

*Dad.*

# Chapter Nineteen

J osie's stomach lurched, and she closed her eyes, willed it to settle. *Goddamn it.* "Clara?"

She grunted, didn't move.

*Throw the paper away. Stop.* "Clara, did you do this?"

*Stupid question. Who else? Except that's not her handwriting. I know Clara's handwriting, and that's not it.*

Josie felt panic swell at the back of her throat. Her vision shook in rhythm with her pulse.

"Did you do this?" she asked again, louder.

Clara blinked, and her eyes scrunched. "Huh?"

Josie showed her the paper, and Clara shook her head.

"You didn't write this?" Josie said.

"No. You know what refried shit feels like? This. It feels like this."

"Seriously," Josie said. "Clara, tell me. Maybe you don't remember, because we were drinking."

"I didn't write that note," Clara said. "Sorry. What's wrong?"

*What's wrong?*

"It's my dad's handwriting," Josie said.

"What?"

Josie waved the paper at her again. Her arm wouldn't stop shaking. "*This.* This isn't how I write. This is Dad."

"Your *dad* wrote that? But ... isn't that what you wrote last night?" Clara's eyes widened, bloodshot, and she pulled herself up, patting at her wild morning hair. "Calm down."

Clara took the paper and tore it in half. When Josie reached to stop her, Clara held the pieces away and ripped them again—and again, then crumpled the shreds in one fist. "I'm tossing this."

Josie watched her leave for the bathroom, tried not to let her thoughts crowd together. Her head throbbed, and her whole body felt dried out and heavy. But that was Dad's writing. *'Find the river.' And a bunch of nonsense babble. What kind of explanation is there for this?*

Clara came back in, held up her empty hands. "Gone. Flushed. And yes, I do love you. But you need to take your pills, okay? I think maybe you forgot yesterday."

*My pills, that's what caused this? I forgot my medications one time and started scribbling in my long-lost dad's handwriting?*

"Okay?" Clara said.

Josie nodded and went to find them. "Yes, sorry. Good idea."

"Eggs and tomatillos will make everything better." Clara searched for clean clothes. "Scientifically proven."

*Right. Focus on goodies, not ghosts.* Or whatever ghost handwriting that was. They pulled themselves together, and in the painful daylight outside the note felt silly. The air tasted like crisp leaves and the smell of sugared almonds from a street vendor at the corner. Walking by clumps of students and a trio of flute musicians, Josie reminded herself that Dad couldn't have written it, because Dad was gone. *It doesn't matter.*

And it didn't.

For twelve years, until, in the second-floor bathroom of their Connecticut bungalow, Josie studied herself in the mirror. *Turning thirty tomorrow. But I don't look* that *different, do I?* Tired lines under her eyes from too many hours spent helping people with real problems. Clara joked Josie's Rutgers Ph.D. was actually in Bullshit Spottery, not Addiction Studies and Chemical Dependency. Still, years spent sharpening therapy tools in her private practice, hosted out of the third bedroom-turned-psychologist-office downstairs, had hardened her jaw a little. And maybe that no-nonsense seriousness took a toll on her youthful demeanor? No getting around it.

"I'm old," she said quietly.

Behind her, Clara said, "Wouldn't have you any other way."

Josie started to answer back, then saw that Clara was kneeling in the hall, both hands up to hold a simple diamond ring. The gold in the band curled around the gem like talons or waves of pointy fire.

"Wait," Josie said.

"No. Josephina Elizabeth Morris ..."

Josie grabbed her, kissing Clara's cheeks and mouth. She held the ring and Clara's fingers tight.

"I love you," Josie said.

At the wedding that summer in Old Saybrook, they got hitched at a new-ish club and walked down the aisle together, sans parents. After the ceremony in a backroom with a wall-length sea glass mural of a woman with red eye shadow and purple lips, an Elvis impersonator direct from Mohegan Sun casinos warmed up, while everyone ate. No Clara foster parents and no Dad or Dad fam. Just Mom and sixty friends and friends-in-law.

"Do we have any family in Europe?" Josie asked Mom. *A stream-of-consciousness tipsy, wedding question.* "We're flying out tomorrow, and only half our itinerary is planned."

Everyone else at the head table was chatting and eating. Mom smiled and sliced her salmon.

"My great-grandparents met in Canada," Mom said. "I don't know any of our relatives in England or France anymore. We're New World all the way, I'm afraid."

"But Dad's family was from Germany, right?" Josie asked.

Mom didn't look up. "Why?"

"Because if we're going to be in Europe—"

"It's not something you should dig into." Mom forced a smile and patted Josie's hand. "Just don't, okay? Not everybody who left Europe, or stayed, was a good guy."

*What? Dad's family were criminals or something?*

Mom watched the center of the room, where waiters cleared tables to create a dance floor.

"Have you ever been?" Josie asked.

The color drained from Mom's cheeks. "Yes. Really nothing to talk about, though. It wasn't my choice."

*This is trauma. The way Mom is avoiding eye contact. Did she get hurt? Did something happen in Germany?* Like the soft shape of a dream, Josie could remember a story about a kidnapping. *Mom was 'kidnapped' by Dad years ago. No, she wasn't. That was ridiculous.*

"I'm sorry," Josie said. "It's okay—let's dance ..."

Josie pushed away from the table and pulled Mom and then Clara up with her. On the dancefloor, Josie took Clara's hand. "First dance, let's go."

People applauded, and the Faux King launched into a slow ballad: 'Love Me Tender.' *Our song, since junior prom, when we slow danced to it at a gaudy midtown hotel, surrounded by people whose names I can't remember.*

When the song ended, the dance floor filled, and eventually Josie returned to her seat for dessert and more champagne. The room was crowded, ear-drum-busting loud with songs about hound dogs and heartbreaking hotels. Like a fairytale from the last century. Josie grabbed a cocktail napkin and pen from the center of the table.

Josie wrote: *'What should I do?'*

Clara was waving to her from the edge of the dance crowd. *Dance. That's what. That's all.* Josie started to set down the cocktail napkin ... There were more words below her question.

*'What should I do?'*

And then, Dad's handwriting: *'Escape ... should have told you ... so that you wouldn't be like me.'*

She pocketed the napkin and forced her mind to go blank. She still took 'happy pills' but hadn't been consistent the last few weeks, with all the wedding prep. *Missed at least every other day. My brain chemistry is acting up again. That's all.*

Later, after dancing until Josie's feet and ankles ached, the wedding was wrapping up, and she still had the napkin. No change. The words were still there.

What did this mean? Dad, again. She scanned the room. Like the dorm room years ago, Dad's ghost hid under my bed and now was disguised at the party?

*This isn't happening.*

*I did it. Simpler explanation. Not a good one, because it means I'm losing touch again, but it's more straightforward, doesn't require a ghost. How long ago was the last note? Years and years.*

Clara came over, stunning in her low-cut, thin-sleeved white-and-purple dress. She rubbed Josie's shoulders. "All good?"

Josie folded the note in her fist. *Today isn't his day. It's ours.* "Definitely."

She didn't tell Clara, and although she kept the note with her—even packing it into her purse enroute to the airport the next morning—Josie tried to ignore it. No good, but maybe it could be normalized. A drunk scrawl on a napkin. And hadn't she been drunk in college, too, the last time?

On the second morning in London, Clara slept in, still jet-lagged, and Josie got up early. She found a bench overlooking the dark blue waters of the Thames River, with early-morning sunlight streaming over the brick and glass towers on the opposite bank. The air tasted wet and fresh from rain the night before. Pigeons cooed and jostled for position on the walk, and she heard the raucous caws of ravens. Josie knew their noise without turning. Bird sounds were still lodged in her brain, even without using the old birding app.

She took out the cocktail napkin and wrote a new question: *'Who is this?'* then put it back in her pocket. No alcohol last night, none today, and she had been taking her medication. If chemicals were causing this, it would stop. A pale face shimmered at the bottom of the river, staring straight up. A spike of adrenaline—but no, it wasn't a person, just a trick of light on the rocks at the bottom of the water. They looked vaguely human but were only rocks. *I'm losing it again.*

Clara called, "There you are!"

Josie turned. Clara jogged over, smiling. *Not so jetlagged.*

"Snuck out on me," Clara said. "What's wrong?"

*I'm delusional or Dad is leaving me napkin messages. Or both. Other than that?*

Josie said she was just tired from traveling, and they walked the shoreline. *Tell her.* More pigeons blocked the path ahead. *The birds aren't in trouble anymore—they won't even clear the pavement. None of us are. The world is fine.* After circling the block to find a coffee, they returned to the rental flat. Impossible for there to be anything on the note, but back inside Josie locked herself in the bathroom—"Two minutes, and I'll be ready to head out again!"—and checked her pocket napkin.

*'Who are you?'*

Dad's writing: *'It's Dad ... my father hid it from me, too ... just like his dad ... all the way back.'*

Josie slumped to sit on the closed toilet. *We have to get going. Restaurants and museums and then a 7:00 PM train to Paris.* Rereading the napkin note, their honeymoon plans suddenly seemed anachronistic, like reviewing a box of old DVDs. Full of important sentiments, sure, but relics from an earlier time, obsolete. *Like the boxes that never existed in Mom's old apartment in Brooklyn. The boxes I imagined.*

"I'm losing my shit," Josie said softly. *Not super professional.* Her voice sounded weak. *Say it calmly. Totally normal to go batshit.*

*No. There has to be an explanation. Those words must have been there before.*

*But they weren't.*

Fingers trembling, Josie wrote another line: *'I don't believe you. Go away.'*

She grasped the pen so hard it hurt her thumb and glared at the note. *Come on, fucker. Talk to me.*

Nothing. No new words.

*Not yet.*

"Fuck you," Josie said. "Talk."

Clara's footsteps in the hall. "Josie?"

"I'm good," Josie called.

But Clara didn't leave. Josie heard her breathing and the creak of the floor outside the bathroom. *She's listening to see if I keep rambling. And I should.* Still no answer on the napkin. *Flush it, the way Clara did with the first one back in college. Or what? Fess up?* Josie imagined a surreal argument in the flat that spilled out onto the sidewalk, pictured Clara pacing with nervous energy when she realized Josie was serious.

And eventually, Clara would insist they call her therapist for advice, maybe look up someone here. 'What was this really about?' they would ask. 'Life changes?' Just like the end of high school. *I freak at transitions—really fucking freak. What would I tell one of my patients teetering on a psychotic break? Check the dosage levels, of course. I would blame all this on brain chemistry, with new prescriptions to save the day.*

*Because that's what it is. I would be right. I can't trust my own eyes.*

Another line of writing had appeared on the napkin. She was still pinching her thumb on the pen, hadn't stopped. *I looked away for a moment, at the bathroom door. That's all.* But there it was, a new bit of Dad's scrawl: *'You're still drowning ... wants to change you ... something wrong.'*

*No. Just no.*

She flushed the note and focused on her breathing as she fixed her hair and splashed water on her cheeks. *Breathe in slow, then an even breath out. Easy peasy.*

When Josie went out into the hall, Clara was waiting with her arms crossed. "Well? Seriously, Josie. Talk to me."

"It's nothing. I'm fine. The flight and time change, I think it's just fucking with my meds."

Clara studied her. *Totally unconvinced.* "Okay to go out?"

They did. Expensive London sightseeing, then a fast, evening train to Paris, and the choreography of the trip found its rhythm again. When they landed on the airport runway back in New York two weeks later, Josie's phone buzzed. The caller ID flashed onscreen: *'Emergency Services.'* Josie answered.

A rushed male voice said, "Is this Josephina Morris? Ms. Morris, I'm calling from St. Luke's Roosevelt Hospital. We have your mother here."

Josie told Clara, and they rushed through the airport terminal to find their car in long-term parking. Mom was in critical condition, a heart attack.

"How serious is it?" Clara asked, as they bounced out of the airport lot in a long loop toward the George Washington bridge back into Manhattan. St. Luke's Roosevelt was in midtown, not far from Columbus Circle.

"Serious."

*Fucking serious.* So serious that when they got to the hospital reception desk, a woman directed them to a quiet room with carpets, comfy sofas, and tissues.

*A room for mourning.*

"We don't know yet," Clara said.

But Josie did, and she was right. And old doctor told them that Mom died on an operating table ten minutes before they arrived. He explained very quietly, using too much medical jargon, that it happened suddenly, and he was sorry. There was really nothing anyone could have done.

"What was Mom doing in the city?" Josie asked.

*Retired now, Mom spends most of her time in Connecticut. Meeting someone, maybe? Why was she here—at this hospital?*

The doctor didn't know, and when he left, Clara cried. Josie only broke down when they stepped into a windowless, bleach-smelling room to see the body. Still dressed, Mom's mouth hung open, and she looked thin, more shrunken. Josie touched her hand, pulled away. Already cool, like a wax figure. A soft-spoken chaplain asked her about funeral homes, relatives, and support services.

In the elevator out, a nurse waved them down. "Wait—ma'am!"

*What now?* Josie held the doors.

The nurse said, "So sorry, I was told you asked about your mother's admitting process. She came here, because an ambulance was called to the park."

Central Park by herself, without telling anyone? Josie and Clara rode the elevator down in silence. Through the ground floor lobby, Josie led them out onto the street, away from the hourly lot where they'd parked. The city was loud with traffic and the thud-thud mechanical noise of nearby construction. Always.

Farther uptown, they passed the familiar shops and crowds of Columbus Circle and approached the park entrance. A tourist family posed for photos by a new bronze statue of a Native American woman at the main path. But inside, as they started on the path, nothing had changed. People sat on blankets on the same green lawn. Dog walkers and cyclists passed. *We never came back here. Never found the old shoebox and Dad's phone on his tree.*

"Do you think she came here?" Clara asked.

*To the park or to Dad's tree?* Josie didn't answer. They followed the shaded path past crowded benches, around the duck pond, where an old couple threw fistfuls of bread to a flock of pigeons, and there it was. A stand of trees at the edge of a more heavily wooded area of the park. Dad's tree hadn't changed. A pair of squirrels circled each other up the main trunk, disappeared in the branches. No barren, ghost limbs or chainsaw stump, the tree looked strong and healthy.

As they approached, Josie asked, "Did we bury a shoebox here?"

Clara smiled. "I forgot about that. Crazy times."

*Yeah.* Josie stepped past a *'Keep Off the Grass'* sign to find the spot at the base of the tree where the box should be. And there was the old carving in the exact right spot: *'Josie'*

*Did Mom come here? Is this why she was in the park?*

Josie spotted a scrap of paper in the weeds behind the tree. *Garbage.* But she picked it up. Words in Mom's handwriting. *'Thank you for watching over her, but she needs to go back. We both do. Take her.'*

The rest was ripped, except for a scribble near the bottom. *'I'll try.' Dad's handwriting.*

"Anything?" Clara asked.

Josie showed her, and Clara studied the torn slip of paper, then flipped it over to inspect the back. *Mom wrote to him, too. And then she died.*

"That's Mom's handwriting," Josie said. *And Dad's.*

"Fell out of her purse, maybe?" Clara handed it back. "It doesn't seem real that she could be gone."

*Maybe it isn't.*

*No, stop it. Mom could have carried this paper around for years, sentimental.* Josie dropped the note in a trashcan back on the path. *So many explanations, none good. Leave the tree—move on.* And somehow, she did, for another year ... until she had a baby girl.

After doctor's visits and plenty of bills, Josie's belly finally started to show, and on Thanksgiving Day she gave birth to Anna Caitlyn Morris, all chubby-pink seven pounds, two ounces of her. Anna was a light that overwhelmed Josie's senses. The first night at the birthing center in New London, Connecticut, Josie, Clara, and Anna slept together in the bed. Josie was exhausted but still alert, ready to slide Anna to her breast to nurse when she snorted and gurgled. Clara smiled and held them both, with her eyes half-open.

"I should have expected her to be as beautiful as her mom," Clara whispered. "Your fault."

In the early morning dark, their room was still, except for a blinking red security light above the hall door. Exhausted and aching, but with the mellow numbness of industrial strength Tylenol, Josie lingered at the edge of consciousness, could still see snatches of a dream. Anna—*my daughter, ours*—grasped the unbuttoned flap of Josie's gown with tiny white fingers. *Hungry again?*

*Hungry. Like another baby in a cavern, on the shoulders of an anteater man.* The thought sent a chill through Josie, and she instinctively clamped it down. An image of Anna's face in a dripping, underground room.

"I'd do anything for her," Josie said. "Silly-obvious, right? But I didn't know how it would feel. They tell you, but I didn't know."

Josie fed Anna and heard a low voice in her mind. *'Burn.'* Her pulse quickened. Anna stirred. She shivered, the room still chilly. *But it isn't.*

"What's wrong?" Clara asked.

*Nothing. A memory of something crazy huffing in Mom's old apartment and hungry things underground. Anna stolen from me by black-legs monsters.*

Josie rubbed the soft fabric of the black hat Anna was wearing. She was dressed in a diaper and onesie blanket wrapped like a burrito, with a hat topper to keep her warm.

*The anteater man with a baby on his shoulder wasn't a man. He blew a bone horn.* The memory of that dream came back in a slow, bleeding rush. A version of her life she knew wasn't real. *But that baby underground was Anna.*

"She's going to be okay." Josie couldn't see Clara's face in the darkness, only her outline and the form of her brow and mouth.

"You should rest," Clara said.

*Not a question. I wasn't asking. I'm going to make her okay.*

"I wonder if this is what he felt," Josie said. "My dad. When he left, he was worried—about me, I think. Like something wanted to hurt me."

*He was ill. But maybe he loved me and thought he was doing the right thing, protecting me somehow. Because something hungry is going to take my baby.*

Not lingering 'waking dream' leftovers anymore, no, this was a certainty that clenched Josie's stomach and made her sit up. Pain swelled in her groin and legs. No surgery and the birth had gone well, but they said she'd be sore for a month, maybe longer. Totally normal. She needed at least a couple days of solid rest. *But something is coming for Anna. That's what drove Dad away. That's what I saw in the caves. A threat to my womb, for children before they grow up to see the monsters.*

"I have to stop it," Josie said.

Clara steadied her hand on Josie's shoulder, like she wanted to hold her down without pushing. "Want me to call the staff?"

"No," Josie said, and she eased Anna off her chest to hand to Clara. "Take her for a minute."

Clara cradled Anna, sleeping again, while Josie crossed to the bathroom. She grabbed a backpack from the wall behind a chair. One of their overnight bags, with a change of clothes, shampoo, car keys. In the bathroom, Josie changed without switching on the light and pocketed the keys. *What's the plan? The stress and hormones of childbirth are scrambling my already over-easy brain. Just electro-chemical noise. Except it's real. It doesn't 'feel real.' It is.*

Dressed, she came out of the bathroom and finally told Clara about the wedding napkin note that she'd taken on their honeymoon. "And a decade before that—at the NYU dorm, remember?"

Clara perched on a chair, frowning, while Josie found a little yellow notepad and ballpoint pen on a side table.

"You're serious?" Clara asked.

"It happened," Josie said. "I didn't imagine it. If you're here, you can watch. I should have tried this in London, but I was worried you would ... I was afraid I was losing my mind."

"All you need is a piece of paper to write to your dad's ghost?"

*Let's find out.* "You think I'm insane."

"No. I'll believe you. Show me."

*'I'll believe you.' Thank you.*

Josie adjusted the pad and wrote: *'Is Anna in danger?'* She showed Clara.

"Now what?" Clara asked.

"Nothing. We wait. If another sentence doesn't ..."

There was already a new word under it: *'No.'*

"Well? I didn't write that," Josie said. "You saw me. You're sitting right there."

Clara came closer, with Anna still against her chest.

"One word," Clara said quietly. "You could have done it when you moved the notepad. And besides, that's a good thing, right? You asked if she's in danger, and she isn't."

*No, bullshit.*

Josie wrote: *'Why not?'* then dropped the pen on the floor. *No way he can give me a single syllable answer to that, and I'm not holding the pen. Explain.*

Clara shook her head and half-sat on the bed. "I think maybe you're overtired. We both are."

"Wait, look. If you don't watch ..."

There was already more: *'Hard to hear ... but none of this is real.'*

Unspeaking, Josie wrote back: *'Why did you leave us?'*

Anna shifted on Clara to squint up at Josie with clear green eyes. She was perfect and soft. *Safe.*

Dad's writing: *'Look around ... I am right here ... you're in the water underground.'*

*The cavern lake by the salt statues. That happened.*

Clara looked over. "Is there more?"

Josie showed her the notebook. "Watch. I'll write more. You can watch ..."

"Stop, okay?" Clara wiped her eyes, her lips trembling. *She's scared of me.* "Just wait. You hear yourself, right?"

*If I apologize, say it was a bad joke, this will go away. Everything normal. Just let it drop.*

*Unless I'm not here. Unless Dad's note isn't a note, and he's with me somewhere else. In the water? But I can't see him. And what did he say before? Something about a river? There's a river not far away, just like the one in London with a face that wasn't a face at the bottom.*

Josie grabbed Anna and ran. *Get to the car.*

"Josie!" Clara shouted. "No—stop!"

Josie made it past the hall security desk and through the lobby, where a guard was coming out a side door with a walkie talkie, frowning like he couldn't decide whether to tackle her or fetch a car for her. "Slow down, ma'am ..."

Outside, Josie crossed the parking lot, Anna burbling, totally cool with the brisk, pine-smelling air, as Josie found her car. She had already installed a car seat—*crazy, overprepared mother-to-be turned just plain crazy.* In a fast buckle-buckle-strap-pull combo, she got Anna in, then started the engine.

Clara ran across the lot behind her, with the security guard. *They'll call the cops. Commit me. Who knows?*

*But I didn't write the fucking words, which means they came from somewhere else. Dad's ghost is somewhere else. And so am I.*

In a haze, she drove fast out of the lot and found I-95, as the sky bled from black to dark blue, streaking red and white on the horizon. Police lights flashed in the rearview mirror. The low *whee-whoop* of a cop siren.

*Pull over. Stop this.*

But there was a suspension bridge just ahead. *It's the 'Thames,' isn't it? The same damn name. I'll hop out and look down at the water—and know. One way or a fucking other. Those notes were real. And years and years of peace and happiness have been so easy. I was afraid of the notes and the water.*

The police siren got louder. She drove up the bridge, a mesh of white suspension wires, steel beams, and pillars backlit by the pink, cloudy sunrise overhead. Josie pulled over, turned off the car. The cop stopped behind her. She leaned into the backseat. Anna watched, serious and sleepy. *My perfect child. I have to know. You're the reason I have to know.*

Josie got out and climbed onto a narrow pedestrian walk on the side of the bridge. Higher than she'd expected, the river was a dark blob below, dotted with whitecaps. Farther out, a fishing boat passed a sandy-lump island crowded with gulls and pelicans. Another stream of seagulls swelled below. Their wings arched in the wind.

Behind her, a man shouted, "Please step away ... back to your car!"

Josie didn't look. *If I see Anna again, I won't watch the water. I'll go back into treatment and stop asking.*

*You did this to me, Dad. Your blood in my veins and now your words. A fucking curse.*

*Unless you're right, and it isn't a curse. It's a debt.*

At the railing, Josie leaned over to stare down. Streaks of gold danced on the fast-moving water. Sunlight.

The cop shouted again, but Josie climbed higher on the rail, leaning farther over the edge for a better look. *There. There is someone there.* The outline of a person with hands reaching for the surface far below. *Who?* Josie eased her whole torso over, legs off the walk. The figure was too distant, but the pale face was familiar.

She went over.

Josie tumbled into a sharp press of air, like the wind wanted to knock her back up. The surface rushed closer—*Jump? Did I slip? Did I...*—and the white glow of a face in the river came into focus as Josie hit the water.

# Chapter Twenty

Josie broke through a surface of dark water, gasping, and was pulled by her armpits onto a rocky ledge. She coughed, her lungs catching with soggy phlegm. A dark, dripping room came into sudden focus. She was in a cavern, on a rock platform above a pool of black water. *The cave, the underground lake. I'm back.* The smell of saltwater and ancient moisture beading on the rock brought fast memories of the fish men and Uncle Don. *We were trapped and swam.* Tracking the wall to her right, the rock ledge backed up to a smooth-cut wall of translucent pale blue, with shadows inside, like bubbles caught in glass.

And there was the glass-face man. Leaning over the water's edge, he hauled a body out. The glass-face man's insect wings flapped, and he braced both hooves to drag the body higher. Uncle Don. *Oh God.* His head lolling down, arms limp, Uncle Don was raised out of the pool and dropped beside Josie, coughing. Uncle Don heaved forward and spat.

"What is this?" he murmured.

"I don't know," Josie said, her voice soft. *We both jumped into the water, didn't we? To escape the fish men—and the glass-face man was there. We swam, maybe into a submerged tunnel, all the way to this room. And that masked monster followed us.*

*All of it real. An entire other life blipped out, snap-snap. No Clara or child. All a brain death delusion in the pool.*

The glass-face man's wings folded down again. He clomped closer, his mask streaming lines of whiteish water, like salt sweat. *The face in the water. It was him.*

*And there's light…*

Climbing to her feet, Josie felt a shock of dull pain. Her forearm hurt, made her wince when she touched it. The burn from before, after the lost days underground in Kentucky, when Clara disappeared. *Jesus, this is—I'm really here again. The cave.* Past the shadow wall to her right, a doorway led away, much too regularly shaped to be natural. A buzzing noise trilled down the hall, like electric cicadas. Yellow light flickered from a room at the far end.

*Wait.*

The shadows inside the blue-ish wall were people. All frozen: a woman stuck in mid-step; an obese man crouched with one arm raised; a child paused, running. Locked inside the stone. Josie still had her soggy bag and phone. No good, her phone wouldn't turn on. *It's waterproof, should still work.* Most of the people were lodged deep in the wall, like bugs in amber—or the dusty jars of preserved insects in Dad's closet. A man with a heavy cloak over a shirt made of metal coins was crying. *Not frozen.* As Josie watched, his lips slowly moved, but his body was locked in the smoky blue stone. *Insane.*

One of the people was right by the surface. As Josie approached, her legs stiffened. Clara. She was inside the rock, locked on the other side with her eyes closed and mouth contorted in a grimace. She looked thin, face still bruised and swollen, but it was her.

Water dripped in the quiet.

Josie pressed both hands to the flat stone wall. *It's her. How did this happen?*

"What is this?" Josie asked. "Clara, can you hear me?"

Clara's mouth twisted in a silent scream, as if she were dreaming.

"Clara!" Josie clapped the wall "I'm here!"

*I'm not leaving you.* No way to reach her, and Clara didn't react, eyes still closed. The buzzing stopped, and the floor and wall rumbled. *Breathing.* Josie hit the stone again right in front of Clara's face, but she just tilted her head, as if she were in pain.

The glass-face man shuffled past, to the cavern passage. "Burn."

Josie didn't move. "That's all you say?"

Uncle Don started to get up, then collapsed again, breathing hard. "Sorry. Give me just a minute ..."

*The glass-face man, the imaginary demon from my nightmares. The thing that broke into our apartment. Monosyllabic monster. it followed us here and pulled us out of the hallucinogenic water.*

"The first time I saw you, you were dragging a woman with your chain ..." *Like you carried Uncle Don out of the water. Saved him. You yanked me out, too. What if you weren't torturing that disfigured woman at our apartment?* She asked the glass-face man, "Who was the woman?" *What if you tried to help her?* "Can I see your face?"

The glass-face man clomped away, deeper into the corridor toward the yellow light.

*It's a creature, not a person. Don't talk to it.*

"Clara is here." Josie tugged twice on Uncle Don's arm. "She's in the wall over there—see?"

"In the *wall*," Uncle Don said, struggling to his feet. "It was the strangest thing. I was alive before all this, lived my whole life, as if none of this happened ..." He paused. "Huh."

"Your voice ..." Josie said. *No more stutter.*

"Yeah." Uncle Don rolled his jaw. "How about that."

Josie looked back at Clara, frozen in the rock. *I'm coming back. You're not alone. I'll find something to get you out. I'll be right back.* The breathing sound pulsed on, and they followed the glass-face man.

*Fuck it.*

*A rock maybe, or some kind of tool—there has to be something I can use to get Clara out. One thing at a time.*

The hall opened into a round, domed room. Three iron bowls were mounted on ledges in the wall, with fires smoking in them. That was the light. Above the bowl torches, empty black hooks dangled from the ceiling. The walls were a mosaic of black, orange, and white shapes and handprints. A throng of charcoal animals that looked like thick, two-horned rhinos galloped alongside a row of horseheads in profile by a multi-colored mishmash of symbols and a drawing of a hairy elephant herd. Mammoths. Bone shards, shriveled plants, and rotting animal hides cluttered the ground to ... more barrels. Three more oil-diesel barrels crowded the left wall, all linked to a jumble of wires that roped up roots in the wall, disappearing into fresh-looking drill holes in the ceiling.

The wall directly across from Josie was cracked, with gray smoke swelling out of it, like a festering wound, and to her right, the ground dropped away into a still black lake. The air tingled, shimmery, like a mirage at the end of a hot highway. It tasted like rotten eggs, and she felt that familiar acidic-chemical sting in her eyes. The breathing sound was louder through the floor. Josie felt it up through her feet and legs. No rocks or tools, though. Maybe she could use a bone. She found a sharp, pointed leg bone, broken at the end. *Will it cut the stone around Clara? Doesn't seem possible.*

"What is this?" Uncle Don asked. "It's like the Chauvet cave. Pre-historic, maybe tens of thousands of years old. Mark left his barrels here ... why?"

Josie watched, as the glass-face man approached the edge of the pool. A deep lake, maybe another aquifer.

"Why not?" she said, and called, "What are you doing?"

The glass-face man stomped, his hooves echoing in a low *thrum-thrum-thrum.*

"Burn," he said and stomped again.

*Not for us. He's calling something else.*

"We have to go." Josie started back for the hall.

Uncle Don didn't move. "Wait. This room ..."

"This room feels wrong, Uncle Don. Wrong like death."

The glass-face man turned to them and dragged one hoof in a slow circle across the stone between them. *Stay. That's what he's saying. Don't run. Trust me.*

"Are you crazy?" Josie murmured. *To who? Who am I talking to?* "Clara is trapped—"

"Burn," the glass-face man said again.

*Burn. 'Run,' you mean.*

But Josie approached the glass-face man and dark slip of water. *He swam after us and pulled us out of the water. Did the glass-face man save us?*

Behind her, Uncle Don asked, "What are you doing?"

"I don't know," Josie said. "Maybe he knows how to get her out of the wall. He helped us."

The glass-face man huffed and shivered, arms slack. Water rolled and lapped behind him. A shadow appeared, slowly growing, something big approaching the surface.

"Can I see your face?"

Still, the glass-face man didn't move. If she reached, she could touch his mask. *It's just a mask. A blank white mask, only eye streaks and a point for the nose. Reflective kabuki demon.*

*But it's real.*

Josie touched it. The mask felt like smooth ivory. With both hands, she carefully felt to the edges, where rough fabric straps held it on the thing's flesh head.

*Don't.*

Josie slid it up to expose a shriveled jaw, lipless mouth, scarred cheeks and up to ...

*Dad.*

She let go of the mask, staggered back.

He was missing his nose, and they'd burned off his lips, all his hair, flayed his skull like a piece of meat—*but those are his eyes.* Bright and wet with tears, not scared. Sad.

Josie felt the same tug in her belly as when he'd walked her to Lake Michigan with hamburgers and milk shakes. Behind them, cars whipped by on Lake Shore Drive, as they stood together watching a flat, endless expanse of water. Josie had tracked it to the right, all the way to the Chicago skyline. The night before, Dad had punched a hole in their living room wall during an argument with Mom. Josie couldn't remember what they'd been fighting about, but she remembered his eyes at the lake the next day. The same look he had now. *'I am so sorry. I failed, Josie.'*

*No. You found me there. You knew I was in the water, and you pulled me out. You were watching. Just like you knew we had to leave Chicago, even if it meant abandoning my friends.*

Behind her, Uncle Don asked, "Josie?"

The black lake shifted past the glass-face man. *Past Dad.*

*What did they do to you?*

"Can you see me?" Josie asked quietly.

Dad shuffled, but his eyes never left her. He didn't reach for the mask.

*That woman, the first time I saw him … what happened to your sister, Abby?*

"Uncle Don," Josie said, "Come here."

*Burn.*

Dad shook with each breath, wheezing through his ruined nostril holes and mouth. Uncle Don approached, then stopped when he was close enough to see the ruined face.

Uncle Don tensed. "What is that?"

"Your brother."

A long silence. Uncle Don shook his head. "No."

*They did things to him, just like you. They fucked him up beyond belief, changed him into this. They were going to do it to us, too. In the water, while we lived an imaginary life. Dad came to kill a dragon, and instead …*

*Instead.*

"That's not Mark," Uncle Don whispered.

Josie studied Dad's shrunken throat and disfigured chin. *It is, though.*

Dad huffed and gasped.

"Can you help us?" Josie asked. "Dad, please. My girlfriend, Clara, is back there. We have to get her out."

Uncle Don came closer. He stretched a shaky hand out again, found Dad's sinewy arm and patted down to ease it up and touch his swollen fingers. No fingernails. Uncle Don clasped their hands together.

"I knew you were alive, Mark," Uncle Don said. "We missed you so much. I shouldn't have brought Josie here, I know that."

Dad shuddered again, but he didn't back away. His eyes flicked from Josie to Uncle Don, then back, again and again, as if he couldn't make them come into focus or didn't believe they were here.

"Everything you did was to protect us." He was nodding. "We understand, Mark."

Josie watched Dad for a response. No change in his raw face muscles or sad, unfocused eyes. *I don't want to understand. Not this. At the apartment, when all this started, the fish man pointed a knife at you, not me.*

Behind Dad, the pool erupted. The shock knocked Josie back and sent the bowl torches bouncing wildly. Shadows spasmed on the walls. Dad shuffled to the wall, ducked sideways, and disappeared into the smoking crack like a spider. *A fucking spider, he left us—just like that. Again.*

Uncle Don had fallen by the doorway. "What is it?"

*What is it?*

A bulbous, whiskered white blob perched out of the water, with two tentacle stalk-arms lined with spiked purple suckers. It watched through a pair of slitted, black eyes, its deep jaw panting and dripping the stink of ocean rot past three rows of shark teeth. Its skin was soft and transparent like a jellyfish, with cords and balloon organs drifting inside. Huge, almost as big as the room.

"You came back," it said. "A monkey with a face."

The voice was new, but it wasn't. *This is the thing that spoke to me underground, that erased my mind. The thing I was talking about in my phone recording.* Josie's lower back ached from the wall impact, but she was okay. *Okay, dragon. Game time.*

# Chapter Twenty-One

The thing groaned, knocking the bowl-lanterns into a dancing spin. Shadows jumped, swelled, and shrank around them. With its two stalk-arms, it hefted itself out of the water and into the room, filling the length of the pool, more of its body still submerged behind it. It wasn't to the doorway yet, and Uncle Don crawled away, shouting at Josie.

Strings of lumpy organs bobbed behind its eyes, and it said, "You belong here. I will save your face, when the world is quiet again."

The stink got worse, a raw, moldy taste in her mouth that made Josie's throat tighten and her stomach burble up. *This is it, isn't it? Not a magic dragon, but actual flesh and guts. It's here and speaks English—or chatters in my brain anyway. I can fucking see it.*

*Now what?*

"Are you afraid to die?" it asked. "I can make it easier."

"I'm not planning to die right now," Josie said.

Its stalk-arms squirmed across the room, feeling over bones and rocks, and its huge body slid closer to the doorway, as it hunched out of the water, like a giant worm or a whale. The top of its head almost reached the chains hanging from the ceiling.

"Run!" Uncle Don shouted. "Josie, this way!"

*Back to the wall, where Clara is trapped. But no—it's right here. How am I supposed to fight this thing? It's too big. Even if it's killable, it's half the size of the room. What can I do?*

"Your time ended," it said and swelled closer, blocking the doorway. "Your life will be a tiny streak of atomic graves and glass in the stone. I know you're scared, but your face ..." It flowed toward her again, the ends of its arm-stalks six meters away, now four meters, two meters ... "You belong here ... you share his smell. Impatient. Angry, always angry. You *will* die. All of you. Very soon, the only memories left will be the faces I preserve in the stone."

*Stay calm.*

Its stalk-arms grasped her shoes. Each of its arms was bigger around than her legs, with suckers flexing and gaping to expose black points, like needle-knives.

"That's why you're doing this?" Josie said. "To *preserve* us?"

No way around it, the thing covered the doorway, and Josie wasn't running for the water behind it. She couldn't see Uncle Don anymore.

*I'm alone.*

"Mark saw. He finally stopped fighting. He wanted to know, and I showed him how, while he could still see."

"How you're *'preserving'* us?" Josie stammered. *Talk. Act—do something.* "Like storing us in the rock is going to ..."

*This is how he did it. Insane, but this—the wall of frozen people, the fossil death everywhere—this is how Dad learned to copy a part of himself for me. He left it. Clara's lucky fossil. So I would find it.*

"Yes. You're food now."

The thing's mouth widened into a stinking tunnel of serrated teeth. A wave of fish-head garbage stink rolled over her. Past three layers of blue-veined pink gums, she saw the dark, reddish maw of its throat.

"You gave my dad a recipe," Josie said, voice too quiet. "I don't understand it, but somehow he learned to mimic a version of ... whatever the fuck this is. Copy himself—at least enough that I might see it." *See him. I have him here with me. Always.*

It was on top of her. If it surged in again, it would have her. *Fight. Stab the fucker.*

*Except. What did he say? Poisonous. Dad was a weapon ... the lucky fossil?.*

*No, that's not a weapon. More than a rock, it's how I speak to him, see his ghost. It's insane, but he's in there.*

*But he's not. Dad lost. Before whatever they did to remake him as that thing, what if he had the chance to pour himself into a fossil. A DNA glimmer-memory, laced with cyanide. One last trick. Of course he did. That was fucking Dad.*

She jabbed with the bone, and a stalk-arm knocked it away.

"My torches burn," it said. "Guide the hungry ones to feed."

Josie bumped back, sloshing the wall barrels. She shuffled her bag around fast, unzipped it. *Dad is in there. He said it. With the fossil, I can see him again, even if no one else can. That version of him that loves me, without any of the horror carnival ruin and insect wings.*

*Fucking poetic.* She closed one hand on the lucky fossil. The creature's stalk suckers jabbed at her shoes, slowly curling behind both ankles. It would close on her and drag her into its glistening mouth as food.

*Of course Dad would leave me like this. The fossil isn't just lucky. Because it's poison. Because it's him. He can't be back the way he was, I know that. I know.*

*I don't fucking know that. All I know is who he used to be is alive in Clara's rock. For me.*

She threw the lucky fossil into the open tunnel of its mouth.

A shrieking spray of dirty water knocked her down, and she wiped her eyes, spat sour grim. The thing flailed and sucked backwards. It lurched past the doorway, then slumped, its black eyes fixed on her.

"No past to remember ..." And its breathing became a wet chortle, stopped.

The room was still.

*Just like that. What the fuck?*

*The lucky fossil did it. Right into its throat, and now the dragon ...*

Black vines grew out of its mouth. And inside, through its transparent skin, Josie watched curling black lines multiply, covering the thing's alien organs like ivy. Not ivy. The vines were metal. Fast-growing razorblades and barbed wire sprouted from inside the dragon, enveloping its face, up over its eyes, then out and across the floor. They spread up the walls. The back half of the ceiling collapsed in a blur of rock that buried the dragon and the water, cutting a rockfall path straight up. A climbing path into darkness overhead.

The cavern cracked, and there was a crinkly, grating sound from the walls, like rock rubbing against a cheese grater. The vines—living wires, taloned with blades—were still growing, pushing deeper into the cave. A torch bowl fell from its wall perch to land between Josie and the rockfall. Yellow flame shimmered from a lump of red rock, blue-hot at the base. *The dragon's torches, guiding the blacklegs to the surface.* If she was careful ... Josie lifted the bowl, then retreated down the hall. Uncle Don was hunched in the tunnel, shaking his head.

Past him, the wall melted. Like a wax mold left in the sun, it oozed into bluish, sticky slop that was already flowing over the landing into the water. Clara's left hand was exposed, the rest of her still encased in rock. Josie watched in the fire-stone glow, as more of the wall slowly peeled away, separating from her. She took Clara's arm across her shoulder and eased her out. Clara stumbled, saw Josie, and smiled.

*It's her.* Josie felt numb. She was squeezing Clara's arm too hard. Behind Clara, more of the wall flowed away, and the armored man's body came out, then broke apart in a mound of dust and bone. *Preserved for too long.*

"You're okay," Josie said and held Clara tight.

*She's here. Right here. My Clara is okay.* The ugly tension in Josie's stomach began to calm, like a slow-fade vibrating string.

Clara coughed.

"What is this?" She took in the cavern.

"A cave," Josie said. "Still in Kentucky. Can you walk?"

Clara wobbled and saw Uncle Don in the hall, muttering. Past him, metal vines rattled and grew.

"My uncle," Josie said.

"Don, right? From your dad's phone," Clara said. "And the note in New York."

*She remembers everything. Thank God—we're here.*

Uncle Don came closer, feeling along the wall.

"He wouldn't do that," Uncle Don told Josie. "Mark wouldn't."

"He did." Josie helped Clara toward him. *Not letting go of her arm, never again. But now what? No going back into the water, not with the fish men and whatever else. So which way? The broken part of the wall, where Dad went?*

"No," Uncle Don said. "That wasn't him."

"What's he talking about?" Clara asked.

"My dad was here." Josie led them back into the smashed cave. "I think. The monster with the glass facemask. We saw him on the boat."

"That was your *dad*?" Clara coughed again, wincing. "How long have I been here?"

"Not long," Josie said. "They brought you down from the hospital."

"Josie, your mom ..." Clara shook her head. "I saw of version of her, but it wasn't ..."

"No, it wasn't," Josie said.

Back in the cavern, the wall opening Dad had slipped through wasn't an option. A slab of gray stone that bristled with white, crystalline knobs had collapsed over it, sealing the gap. *It was Dad. I know it was.* The ruined room was filling with moving metal vines.

Uncle Don pointed up the rockfall. "We have to go. Can you both climb?"

Josie raised the half-bowl, adjusting the burning stone for a better look. The broken mound rose farther than the light could reach, but it didn't seem to lead out.

*Go where?*

Uncle Don started climbing. No way of knowing if the rockfall path would smack into a roof of stone spikes or trap them in a tight shelf of debris, but Josie and Clara followed him, their hands clamped together. *Safety lines in the darkness. If one of us goes down, we both fall. Not losing you again.*

"I don't remember what happened." Clara climbed beside Josie. "We went into a club, to a stone basement, and then ..."

Through the drifty dust, they found solid stones, testing rocks, sharp-edged corners, and smooth, half-buried boulders to be sure they didn't wiggle. *Just like the creekbed ravine. No fossils this time, though, just us.*

"I remember a presence." She paused on a ledge, rubbed her neck. "Your dragon, he laughed."

*The dragon didn't laugh.* But Josie didn't say anything.

"And torches," Clara said, nodding to Josie's bowl flame. "Fires to end the world ... or something."

Josie tried to steady her heartbeat, couldn't. Feeling for handholds and finding places to grab and pull wasn't hard, but to where? *Just keep climbing. Say something to make her okay. We're together. The dragon is dead. We'll figure out an escape.*

Clara watched Josie, as if she were desperate for an explanation. "I don't understand any of this."

"I killed it," Josie said. "These things try to confuse us. In the water back there, I woke up in a mental hospital, and we lived an entire other life."

Above them, Uncle Don slipped on an uneven jut of rock, then kept going. No sign of light past him. *A dead end, probably, locking us in. Insane to hope for a way out from the collapsed roof of this deep cavern, but what are our options?* The rockfall climb rose to a cracked but mostly intact curl of deep brown stone overhead. Clara pulled Josie closer, wrapping Josie's hand around her back. *Maybe to steady her on the ledge. No, to hold on.*

"And what happened to us?" Clara asked.

"You became a lawyer."

Clara made a face. "Gross. That should have told you right away it wasn't real."

"And we had a little girl named Anna."

Clara's eyes softened. "Really?"

"No—it wasn't real," Josie said. "They did that ..." *I don't know why.* "... to keep me here." *Distract me, while they change me into something else, like they did to Dad.* She called to Uncle Don, "No opening up there, Uncle Don!"

He patted along the brown rock ceiling, as if he expected to hit a hidden trigger mechanism, maybe open a secret hatch. In Josie's hand, the fire stone flickered twisty light across the rock pile. When the cave collapsed, it opened this path, but it didn't dislodge the entire shelf of stone above it. Not to the surface.

"I can't believe we would just be left here to die," Uncle Don said.

*We have to swim. We got into that room in the water, so there must be a submerged passage back out. But what if I disappear again and wake up in a hospital? What if I don't come back next time? Stay with the fantasy.* Josie touched Clara's cheek, and Clara blinked, smiling back.

"I'm not going anywhere," Clara said.

*Right, because I won't let you.*

A metal vine burst through the debris on their right, dividing and splitting and splitting again into black arteries that flowed over the rocks and moved up. Pointed shoots of barbed wire and razors appeared on the vines, like artificial thorns, and when the vines hit the roof, they crunched in, with a ripple of cracks and fissures that zig-zagged overhead.

*It's all going to collapse. We're about to be crushed.*

But Josie and Clara climbed up beside Uncle Don. Overhead, the vine dug openings in the ceiling. The metal was growing. Vines that had been the size of Josie's fingers a moment ago were now as big as her wrist, straining the rock as they expanded. *Like it knows and is helping us.*

Uncle Don pointed to a main network of vines in the roof. "Look."

The vines were opening a fissure, like a narrow chimney, with a speck of white in the high distance.

*Daylight.*

"Holy shit," Josie said.

"How are they doing that?" Clara asked.

*They're alive. Living, breathing tendrils of metal.*

Uncle Don reached to help Clara up, closer to the vines, and she looked back. "Wait. Your mom—I mean, your real mom ..."

"Not here," Josie said.

The metal vines flexed, jarring the rock chute open in a shuddering explosion of dust and falling pebbles.

"I don't believe this," Josie said.

"Can you both fit?" Uncle Don asked.

Following Clara up, Josie grabbed the vines, driving sharp metal points into her hands. She stepped onto a razorblade, felt her shoe bend and give. Wincing, Josie climbed, shivering when sharp metal jabbed into her feet, shoulder, and fingers. *But the hole is wide enough. Knife vines grown from a dead sea monster.* They didn't stop climbing until they broke the surface into a concrete pipe. Some kind of drainage tube. The vines had gashed the floor, flexing out now in a crinkling spread toward a circle of soft, white daylight at the far end.

Josie waited for Uncle Don to come up, and then all three of them tracked the pipe to a ragged stone embankment at the side of a wide river. Black metal vines covered the concrete pipe and flowed over the hillside like weeds. The sky was hazy. When Josie tracked the river to the left, she spotted a railroad and highway bridge and the buildings of downtown Louisville, not far off. Four years since she saw the small cluster of domed and glass-block towers. Squinting, bulbs of fire came into focus above the bridge: bodies. More people hanged and now lit into smoking, mid-air pyres on the suspension lines of the bridge.

Josie helped Uncle Don and Clara out of the drainage pipe, all three of them caked in white-brown dust that made Josie's breathing chalky, scratching her throat. Uncle Don slumped onto his side, gasping and slick with sweat. Beside him, Clara turned in a slow circle, watching the vines spread. *How far will they grow? Where will they stop?* In gaps between the black-metal vines, the stone riverbank was checkered with shells and tiny, segmented jots, like pieces of crystalized pasta. More ancient fossils, of course, now quickly covered by black metal.

Josie started toward the city. Uncle Don staggered after, and when Clara fell into step beside her, Josie told her about tracking down Uncle Don and Grandma, finding Not-Mom—and everything that had gone wrong since.

"If the glass-face man, that thing, was your dad," Clara said, "then it was him. Had to be."

"What was?" Uncle Don asked.

"Your dad brought us here," Clara said, watching Josie's muted reaction. "If he's alive, he found the shoebox, his old phone—who else would remember the tree in Central Park?"

*Dad is gone. My last connection to him—the real him—disappeared when I chucked the lucky fossil into the dragon's mouth. And started this.*

They passed a vacant park and riverfront playground, almost to the bridge. Around them, more vines poured over the landscape. Josie sidestepped around the razorblade vines, but as they neared the highway overpass, it was getting harder. The vines grew faster than the three of them could walk. The river was lower than it had been four years ago, and dead shapes—glistening sacks, feathered lumps—flowed with the current.

Josie slowed, as they neared a concrete rise up to an empty railroad bridge, just above the floodwall. *This is where we met.* Josie took Clara's hand.

Uncle Don paced, confused. "What's wrong?" he asked. "Why are we stopping?"

*I don't know what to do. I'm lost again. I'm fourteen years old and lost in a strange city at a riverbank, searching for my parents.*

Clara rubbed Josie's shoulder. "This is where I found Josie. Back in the day."

*Same river and railroad bridge, new living razorblades and corpse glowlamps, though.*

"You were too cute to leave then, too," Clara said. She tugged Josie's arm, and they kissed. A long taste of Clara blotted out the chaos. "Thank you for coming back for me. Both of you."

"You don't need to thank family for being there," Uncle Don said simply, then to Josie, "Where would he take Caitlyn? Do you have any idea?"

*Caitlyn. Still weird to hear him call Mom by her first name. But he knew her long ago, maybe better than I do.* "I'm not sure."

Josie adjusted the fire bowl to watch the flame shudder in the wind. A molecular fire, the kind of flame that would burn through a hurricane. As she shifted the stone, the vines spiraled around them. Subtle, but the movement matched her, almost a dance. Like a stop-motion mosaic in sand or stone, but made of shiny razors and knives.

Behind them, the black vines snarled up onto the highway overpass and were already swarming the office buildings in a squirmy, glistening mesh of coils and knives.

"They're attracted to this," Josie said, holding up the fire. "Do you guys see that?"

They all watched as Josie slowly mounted the incline up to the edge of the railroad bridge, almost over the water. No bodies hung here, they all burned further out, at least fifty meters up in the air over the middle of the river. Glistening metal sprouted in concentric curls with each step Josie took.

"I think ..." *This is insane. No, it's happening, so it isn't.* Guiding the fire stone back and forth, Josie felt the surreal sense of the actions *clicking,* like pressing a Lego piece into place, according to the directions—but more than that. Her movement, right here at the ledge of the railroad bridge, where Dad's ghost spoke from the lucky fossil for the first time four years ago ... each footstep was an echo. *He did this, too. Not when I was here. I am moving where he moved. He held a fire stone here, exactly like this.* The certainty of it made Josie pause—and the vines stilled, too.

Vines still smothered the city, the highway overpass shimmering now, buildings turning to black boxes in a riot of overlapping metal links.

"I see what you mean," Uncle Don said. "You aren't controlling them exactly, but the metal vines respond to that."

*Dad stood right here. This is where he left the lucky fossil for me to find. Why?*

"The fires ..." Josie closed her eyes, waiting for the manic pieces to settle into a coherent picture. Explosive events into a narrative. "My dad wrote down where all the torches are." She looked again: Clara and Uncle Don both waited below, weak and dirt-spattered, but trusting. *They believe there's an answer.* "The fires are important. And that's all he said, isn't it? 'Burn.'" Neither of them answered. *So that's it? Find the fires and burn away the blackleg vines and monsters?* Josie knelt to place the fire stone in a nest of growing metal, and the tips of blades sprouted toward the flame, not away.

*No.*

She stood with the fire again. "These things live on fire." Josie glanced at the burning people behind her and over the city's other bridges, further down the waterfront. Meaningless brutality. *The same way it ended for Dad.* "The torches woke them up. If there's any sense to this," Josie said, "then that's what this is." She held the fire stone to the edge of the bridge. *And what I saw in that other place, the version of my life that never happened. Dad pulled me out of there, too, didn't he? He wanted me to see that path out. Over the edge. Into the water.*

"What if we have to put them out?" Josie said, and she let the fire stone drop, with that flicker-mirror sensation that this was a scene repeating. *Dad did this, too. To test his theory. If the fires bring them to the surface, then the torches underground all need to die.*

The fire stone puffed out into the river in a spurt of white smoke, already gone under the waves. A crinkling whine echoed under the overpass. Vines collapsed, peeling back in a mass of grainy black. Closer, she watched layers of knives and razors come apart like clay. No longer shiny, they disintegrated into a dry mash, already whipping away as dust in the hot riverfront breeze. But the bodies stilled burned. *The monsters are still here.*

"That was easy," Clara said.

Descending from the railroad bridge again, Josie said, "Yeah, except how many more are there? I saw two more torches in that cavern underground, and there were I-don't-know-how-many on Dad's maps."

"Dozens," Uncle Don said. "At least."

"This won't stop until we put them all out."

Clara shook her head. "No. We're not going back down there. Josie, no."

"My dad ..." A strong gust of wind tossed black-vine debris into a momentary whirlwind, clearing the onramp to the highway. Black flakes gathered in tidal curls on the windows and roofs of empty cars. "His plan wasn't to try to drag all the torches to the river and put them out. Maybe he did it once—like I just did—to see if it would work, if ordinary water would stop these things."

"Mark arranged barrels underground," Uncle Don said, nodding more quickly. "Wired somehow ..."

*To the fucking trees.*

"I know what we have to do," Josie said.

# Chapter Twenty-Two

"Those electrical wires ran up the tree roots," Josie said. "You saw them, Uncle Don. Dad rigged them into the cave ceilings, somehow *through* the rock."

"From deep underground? How?" Clara asked.

"I don't know, but we saw it."

Uncle Don started pacing again, just like at the house, both hands patting his legs, as if keeping time with the accelerating rhythm of his thought. "Right, right," he said. "Mark was a tactician. And in his writing, he always talked about the trees."

"About how they would protect me," Josie said, watching for Clara's response. "If he took Mom's phone—probably brought her here, too, maybe even in the tunnels—then what if he was trying to show us, right at the beginning, how to stop this?"

"The tree where we found your mom's phone? In the fossil park?"

"Yes," Josie said, pointing at Uncle Don. "You said Perryville is near where I first grew up. That steamboat restaurant was where my first birthday party happened, right? That was Dad's first tree for me."

"Okay ..?" Clara said, shaking her head. "I'm sorry, I still don't ..."

"There's a bomb under it," Uncle Don said and stopped moving. "Let's see if any of these cars have keys." He started off to a line of cars below the highway overpass.

"Really?" Clara asked Josie.

Josie gestured at the layer of black crud around them and the burning bodies further out. "Look at how different the world is now. I wouldn't have thought this—not when we started. But now?"

"Now, you're talking the way he wrote," Clara said and forced an uneasy smile. She took Josie's hand again. "I'm here for it, though."

"No wonder everybody thought he was crazy."

"You're right," Clara said, and they walked down after Uncle Don, who ducked, half-in the front seat of an unlocked minivan to search for keys. Finally, he gave up and continued down the street, checking more cars. An alarm went off on a locked black sportscar, but Uncle Don didn't even slow, jogging faster from car to car, closer to downtown. "He seems good," Clara said.

"Better anyway," Josie said. "That skinless thing killed his mom, my grandmother. He has a gun now, but I don't think that would have mattered."

"He has a gun?" Clara slowed.

"It's okay. I think. We don't have a choice, do we?"

"Of course we do."

*She's right. We can walk away. Mom will come back. Somehow, she will ... no.* Those thoughts felt forced, the 'rational' ideas behind them flimsy. Half-remembered jokes with no punchline.

"We don't, though," Josie said at last.

"No," Clara said. "I know. But that tree—the one with your name on it at the battlefield fossil park—if your dad *did* leave your mom's phone there for us ... why wasn't he there?"

*She's right. He wasn't.*

At the end of the block, directly adjacent to the highway onramp, Uncle Don hopped out of a blue Ford sedan, with both hands waving.

"Found one!"

A Ford sedan, like the car that Dad drove to the gas station. *Stop it.*

Clara brightened, hurrying faster. "Hell, yes. That's ..." She noticed Josie's slack stare. "What's wrong?"

"Nothing. You're right, I don't know why he wasn't there at the tree ..."

"That other thing was," Clara said. "You saw it. That's all I'm—*it* knew we would go there."

The skinless man, Not-Mom. "It's going to be waiting for us, isn't it?" Josie said. "Uncle Don has a gun, and ..." *And what? They couldn't fight Not-Mom before. Would a pistol matter? Dad said 'no.' Again and again in his notebook, he talked about guns not being helpful to fight them. Bullets weren't enough.*

The driver's door open, engine already running, Uncle Don slapped the top of the car, as they approached. "A quarter tank of gas," he said. "Should be enough, but it's not a lot for the return trip."

"Let's just get there first," Josie said. *No gas stations. Not here.*

She climbed in up front, with Clara right behind her, and when they buckled in, doors closed, Uncle Don pulled out and up to the highway. He talked about how lucky they were to find an unlocked car with spare keys, how he'd thought they would be searching for hours, maybe even have to walk back to the hospital for the rental car. Past the highway, the sky turned a soft gray, then streaky red at the horizon. Sunset. Uncle Don kept their speed low, as the light faded.

Beyond downtown, a University of Louisville billboard with an angry-looking cardinal bird mascot appeared on the right. Closer, it read: *'Visitors must wear identification at all times. Absolutely no residents beyond this point.'*

*No.*

Josie looked away, shivering. *No, Goddamn it.*

Clara noticed. "What?"

Josie shook her head. *Say it's nothing. Lie.* "The sign out there—you see it?"

They were already past. Clara swiveled around to squint out the back. From this angle, it was turned crooked, impossible to read in the fading daylight. "What was it?"

"Writing for me, like before in the caves." Josie was breathing fast, felt her pulse in the squeeze of her fingers on the dashboard. "I know it wasn't real. I know this is happening right now."

"I don't understand," Clara said. "What writing?"

"When we were in the caves," Uncle Don said. "Josie saw writing on the walls that was put there to make her think she was someplace else. If it's starting again, we should take it seriously."

*He's right. It's directed at me. Something put those messages there. The same something that's waiting for us at Dad's tree.*

"What if it's there?" she asked.

Uncle Don's fingers tightened, and he turned the wheel. Still no one else on the road, just vacant cars on both shoulders. "The blackleg thing," he said. "The one you call 'Not-Mom.'"

"Yes, it was at the tree the first time Clara and I went there. It was waiting for us."

From the backseat, Clara said, "It might be again."

*"Will be,"* Josie said, and to Uncle Don, "What do we do?"

At the suburban outskirts of Louisville, the sky faded twilight blue with rainclouds. Ahead, the interstate darkened. Old-fashioned nighttime on the endless empty without cars, streetlights, or people. Whatever was happening, it wasn't done. The world wasn't back. It started raining. Not hard, just a steady beat of water that made Josie hunch forward. *Stay alert.* Past the lull of the windshield wipers and headlights, water sluiced along the shoulder. No lightning, no thunder—just rain.

"I'm not sure," Uncle Don said at last. "If the barrels, explosives, whatever—if they really are wired up to the tree, then Mark must have left a trigger. Something we can find." He blinked, smiling suddenly. "Josie, in your bag ..."

*Dad's notebook.* She shifted her bag to unzip it, the fabric still damp from the cavern pool. *If it isn't ruined.*

"There was one more entry," Uncle Don said. "Earlier, I didn't have time ..."

Josie found the notebook: still mostly dry. Her fingers separated the pages, and—Mom's phone rang. Josie jumped, dropping the notebook. Mom's phone flashed in her open bag with a robotic chime.

"What is that?" Clara asked, one hand on Josie's shoulder.

"The police, maybe," Josie said and lifted Mom's phone out. Not the police, Mom's phone displayed two word: *'Unknown Number.'*

Leaning in, Clara asked, "Wrong number?"

"Who is it?" Uncle Don asked.

Josie let the call go to voicemail. Mom's phone was dark and silent again.

"Nothing," Josie said. "It wasn't ..."

It rang again: the same *'Unknown Number'* incoming call display.

Uncle Don craned around to see. "What is ..." His hands slipped, and they swerved, jostling back and forth in the lanes. "Sorry."

"Ignore it," Clara said.

Her hand pressed harder on Josie's shoulder. Josie tapped to answer, putting Mom's phone on speaker. *No.*

"What are you doing?" Uncle Don asked. "Don't."

"They won't stop," Josie said, and into the phone, "Hello? Whoever this is ..."

Whimpering on the line. The sound of someone's muffled crying, like lips quivering against a gag.

"Who's there?" Josie asked. "You called me on ..."

The crying amped into a startled cringe of pain, then shaky, non-verbal pleading. *Mom. That's Mom's voice.*

Clara said, "Josie, I think that's ..."

The rain was picking up, foggy in the headlights. Clara rubbed Josie's arm—*and that's real.* That feeling of warmth cut through the terror knot in Josie's stomach. Out of the corner of her eye, Uncle Don hunched closer to the windshield. They sped up, stalled cars and black trees flashing faster out the windows.

"Stop," Josie said into the phone.

"Ignore it," Uncle Don said.

"*Ignore* it?" She turned on him. "Are you joking? Do you hear this?"

"You don't know it's real, Josie."

Sobbing on the phone, and a shaky, garbled vocalization. Pleading words scrambled under a mouth gag.

"Turn off the call," Uncle Don said. The engine roared louder, as they surged. The median lines were a white blur on the rainy highway, windshield wipers flashing faster.

Speeding alone on the road, they were already almost there, but impossible to see much in the nighttime trees and fields outside.

"You have a choice," a calm, male voice said on the phone. "Your family is worried about you, Josie. They miss you. Do you remember Clara and Anna?"

"Yes," Josie said.

"No," Uncle Don said. "Josie, don't talk to it."

"They're waiting for you," the skinless man said on the phone.

The car slowed, and Uncle Don took the turn, and the next one, and in the swipe of the windshield wipers, the headlights illuminated the battlefield welcome sign at the gravel road. *The visitor's center is just up that hill.*

"You can return to the treatment plan we discussed," the skinless man said. "You suffered a break. A crisis. You scared us all, with that jump, Josie. You really did." He laughed. "But you hear me now, so that's progress."

*It's not real. That other version of the world, the one without demons and metal vines.*

They pulled onto the gravel drive. The car's jumpy movement felt distant, and now even the tap of rain on the windshield seemed farther away, like Josie was drifting deeper into her skull.

"Are they really there?" she asked.

"Stop it," Uncle Don said.

*I know I'm here. I just want to hear the answer. I know it's not real. But let me talk to it.*

The air was too thin, hard to breathe. Josie took a shaky gasp. The low shadow of the battlefield visitor's center and empty parking lot appeared ahead. *Get out of the car.*

*I'm mad in a hospital somewhere. I've been delusional my whole life, just like Dad.*

A brief memory of the glass-face man's disfigured face and scars. Dad's face. She blinked that away, as they slowed into the lot. Uncle Don turned off the car.

"You can come back to us, Josie. To your family," the skinless man said. "All you have to do is stop."

"Come on, Josie." Clara opened her door.

Clara's voice was far away. *No, she's right here. So why does she sound like she's behind a wall?*

Uncle Don opened his door and stepped out in a rush of thick, rainy air.

"Stop," Josie repeated.

"Yes," the skinless man said. "Tell me where you are. Are you back at the killing fields? Stay there, and I'll come to help you."

*Yes, I'm in a car at a battlefield cemetery.* "Okay," Josie said.

Outside, Clara and Uncle Don watched through her window. *Both waiting for me.*

"Would you like to see your family again?" the skinless man asked.

*Why is it so hard to breathe? Why won't my lungs work right?* Josie's chest clenched for too long every time she sucked in air. "What if I say 'no'?"

"Josie ..."

"What if I don't want to tell you where I am? What if I decide this ..."

"If you choose to continue with this delusion," the skinless man said, "then this fantasy will play out in all the messy, painful ways you're afraid of. You'll watch your friends and family die." The distant sound of Mom's muffled crying on the line again.

Uncle Don knocked on Josie's window. "End the call."

Clara waved at her impatiently.

"Ask yourself that question again," the skinless man said. "What's really more likely to be true? That monsters are real, and only *you* can see them? That the whole world is dying, and *you*—only you again—have to save it somehow?"

Josie didn't move, listening to the slow rain. *It doesn't matter what's more likely. 'Likely' isn't how the world works.*

"Or," the skinless man said, "that you're unwell. And that you can get better? Doesn't that sound just a little more plausible? Where are you, Josie? Tell me, and I'll come to find you. I'll bring you back ..."

"No," Josie said. She stabbed off the phone and kicked open her door. "We need to do this quickly."

"Which way is the tree?" Uncle Don asked.

*That's right, he doesn't know.* "That way." Josie shrugged her bag onto her back and stepped out into the rain, her vision already adjusting to the gray and black nighttime blobs. "What happens, when there's nothing there?" she asked.

*And Mom is killed, because I didn't find a way to help her. But we can't stop. I have to finish this.* The call was desperate. It meant the blacklegs were afraid, grasping at traumas to stop her.

The three of them followed the squishy mud path into the park. The warm slog of rain made Josie's legs heavier. When did she last rest or eat? The thought prickled a biting ache in her stomach. Not hunger, this felt deeper and more animal, like the feeling normal hunger was imitating. She was fucking wiped. *Don't stop. Almost there.*

They walked in a quiet line through the wet darkness, past the battlefield monuments, and up a hill that should overlook a pond. Just blotchy shadows now. *Not much further.* Over the next rise, the hill would dip again. Josie tracked the curl of the path to where it sloped down to the field and leveled to meet the forest tree line.

Sentinels burned at the edge of the woods. Human pyres.

# Chapter Twenty-Three

S keletal shadows of people shimmered inside whooping flames at regular intervals, blocking the trees, and in front, backlit so their shadows danced across the wet grass: five fishmen. Dozens of burning people—she counted thirty-seven—with a semi-circle of fishmen in front, all decorated in sheathed clothing. Two wore stiff flags on poles in their backs, just like the cave.

"What is this?" Clara asked.

She stopped with Uncle Don, but Josie kept going, feet moving fast to keep from sliding on the slippery path. Rain pattered her face, clothes already clingy. Josie's hands trembled at either side. The rain tasted hotter, as she neared the fires. She felt it coat her throat and nose.

"Josie, stop," Clara said. "Are those *people*? In the fires ..?"

*What am I doing?*

She kept going, heard Clara and Uncle Don following behind. Clara tripped, caught her footing in the muck. Josie took Clara's hand, then kept on, almost to the bottom of the hill. Wind tossed the moist smell of barbeque and burning hair. The people on the poles were dead, already gone. Josie spat, tried to wipe the taste of the smoke out of her nose and lips.

Hitting the grass, closer to the formation of fishmen, she heard drums. Music sounded through the trees behind the fires. Voices sang and pitched too high into shrieks, mixed with rougher sounds. Cracks and snaps. Under it all, the drums and a horn—like the cavern, and the apartment in New York, so fucking long ago. The first time one of these things broke into our kitchen, when Dad tried to protect me. *Is that what he was doing?* I heard a melody in the hall then, too.

"Josie ..." Clara's thumb pinched Josie's palm, as they stomped closer, Uncle Don's footsteps right behind. The fishmen were armed: one held a fire poker, another a cleaver, another a short blade, and that same blunt shovel weapon, and a three-pronged poker. All ready to stab her to death, sparkling in the dark rain and firelight, with fucking devil music under it all.

"What is this?" Clara said, close enough that they could hear.

"Yes, what is she doing?" the poker fish man said, murmuring, "Off her medications ..."

The cleaver one said, "No, she doesn't listen to reason anymore." He stepped up, aimed the weapon at Josie's head, as she continued forward, not slowing. The same cleaver from the steamboat. The one that lodged in the waitress's neck.

*No. I'm not afraid.*

Behind her, Uncle Don said, "Josie, move ..."

Josie spun—he aimed the gun—and she pulled Clara aside.

The fish man with a knife chortled, its head bobbing to either side. "He thinks he can—

The gun flash-cracked, and part of the cleaver fish man's head blew off. The cleaver fish man spun in a tilting twirl, like he'd been shoved, and the other four all turned to watch, as his head flopped forward awkwardly, blood splattering from a ragged hole where his left eye had been.

"Thinks he can hurt us," the cleaver fish man said. His mouth sucked, spurting bubbles in the rain, and he raised his cleaver at them. *A big 'fuck you, Uncle Don.'*

The fishmen focused on Josie again.

"I was aiming for the other one," Uncle Don said quietly, the gun still raised.

*Shit. Dad was right about this part, too.*

"The other what?" Clara asked.

"Fish man-demon-thing," Josie said. "They're right here."

"She won't listen to reason," the wounded, cleaver fish man said and stepped to the front. Blood splashed out of the gaping wound in its head in steady beats. It wasn't healing, it just didn't care.

Clara pulled back, tugging Josie's hand. "Josie, think."

"I am." Josie didn't move. *Trying not to, but I am. They're afraid of me. Everyone says it. Dad said it, and Uncle Don—that's the entire fucking point. Lure me into a cavern, trick me with visions of a beautiful life I can't have. So they don't have to stand here with me in the rain. Why? Why don't they just murder me like everyone else?*

The wounded fish man shuffled closer, its head drooping sideways on one shoulder, so blood flowed down its torso and arm.

"I see you, dear," he said.

But it stopped, still five meters away, out of reach.

Clara said, "The gun ..."

"Don't start shooting," Josie said, glaring at the wounded fish man.

"You believe what you see now?" he asked. "Do you?" He leveled the cleaver at her, crept in, body low and tense, but still half-stumbling, like he wasn't used to walking in the open. *Or is afraid to be out here.*

"Why did you do that to those people?" Josie asked, nodding past him to the line of pyres.

"Vision," the wounded fish man said, two meters away, almost close enough. If he dove in, could Josie move in time? "To help you see."

Clara pulled again, but Josie slipped her hand free, still facing the fish man.

"Your friend is very pretty on the outside," the fish man said. "Does she ..."

"Don't threaten us again," Josie said and moved in. The wounded fish man froze, cleaver still raised. This close, he smelled of dead fish, with an oily tang. "No."

"She is the daughter," the poker fish man said.

"Passed into her blood," the knife one said.

"Mental illness," Josie said. "I know." She eased her arms apart, legs tight. *Fuck this. You don't threaten us again.* "But that's not me."

She lunged, ducking to dodge the cleaver, but the wounded fish man stumbled and slid in the grass. He lost his footing and went down. The other four backed away, gasping, and Josie dove on the wounded one on the lawn, using both hands to catch his cleaver—"No!" he screamed. "Please!"—and when she touched his wrist, the wounded fish man burst into flames. Hot fire knocked her back, and the thing screamed, flailing in the mud. Behind Josie, Clara caught her.

"What the fuck?" Uncle Don said.

Shaking, hands and legs—all of her—soaked on the lawn, Josie's heart thudded up her neck. The other four fishmen were gone. Movement flashed by the pyres, into the trees.

"What happened?" Clara asked.

The wounded fish man stilled, its body collapsing into dark, burning ash. Its fire dwindled into a charred pulse around a figure in embers, and then a shadow that muted away in the rain.

"It burned up," Josie said. "I touched it, and it caught on fire."

"The fish man," Clara said. "The monster—you just touched it ..."

"Yes."

Uncle Don came to inspect the depression in the slick grass where the fish man had been. "I don't believe it."

"This entire time," Josie said. "But that didn't happen with the other one, Not-Mom ..." *I grabbed the skinless man, when he pretended to be Mom. I tried.*

"It was wearing fake skin," Uncle Don said. "Pretending to be your mother. Maybe that protected it. Mark always talked about something in our blood that makes them afraid. Something inherited. I always thought ..."

"It isn't just that we see them," Josie said. "Can you do that? If you touch them ..."

"What you just did?" he said, as if it were absurd. *It is.* "Set them on fire by touching them?" *Make them burn.* "No," he said. "Not at all. I've come into contact with them before, and ... no."

*Dad could. Somehow he could, and he knew I could, too. These things here to butcher the world, and all we have to do is touch them.*

"Into the trees ..?" Josie checked Clara, the yellow light of the pyre fires quivering the edges of her mouth and eyes. *Like she still doesn't believe it.*

"Why couldn't I see them?" Clara asked. "I saw the glass-face man."

"I think maybe you saw him," Josie said, "because he's my dad—he used to be a person. Not like the others."

They passed between two pyres. Bonfire heat flooded in on either side, and Josie held her breath, watching the slick ground, not the corpses at the center of the fires. On the other side, she led them into the trees and swallowed the taste of char and wet wood. The forest shivered in the rain, barren branches ticking and dripping. A bed of mist still wrapped depressions in the ruined foliage, and when they turned off the path in a sideways course to where Josie remembered the creekbed, the drums echoed louder. The chanting, screaming voices were almost close enough to understand.

The ground rose to the top of an embankment. At the bottom, the fossil-bed creek hadn't changed, the shallow, fast-moving water shimmering. Further downstream, a mass of people seemed to be crawling or running at a low tilt in a circle through the stream, up one bank, then back around into the water and around the other bank again. Small figures patrolled the perimeter with whips, long poles, and knives. The guards were little men in insect masks with hooved feet and flags mounted on their backs, and one was beating a wide leather drum in the center. The circle-people sang, "... *a song for whiskey smoke ...*" The ground slithered on this side of the creek. Not a trick of the light: vines. More black metal vines.

"There it is." Clara pointed across the stream to a tree on the opposite bank. The carving was still there, but from here, Josie couldn't read her name. She didn't have to.

"They're bringing them up," Uncle Don said, as if he wanted to be told that no, what he was seeing wasn't happening. "The knife vines, like before."

They climbed down to the creek. Clara was the first across, shaking water from her shoes, as Josie and Uncle Don stepped to the tree with her. Here, even in the dark-dark, the name was visible: *Josephina Elizabeth Morris.*' Josie glanced down the length of the stream: no change in the chaotic movement and song. The circle of moving people was hunched forward with their naked backs and legs in the air, but they weren't crawling. They were *rolling*. The people had wheels for hands, stomping bare, horseshoed feet to heave on the path around a gash in the hillside. *A cave.* A hundred of them at least—men, women, even children—all nude, sang and shouted, their bodies slick with bloody whip lines.

Flowing like ivy ink, glinting blackness bulbed around the mouth of the cave, already filling the hillside by the circle. Pointy tendrils glistened over the rocks at the edge of the creek.

"When we lost time, after going into the Cadillac Club, that cave is where I came back with you," Josie told Clara. "I didn't realize it was so close."

"They haven't seen us," Uncle Don said, and he felt along the grooves of Josie's name carving. "What are we looking for?"

By the cave, an insect man cracked a whip over a wheel woman's back, and her scream blended with the song.

*"... oh! No chain, no fire, no rock from heaven ..."*

The noise made Clara look back, shaking her head. "What are they doing?"

"How much of it do you see?" Uncle Don asked.

The song continued:

*"... no steel, no fetus, no faith eternal ..."*

"I see people screaming in a circle. Hurt, with *parts* attached to them ..."

Josie went to the tree, both hands testing the bark. She moved in a quick circle around it, ducking a low branch on the far side. *And I'm expecting what? A secret door? A magic switch Dad somehow hid? There's nothing.*

*"... take the prayer, whiskey-smoke, and seed ..."*

"You don't see the men with whips and poles?" Uncle Don asked, then noticed Josie circling closer around the tree.

"I only see the people," Clara said.

"Just like the glass-face man," Josie murmured. "My dad is still some version of human. That's why you saw him." She stopped back at her name carving. "I can't find anything."

Uncle Don stepped in, craning to look up into the tree's expanse of bare branches. "I've never seen this carving before. But if this was Mark's first tree for you, it makes sense it would be here."

Josie sagged back against her name. She half-expected the wood to clack and reveal something. It didn't. "This can't be nothing."

"I'm sorry," Uncle Don said. "But we have to do something. They're bring the black vines to the surface. We have to stop them. Josie, if you can kill them, just by touching them ..."

"She's not going to *fight* them," Clara said. "No."

"Why not?" Uncle Don took out his gun, one hand already up to placate them. "Look, I know that it walked and talked after I shot it, but the bullet *did* work."

"It blew a hole in its head," Josie told Clara, and to Uncle Don, "But that barely slowed it down. No, Uncle Don. Even if I *can* do whatever I did—even if I can do that again, to all of them, what about you? Both of you? All it takes is one of them with a knife Clara can't see, or a machete that hits you from behind ... or who knows what. No."

He lowered the gun and closed his eyes, as the circle of people screamed louder:

*"... he is the point of a broken star .... not alone, not alone anymore ..."*

Josie pushed off the tree, squared up to it again. *This, right here, is where they found Mom's phone. Where he left it for us. Dad was trying to tell us then.*

"We all thought there was a chance." Clara rubbed Josie's arm.

"Why would he bring us here? If there's nothing ..?"

"How did he show you?" Uncle Don asked, and when they frowned, Uncle Don shrugged. "Sometimes with Mark, the form is as important as the function. A message on a tree isn't just about the message, right? It's about the tree, too. How did you know your mom's phone was here? If that thing in the mask is really him, he's not exactly calling you on voicemail ..."

"It was a birding app," Josie said.

Uncle Don shook his head, as if unsure what that meant. "Birding?"

"Yeah, Dad was into birds. Mom had the app on her phone, too, so he must have taken a picture, or let Mom take ..."

Clara stepped up to reach for the tree branches. "What if it's in a nest?"

Uncle Don tried to shake away a smile. "That would be like him. I'll check the other side ..." He wandered around to inspect the lower branches on the back of the tree, even pulling himself up to shake two of them. The tree was maybe ten meters tall, but the dry foliage thinned like capillaries that shrank from the larger arteries of the trunk and central branches. Too small to support much of a nest. Still, Josie didn't move. Hiding something in a bird's nest would be on-brand for Dad. Old Dad, from before.

"Anything?" Uncle Don called.

Clara slapped an empty branch and checked Josie's expression. "Nope. It's nest-less. Josie, what do you think?"

Behind her, the song continued. When she glanced back, the snaking black vines had spread closer, into the creek and along the opposite bank. *The woods will be covered in knives, razors, and barbed wire. Then the fields. Cities. Then the rest of it, whatever's left.*

"Fuck." Josie let out a breath that made her cough, eyes tearing. But not from the smoke this time. She tasted tears in her snot and on her tongue, when she swallowed. She shivered, hugging her arms, until Clara stepped close. "No wonder they don't care about this tree," Josie murmured. "We lost."

Uncle Don came back around, the gun ready. "We can still try."

"It won't work," Josie said.

Clara took Josie's hands. "What can we do?"

"I have enough bullets," Uncle Don said. "If I knock them down …"

"No," Josie said and returned to the carving. *One last tree.* "My dad said bullets were useless. Guns, weapons, that's not the answer." *He gave me the answer, I just don't see it. If it's not a fucking nest in the tree branches, it's …*

A roundish bowl-shaped clump of leaves and sticks came into focus near the base of the tree, half-hidden in a nearby bush.

"I didn't see it," Josie said and crouched to inspect the shape. "I can't believe I didn't see it."

"What is that?" Uncle Don asked.

"A nest," Josie said. "Probably a grouse, maybe a Kentucky warbler."

Carefully, she lifted the patch of organic debris … it caught. Something snagged on it from the bottom.

"I didn't know birds make nests on the ground," he said.

"They do."

They both watched, as Josie leaned the nest away: white-and-red wires looped into the belly of the bird's nest. Electrical wires. Josie pulled, and the end came out of the dirt with a simple plastic attachment for a docking port.

*Dad's phone.*

Josie swung her bag around, feeling for it—*there*—and took out Dad's phone to tap it on. The screen brightened. No signal, but it worked, and the opening at the bottom matched. The wires clicked into the phone, like they'd always been there.

Clara murmured, "Holy shit. From the shoebox."

*He showed us. Every step of the way, Dad laid it all out.*

"That's Mark's phone?" Uncle Don said.

"It is," Josie said.

A box appeared onscreen:

> *'Would you like to save the world (trigger C1-10)? Y/N?'*

Her body sore, limbs weak and dripping in the rain, Josie still felt a short laugh rise from her belly. "Goddamn it, Dad."

"Don't you dare click 'no,'" Clara said.

Uncle Don gestured at the wire. "The wires look the same as underground."

"Yep." Josie checked with each of them. "I'm doing it."

Clara tensed, and Uncle Don nodded. Josie pressed *'Yes.'*

Nothing happened.

The phone screen blinked:

> *'Connection interrupted. Repair for trigger activation.'*

"Do we know what that means?" Clara asked. "Is the line cut or there's a problem with the phone?"

Uncle Don gestured at the cave and screaming people with his gun. "It means it doesn't work. The black vines are spreading. We have to stop those things."

"No, wait," Clara said. "Let's think about this."

"We don't have time," he said. "Look at what's happening. You can't see all of it, but you see the people being hurt." He nodded to Josie. "Josie, we can do this."

"You're not throwing her at those monsters," Clara said.

"*Throwing* her? She can kill them, just by—"

"She killed *one*," Clara said, straightening to face him down. "And another one—the one that killed your mother—she couldn't hurt at all."

At the mention of Grandma, Uncle Don shifted his weight, hand flexing on the lowered gun. He looked away at the people and the cave. Josie set Dad's phone in her bag again and felt along the red-white wire. A length came up out of the dirt along the top of the embankment. They were buried shallow.

"They're right there," Uncle Don said. "We can *see* them. We can kill them, before this spreads."

"You don't know that," Clara said. "Josie might have gotten lucky before. We can't count on that happening again."

Crouching, Josie followed the wire, pulling more up, and more, away from the tree. The direction of the wire turned deeper into the woods, away from the stream and cave song.

"Josie?" Uncle Don said. "Please ..."

She paused, the wire in one hand. She coiled the wire that attached to Dad's phone into her bag. *This was his last act, wasn't it? Wherever this leads.*

"No," Josie said. "Uncle Don, I told you, we can't kill them all. Not like this. I can't stop you, if you want to run down there, guns blazing—but don't."

Clara came after Josie. "Where does it go?"

"I think it's cut," she said. "Somewhere along the line. I think it's that simple. Repair the wire, and finish what my dad tried to do."

"*If* the wire is cut," Uncle Don said, "how are we going to ..."

Josie dug the roll of electrical tape from her bag to wave at him. Uncle Don shook his head again, with an involuntary smile. "Mark would do the same thing."

She led them into the woods, threading the wire with both hands, like a guiding line. Ahead, more and more wire sprouted from the leaves. Josie wound it into her bag ... until the trees opened, and they emerged at an empty roadside. Past the gravel, the gray grass on the far side ended at the dark curl of a river. No steamboat this time. Josie didn't slow, following the wires in a neat path along the edge of the road, until the drums and singing faded behind them. This was the opposite direction Josie and Clara had followed the last time.

"Why would he do this?" Clara asked. "Your dad—why take this all the way to that tree?"

*For me. So if it didn't work, there would be another way. A Plan B.* "The same reason he dug up the phone for us," Josie said.

She kept walking in the dark quiet. No more rain, the air was still and silent, except for the crunch of their shoes in the dirt. Around a turn in the road, lights appeared on the roadside ahead. Not a fire, that glow was electric. Someone still had power. A squat, nondescript building and parking lot, alone by the river, surrounded by empty fields and more trees, further off. The wires crossed the road, leading them closer to the river and the lit-up building. A bright yellow-white sign came into focus, and Josie slowed, stopped.

*'Last Chance Discount Gas Station'*

# Chapter Twenty-Four

"I see it," Uncle Don said.

Josie's hands closed on the wires, but she couldn't make her legs rise again. The gas station was maybe one-hundred meters away, directly ahead, between the road and the riverbank. One car was parked at the pumps, too far to really make out. But it was blue, just like their car. And Dad's.

"What is that?" Clara asked. "Josie, what's wrong?"

"That's it," Uncle Don said.

"It—what?" Clara asked.

When Josie still didn't answer, Uncle Don said, "The service station where Mark died. It's right there."

*This is what he was doing when they killed him. Laying wire. Preparing this, whatever it is.*

"There shouldn't be any lights," Josie said softly. *Walk. Keep going. I am not afraid.*

Her feet too heavy, she dragged the right one forward, then the left, and more wire passed through her palms, ripping free of the dirt along the road. *Four years it's been here. Four years since he did this.*

"They must have a generator," Uncle Don said. "Or ..."

*Or.*

"This is where it leads?" Clara asked, voice rising a little too much. She could see, the same as them.

Fifty meters away, the gas station came into clearer view: two simple pumps, and a bright-lit convenience store, with an *'Ice'* cooler by the empty parking spaces. The skinless man stood by a blue Ford sedan at the first pump, his bloody figure shiny in the glare of the lights on the overhang above him. Someone was in the front seat of the car.

"There's someone there," Josie told Clara. "The thing that pretended to be my mom."

"Where, by the building?"

"No, the car. He's standing right there."

Josie continued closer, the wire still tugging up in a straight line to the gas station. *Keep going.* Her legs moved automatically in time with her breathing. *Don't think.*

Ten meters away, the skinless man lifted a gas nozzle from the pump, then walked to the driver's door. The window was down. Inside, someone shifted in the driver's seat. Josie walked faster.

"Oh my God, Josie. Is that your ..."

"She's not alone," Uncle Don said. "It's there with her."

Josie's legs numbed, her pulse fading out, along with the black fields and road, the river, even the wire she still pulled up with both hands—all of it muted around the focus on Mom in the car. Mom's mouth was duct taped closed, wrists wired to the steering wheel. When Mom saw them, she jolted, straining and tossing. The car shook and bounced. Forty meters away, now thirty, Josie felt her pulse slow, as if she were approaching a rare bird and didn't want to spook it. *Take a photo. Preserve what I see. Like a grainy security camera would.*

The skinless man held the gasoline nozzle in one hand, an arm's length from Mom's open window.

"I can take a shot," Uncle Don murmured.

"At a gas station?" Clara said. "Are *you* insane now?"

"We don't have a choice." He watched Josie.

She dragged another long length of electrical wire up, and it came free at a ragged end by the edge of the gas station lot. *Here. This is where his line was cut. Because of course it was.* From the edge of the pavement, she spotted the other severed end of the wire by the gas pump at the skinless man's feet, where it looped into a metal grate. *This is where he finished prepping. Dad wanted to use the gas station. The gas station and the barrels of fuel—all of it one big, networked line of explosives. Until it was cut.*

"Here we are again, Josie," the skinless man said.

Still holding the broken wire, Josie stepped closer. The skinless man jerked the end of the gas nozzle into Mom's window, so it aimed at her face. She braced, eyes close, shaking in the seat.

Josie stopped. "Don't."

"Do you believe in this?" the skinless man asked. "Do you believe that you're standing at a gas station, about to watch your mother burn to death? Here." He reached in with one hand to unwind the wire from Mom's left wrist, then yanked it free. Mom watched her own hand, startled, as the skinless man planted her fingers on the gas nozzle, like a gun, her index finger light on the trigger. Still facing Josie, the skinless man pressed tight to clamp Mom's hand on the pump. If he squeezed, she would spray gas on herself through the window. *She can't see him, can she? She doesn't even know.*

Mom looked at Josie, eyes huge and terrified. Shaking her head, Mom's face pulled uselessly at the duct tape over her mouth.

"It's doing that?" Clara asked quietly.

"Yes," Uncle Don said.

"How do we stop this?" Clara said. "Josie ..?"

"We can't," Josie said.

"Let go of that," the skinless man said, indicating the wire in Josie's hand.

Josie eased closer. "No."

The skinless man tensed. Mom's finger tugged, and gasoline spurted over her. She flailed, trying to move away, as the foul-smelling liquid splashed over her face and hair, down her neck, soaking her shirt.

"Stop, stop!" Josie stepped back, let the wire fall.

The gas stopped.

Mom shuddered and dripped in the front seat, one hand still locked on the nozzle, the other on the wheel.

Clara pulled at Josie, frantic, and Uncle Don shouted questions, waving his gun, but there was only Mom and the skinless man. Nothing else.

"What do you want?" Josie asked.

"What do *I* want? I want you to be well again," the skinless man said. "I want you to stop fighting your treatment. No more living in a reality that's so upsetting and implausible. I want you to acknowledge what's real and what isn't. To really believe."

"You want me to give up."

"On this? Yes." The skinless man waved in a broad stroke to indicate the gas station, the river, Uncle Don, and Clara. "You've done it before. You can return to that again. To real life. I care about you, Josie. Can't you see this world is madness?"

Josie tasted the acid stink of gasoline, drifting out of the car. *I've done it before, he's right. I have. A world without demons. No fire in Chicago or murder in New York. None of this. I'm in a hospital right now, my medications unbalanced.*

"You see it, don't you?" the skinless man said, nodding. "You know I'm right."

"Or you're afraid of me."

"Because you can see me? Because your cells are part of the one percent of one percent of one percent that trigger a chemical reaction when they come into contact with the molecules of other, more ancient organisms?" He waited, the gas nozzle still poised. "Does that sound believable to you?"

"'Believable' isn't how it works," Josie said quietly. "Reality doesn't care what I believe, it just is."

Movement behind the skinless man. Something darted in the darkness past the gas station, gone again in the electric-white glare. *More blacklegs creatures. The fish men, probably.*

"Okay," the skinless man said and closed Mom's hand on the pump trigger again.

Gasoline sprayed over her, hitting Mom in her seat, and Uncle Don and Clara started forward, shouting.

"Wait!" Josie yelled. "Wait, please!"

The pump stopped. Mom was drenched now, trapped.

"I can't stop you," Josie told the skinless man. "And even if I could—even if the fire worked again, I can't ..."

"No," the skinless man said. "This isn't an ideal situation for flammable materials, is it?"

"So let them live."

"Your friends and your mother?" The skinless man nodded, musculature shifting tight, then loose around his jaw. "Until the end. The very end. When the earth quiets again, and there is no more food. Until we go back into the stone. That may be longer than their lifetimes anyway, Josie. And I agree. They can live."

"You can't bargain with it," Uncle Don said.

"Josie, what are you doing?" Clara asked. "What did it say?"

"They don't trust," the skinless man said and began to lower the gas nozzle, loosening his grip on Mom's hand. "But you do. You'll go back? Whether you believe in it or not, you'll go back, won't you, Josie?"

"No," Uncle Don said and moved between them. "She won't. She's not …"

The gas nozzle twisted up and sprayed him, knocking Uncle Don back a step. He spat and pawed at his dripping face.

Still using Mom's hand, the skinless man lowered the nozzle again.

"I give up," Josie said. "No more." She stepped closer.

The skinless man raised the nozzle back into the car window.

"No!" Josie said. "I told you. You win. Don't hurt her."

The skinless man watched her approach. "I'll take you back. You'll be safe again."

*And none of this will be real.*

Mom spasmed in the car, trying to scream through the tape. Uncle Don yelled behind her, and Clara came after Josie, took her arm.

"Stop it," Clara said. "Whatever you're about to do, don't."

"I can't," Josie said, voice too weak. "I can't let this happen to Mom and you …"

*Loss. Don't be afraid of loss. Fear pain.*

*But I am afraid. I can't.*

"Look at me," Clara said, blinking away tears. She pressed close. "I won't let you go. I told you that, right? You came back for me, and now …"

*You'll be there. Another version of you. It'll be okay.*

Josie started to turn back to the skinless man—fast movement behind him, a figure approaching—and Clara spun Josie back to her for a kiss that broke her resolve. The detached pull in her chest drained away.

A voice said, "Burn."

When Josie looked, the glass-face man—Dad wore the mask again—dove into the skinless man from behind, knocking them around the pump and into a tumbling ball of flame. Josie's legs locked. Uncle Don dashed past, into the passenger seat of Mom's sedan. Dad held the skinless man in a rolling embrace, their bodies swelling with hot yellow fire. Fire swam and spread on the pavement, sizzling onto a streak of gasoline. *The car.*

Leaning across the front seat, Uncle Don somehow unlocked the brake, and the car rolled forward, forcing Josie and Clara out of the way.

"The wires, Josie," Clara said, and she found the end Josie dropped, then ducked to feel for the severed end. Blue-hot fire snapped and smoked in puddles by the pump. *Any moment, this might—we can't stop.*

In the corner of Josie's vision, Dad and the skinless man settled into a writhing, burning pile.

*Dad.*

Clara found the missing end of the wire, and Josie whipped out the electrical tape, tearing a rectangular sliver, as Clara—one eye on the spreading fire and the pumps—put the two ends together. *We only need it for a moment. It's already activated.*

"This will work," Clara said.

Josie bound the tape tight, wrapping the severed electrical ends together, started to say that nothing—

The concrete shuddered, tilting the gas pumps. Glass exploded from the store windows, and Josie and Clara pounded off the lot to where the Ford had dipped into an embankment across the road. On the opposite side of the car, Mom caught Josie in both arms, hot and wet with gasoline, but still that same Mom-scent under it.

Uncle Don said, "Is it ..."

The pumps exploded in a fireball that flashed to sting Josie's eyes. The tremor knocked them back in the wet grass, with the car between them and the now-burning station. The pavement cracked, opening a jerky fissure down the center of the lot and across the far dirt to the riverbank. Josie pulled herself up on the hood of the car, the air thick with chemicals, smoke, and burnt plastic smells. Uncle Don shouted for her to get down, it wasn't safe. Bits of metal and burning rock burst across the road, denting and pockmarking the side of the car. But it shielded them from the shrapnel.

Another low rumble, like tiny thunder, sounded from somewhere far away. As Josie watched, the edge of the riverbank cracked, giving way into the lip of the explosion fissure. A trickle at first, the flow of water expanded over the top, washing it down, until a torrent poured down into the hole that had been blown out by the fires. No sign of Dad or the skinless man. The entire lot was a confusion of curled metal, broken glass, and smoking wreckage. The convenience store hadn't collapsed, but it leaned sideways, ready to go at any moment.

Mom held Josie, pressing her head hard to Josie's neck. "I'm so sorry," Mom whispered.

"It's okay."

"I don't remember how I got here. I couldn't control my hand—you saw ..."

Clara and Uncle Don came to watch the fires, and the river water rushing into the hole. Wider and faster, it didn't stop.

"Where is it going?" Clara asked.

"Filling the tunnels," Uncle Don said. "Putting out the torches."

Mom shook her head and spat gasoline. "I have to sit down. I can't ..."

"Me neither," Josie said.

*Can't walk. Can't magic this situation, not now. Not a dream or a mistake in my brain, though.*

*It just is.*

# Chapter Twenty-Five

—————————

**M**om held Josie and Clara tight. Uncle Don said he wanted to check the cavern at the creek, see if the circle of people—all of that—was gone. They didn't argue, and he promised to be back in one minute.

"I'm counting," Josie said.

Josie, Clara, and Mom retreated further from the road. The entire gas station was burning now, flames flaring out of the ground and into the convenience store, hot enough to feel on Josie's cheeks, even in a field of high dark grass across the road. The river still poured underground. *This is what he did. He extinguished it all. Did we just win? Is this what it feels like?* Josie wiped tears from her face, but her eyes still stung from the smoke, and her ribs squeezed, turning every breath into a cough.

*What do we do now? Go back to our lives? What's the world now?* Josie's guts twisted, and she swallowed sharp bile. *Going to puke. Dad is actually gone. All of him.* Her arms shook, and Mom and Clara held her. *Like it's freezing, but it isn't. It's warm.*

Josie cried. She didn't mean to but couldn't stop, and even as weak as Mom was, she held Josie, stroking the back of her head.

"It's okay," Clara said.

Dad, ruined and disfigured, had burned with the skinless man. *I saw their torsos burst with light. He wasn't alive. Not really. But erased now from even the memory of a ghost. Nothing left but what's in my head, like wounds.* Yellow-orange flames bellowed out the store windows. The air was sooty with an unnatural stink like a garbage fire. Part of the roof collapsed.

Uncle Don returned to say that the fossil creek was empty, the cave abandoned. No sign of monsters or tortured people or black vines. Mom listened, shaking her head, but she didn't ask.

An hour later, the road filled with flashing lights, when a bulky firetruck, two police cars, and an ambulance appeared. Smoke swirled red and white in the lights. The ambulance took them to a quiet, rural hospital, and after a blur of exams, they called a taxi in the early dawn.

Josie's phone was working again, and as they returned to the Tyler Lane house, Josie and Clara checked news reports.

"A gas leak from a limestone mine," Clara said in the back of the taxi, between Mom and Josie. Uncle Don was up front. "Dangerous fumes, hallucinogenic and flammable. That's the explanation. And the drought is over. After the storm yesterday, everything is already rebounding—look at this ..."

Josie  stared out at the highway cars and tried not to think. *No more metal vines or blacklegs or Dad. All of it over.* Finally, she looked at her phone again. According to the newspapers and social media, most people everywhere were back like they'd never gone. Never been hypnotized, brutalized, or killed by the blacklegs. Yes, there were stories about disappearances—entire families and communities that had gone missing—and deaths, too, but those were exceptions. 'Global hysteria,' the media called it. Most people couldn't remember and didn't care why their memories went to static over six hours of missing time. And that's all it was. From the house to the gas station, that's how long the end of the world lasted.

"I want to go home," Josie said.

But they returned to Uncle Don's house first. Grandma was gone. No sign of her body, but the walker was right where it had fallen on the living room carpet. In the quiet kitchen, Mom and Uncle Don made pancakes, while Josie and Clara continued to flip through news apps. Except for the sizzle of batter and chirping of birds in the backyard, the room was silent. *No Grandma. And now we're supposed to just slip back into our old skins and walk around like—what? Everything happened so fast, then crushed us, like test dummies against a concrete wall.*

"It happened, didn't it?" Josie asked.

"Yes," Clara said.

Mom fussed with the stove, didn't turn. "I agree. Yes, it did."

"No one knows," Josie said.

"They didn't before, either," Uncle Don said.

"Your father was frustrated for so long, Josie." Mom came to sit with Josie and Clara. The color was returning to Mom's cheeks, but she still looked weak. "I never really understood it before—how something so big could happen, and then ... nothing."

"But my dad ..."

"We lost Mark four years ago, Josie," Uncle Don said. "Not last night."

*That shouldn't have happened to him. Even the worst version of Dad didn't deserve to become that thing. We finished it. Followed it through. I did everything you would want, Dad. But that didn't make it easier. Right now, I can handle it, because I don't have a choice.* The thought didn't bring him back, though. Dad had been scratched out.

*Still, I slayed the dragon.*

"At least it's dead," Josie said.

Uncle Don finished the pancakes and brought plates over. A blackbird perched on a tree outside, watching in through the backyard windows. *No tagging him. I don't want to count anymore birds, even if they're alive again.*

"You saw it?" Uncle Don poured syrup on his pancakes. *Like it's the most normal thing in the world. 'Oh you met Satan? What car does he drive?'*

Josie stared at her food. The throbbing twist lingered in her belly. *This is my life now. Always nervous, with this feeling. Dad was like this, too. And that's okay. It has to be, doesn't it?*

"Yeah, I saw it," Josie said.

Mom and Clara started eating.

"We should have added blueberries, I forgot." Mom noticed Josie's tense perch. "You're so resourceful. All of you."

Josie tried to focus on the pancake batter smell, then shifted to look out the glass back doors at the wooded yard. *I want to remember Dad before, watching birds.*

"It cost a lot," Josie said. "The trip, I mean. Airfare was expensive."

"This house belongs to you," Uncle Don said. Mom started to protest, and he shrugged. "I don't want it. My mother isn't coming back, so it should be yours."

"We don't need ..."

"Then sell it," he said. "Whatever you want. Get it out of our family, along with everything in here." He gestured to the blackbird in the backyard. "He looks hungry, too. Help me fill the feeder?"

*No, I just wanted to sit here.* But Josie nodded and stood with Uncle Don to find a bag of birdseed under the sink. Clara squeezed her arm, smiled. Uncle Don carried the bag to a thin door that opened onto the back patio. The bird didn't move as they approached the tree, and Josie noticed a dangling wooden bird feeder on a lower branch. She was still carrying her own bag. Force of habit at this point, she should have left it inside.

"Your mother wouldn't want to hear us talk about it," Uncle Don said. He took the feeder down and unscrewed the lid, while Josie dumped in a swirl of multicolored birdseed. "Still, now that it's dead, I can answer your questions. You aren't in danger now. First, though, tell me: what did it look like? Mark described its red scales and the fire in its teeth."

"It didn't ..." Josie shook more birdseed in, almost half full. *Uncle Don saw it, too, didn't he? Why is he asking like this? He saw that bulbous, jellyfish monster swell up through that ancient room.* Her mouth felt too dry. "That's not what it was. Is that what my dad said?"

Uncle Don nodded, watching the feeder, not her.

"Yes. Scales, fire-breathing." He waited, and when she didn't answer, said, "That's what you get with a dragon, isn't it?"

The birdseed filled to the top, and Josie lifted the food bag away, while he fixed it back in the tree. The blackbird hopped down, closer. Its feathers bristled.

*That's not—it wasn't ...*

Josie dropped the birdseed bag and tapped her phone to find the audio file again. *The recording of me.* She pressed 'Play' and scrolled to the babble about the first extinction and ... *the water people.*

*The dragon was collecting us to preserve us from extinction, isn't that what I said? That's the purpose. The dragon wants to save our memories in the fossils. And it made other animals into monsters, just like Dad. Kept them alive after the last extinction events.*

*Like the water people.*

*The thing I killed with the lucky fossil.*

"If you don't want to talk about it, that's okay, Josie." Uncle Don grabbed the birdseed bag and started for the back door.

Still watching her phone, Josie followed—her right foot twisted sideways on an uneven tree root. White pain flashed in her vision. She hopped, holding her leg. Wincing, she smiled, when Uncle Don looked back. *Un-fucking-believable. After everything, I twist my ankle here.*

"Are you okay?" Uncle Don asked.

Josie nodded. She crouched to test her foot. Pain streaked up her calf. "Fine. I just ..."

A low line of smoke drifted around the pine needles by her shoes.

*That jellyfish monster didn't have scales. It didn't breathe fire. Or laugh.* Josie closed her eyes. The cave paintings of long-dead horses and mammoths came into focus in her mind ... and that smoking gash in the stone. *Dad ran that way. He wasn't abandoning me. He was trying to lead me to something else.* She imagined the smoke pulsing, as if something panted inside that tear.

"What's wrong?" Uncle Don asked.

Eyes still closed, Josie heard him approach, felt his hand on her shoulder.

"Did you twist your ankle?"

*What's wrong.*

In Josie's mind, that underground smoke wasn't breathing. It was laughing at her.

"What if I didn't ..." Josie stopped herself. *It wasn't ...*

*Don't.*

She flipped the bag off her back to find Dad's notebook, traced to the last entry—much longer than the others. It went on for multiple pages, and they never got to read it.


*'Each time the world dies, something survives. The tiniest scrap of life.*

*During the Permian Extinction, the so-called 'Great Dying' 250 million years ago, ninety percent of all life died. That's a hard num-ber. It didn't happen in a day or a year. But it was fast. So fast that we still don't fully understand. It's hard to make sense of ninety percent. Volcanoes exploded smoke plumes to clog the air, until it sweltered, and the oceans clotted to acid. Creatures that had thrived for millions of years crashed and broke. Entire races of animals that we would never recognize as terrestrial—because they no longer exist—were erased from the land, water, and sky.*

*'But, but, but: like the genetic mutations that marked the natural sur-vivors of the Black Death and smallpox, a miniscule fraction kept going. In every species, even those that were obliterated entirely as if they'd been standing at the center of a mushroom cloud, life con-tinued. In ones and twos, yes, but their blood didn't stop. Immunity to extinction. An inheritance, sure, a glitch in their cells that would never have been noticed if they hadn't been born at the end of the world. Many survivors probably lived on in darkness, carrying that lonely debt without hope, only to feel the warmth flicker out. Ninety percent is a hard number. Today, we mourn (rightly) the white rhino, the passenger pigeon, the sea cow, and countless other crawling, flying, swimming creatures that vanish around us. But how many have we lost? Five percent or ten percent or maybe even as high as fifteen percent? What does ninety percent look like? Look outside at the trees, birds, bees, grass even. Scrub it all away, until what's left you can hold in your hand. That's our future. That's why they're here, Caitlyn. I'm so sorry.*

*'But people won't vanish without help. They know that, too. We're too resourceful, too angry and willing to suffer. Even if the entire world melts into a poisoned rock, we'll go on in the catacombs at its heart, singing songs about our bravery. Our imaginations are too big to be erased by chemicals and smoke. So they'll help. The blacklegs have*

*done it before. Species that were different. Over hundreds of millions of years, we can't be the only ones to believe and invent and love. And people won't see them coming. They literally won't. The blacklegs will enter our houses and churches and schools, our offices and stadiums, and they will cut. And they will burn. And they won't stop, until we join the rest of this planet in silence and return to the stone. They won't let us hide in caves or fly to outer space. They'll murder us in our beds, and we won't even see it happen. We will watch ourselves grip the knife and the gun and the box of matches. Sure, we can scream and cry and beg, but they'll slaughter us in rituals or remake us as pets or bury us alive in wet mud. Until the last person stares back at the dragon who brought the blacklegs here—until that last human being on Earth cries, "Why?"*

*'And the dragon will laugh. The same way he laughed at me, when I tried to fight. Just like that, the world will go quiet, and everything we've built will grind down over hundreds of millions of years into a line of sediment the size of a pencil somewhere in the mountains or under the ocean. Areas will glow with strange, unexplained radiation, yes, but do you know what the fossils will say? What they'll call it, whoever comes after us? They won't remember us. There won't be enough of us left. They'll call it the age of the bird.*

*'Caitlyn, this isn't how I save the world. I can't. But we will have a chance, if I can drive them away. That's my debt. Make their fires go out. Do you know what I want you to tell Josie? The answer to meaninglessness? Nihilism is exactly why it matters. This only matters, because it doesn't. This isn't a prayer for the end of the world. Or to my own death. I'm praying for a release of our debt. Debt means there's a hole in the center of my chest, inside the depression where my bones meet. That's what I fill with bourbon. That's what burns when I swallow. I can never pay it off, only pass it down. Was it cruel of us*

*to bring a child into an age of extinction? Yes, until I saw her. Then, I realized there's no world without Josie. What does the world mean without her? She is the reason I push through the dried ache behind my eyes in the morning. You can smell the life on her, electric in the air. It's obvious and cheesy, but I love her. Every generation goes extinct. Ours isn't any different.*

'So now I have to go burn a hole in the world. Ninety percent is a hard *number, Caitlyn. I love you.*

'For Josie.'

Finishing the letter, an icy thrill spiked up Josie neck and shoulders. Out of the corner of her eyes, the mist shivered too.

9 780999 771532